Your Pick

Selected Stories

V.S. Kemanis

2019 Eric Hoffer Award
short story/anthology category
2019 Montaigne Medal Finalist

Cover design by Valdas Miskinis

The stories in *Your Pick* have been selected from the following story collections by V.S. Kemanis:

Love and Crime: Stories (Top Shelf Book Awards 2018 Finalist): "Rosemary and Reuben" and "Journal Entry, Franklin DeWitt" (originally published in *Ellery Queen's Mystery Magazine*)

Dust of the Universe, tales of family (Commended—SPR Book Awards 2014): "My Latvian Aunt" (a *Glimmer Train* Top 25 award winner), "Like Love," "Reckoning," and "Dust of the Universe"

Everyone But Us, tales of women (The Kindle Book Review Awards 2013 Nominee): "The Cost of Ice Cream," "Pianissimo, Fortissimo," and "The Missing and Uninvited"

Malocclusion, tales of misdemeanor (B&P Readers' Choice Awards 2014 Nominee): "Malocclusion," "Gray Zone," and "Fractals"

ISBN: 0999785036
ISBN-13: 978-0-9997850-3-4

℞ **Opus Nine Books**
•**New York**•

For my readers, always

.

CONTENTS

Introduction

THE DOZEN STORIES in *Your Pick* are reader favorites, carefully selected and handpicked from my four collections of short fiction. I wrote these stories at various times over the past twenty-five years, and readers have responded to me with their personal insights, enthusiasm, and praise. These twelve stories have inspired deep emotional reactions, bringing tears and smiles, wonder and discovery.

Dear Readers, I've listened to you and learned from you. These are your picks. New Readers, take these stories and escape into worlds unknown yet familiar, imbued with universal situations, conflicts, and emotions. My characters are everyday people navigating the breadth of human experience: love, loss, attraction, repulsion, rejection, acceptance, despair, joy, temptation, loneliness, creativity, self-discovery, failure, success. Enter the lives of these characters and let them stir feelings deep within you.

Imagination is my refuge, conception and creation my delights. I wish the same for you.

V.S. Kemanis

Autumn 2018

My Latvian Aunt

AUNT MIRDZA DIED in 2004 at the age of seventy-seven. I'd known her only ten years. My father's sixty-fifth birthday party was the occasion of our belated meeting, owing to one of those epiphanies that strike at the threshold to the sunset years—in Papa's case, a sudden regret at having shunned his sister ever since her scandalous marriage to an older man at the DP camp in Würzburg, 1947.

Mirdza and I were coaxed into attending the distant celebration with invitations we knew better not to decline, sent along with plane tickets to L.A., hers from Toronto, mine from New York. There were follow-up phone calls. "Your sister is coming—*and* your Aunt Mirdza." Papa was confident. "I also booked the Stanley Pendleton Trio." A big to-do, March 15, 1994. I went alone, leaving Marcus behind for a few days to get the kids off to preschool and kindergarten.

Years have passed. There's a Baltic look that sets in particularly hard from middle age on, when the eyes sink into the skull, the hair becomes thin and brittle, the face lengthens and yellows, and the jowls dip below chin level.

You'd think that I, being of mixed breed, would have been spared, but certainly, it isn't so. The other day in a health club locker room a young woman, a complete stranger, looked me dead in the eye and started to lilt happily in Swedish. It took a moment to register before I muttered something about, "just across the water," neither in Latvian nor Swedish.

I'd never learned my father's mother tongue. Upon landing in the States in 1950, Papa was so grateful to his new country that, when he married a coed from Bakersfield Junior College and started a family, he found no utility in passing along a language and culture that lay buried in the rubble he'd left behind. This hole in my upbringing dawned on me during college in the mid-1970s, spawning a righteous period of visceral indignation inspired by the newly emerging roots fad. The phase slowly dissipated, replaced with a misty-eyed swell at any mention of Papa's Atlantic passage by steamer. He is now gone, since 2001, my mother long before him, 1992.

The moment I first saw her is untouched in memory. Aunt Mirdza sat on a corner of the couch in Papa's living room, surrounded by aging Americans, most of them several generations removed from their European ancestors. Her identity jumped out in that quiet Latvian way just as Stanley Pendleton was finishing his Bill Evans-style piano solo in "What is There to Say?" My mystery aunt was stamped from the same press as her brother Karlis, the man who'd raised me, her countenance offering a preview of my own, thirty years hence.

Half of that thirty is now gone, time a witness to my face, gently sagging, revealing her in me.

*　　*　　*

*June 13-14, 1941, Night of Terror: Soviet Central Government
Deports Anti-Soviet Element, 15,500 Latvians*

"I was at the farm that day."

"How old were you?"

"Fifteen. Our neighbor to the south came over and said all sorts of people were being arrested. My parents and Karlis were in Riga. I wanted to call and warn them not to come, but the phone was cut off, which kind of scared me. Of course, I didn't know the same thing was happening in the city. Later we heard all kinds of horror stories. There were people we knew—the parents were taken and their new baby left behind, alone in the crib. Just shut the door on it. Things like that.

"The other neighbor, the one to the north, was somewhat on the pink side, a Socialist. I figured there's a safe place and his phone will be working, so I jumped on my bike and went over there, but a big truck was standing in the middle of his yard, the military police. I sort of blustered something about coming over for potato seeds or whatnot and rode out of there as fast as possible."

"Russians were deporting a Socialist?"

"Nothing made any sense. They owned their farm, so naturally they couldn't be Communist because they must be rich. If somebody didn't like you they informed against you. I still don't know why we weren't taken. My father was in the Latvian border guard and we owned a 300-acre farm. They took most of our land in 1940 and left only thirty acres, but they didn't take us.

"They were disorganized, and that could be the only

reason we didn't end up in Siberia."

Vilnis was her love, a man seventeen years her senior. Mirdza was a few months shy of twenty-one when she told her parents that they might as well approve the marriage because soon enough there would be nothing they could do to prevent it.

This was the story she told, anyway, during the first of my yearly visits to her Toronto apartment. Having met, finally, at sixty-seven and forty, we latched onto all those wasted years as an excuse for silent anger at my father, a subterfuge for the disappointment we might have directed at ourselves. Easily, long ago, we could have arranged a meeting on our own. The grumbling, estranged siblings, Mirdza and Karlis, had never, really, lost touch. They habitually gossiped about one another with mutual acquaintances from DP camp days and occasionally exchanged preprinted Christmas cards, just to confirm the still-beating heart and unchanged address at the other end.

Not very difficult, then, for Mirdza or I to have asked Papa for a phone number or address, but we outwardly denied our choice of scapegoat, dropping hints with nasty little digs over coffee. "Here we sit together. Let's just call him up now, shall we?" Mirdza mused. "Let's not," I answered. Mean. We locked eyes and smiled because, although she'd surrendered to curiosity and swallowed her pride to attend the sixty-fifth, she certainly hadn't forgiven him for the original injury, his arrogant rejection of her lifeblood.

As children, the siblings had never gotten along, well

before Vilnis so shockingly robbed the cradle. When asked to explain, Mirdza always gave the same answer, reducing their intractable conflict to a comfortable platitude: "Your father was a city boy and I was a country girl." Their family had an apartment in Riga and a farm thirty-five miles outside the city where Mirdza spent every possible moment, weekends, holidays, and summers, tending the pigs.

June 22, 1941: Nazi Invasion Interrupts
Soviet Deportation of Latvians

"It was only a week or so later. The Germans came in the middle of the night. In the morning there were fifty or more of them settled in the yard."

"Were you terrified?"

"Actually, we were happy. In a few weeks they occupied the whole country. There was no fighting, the Russians just ran, and we didn't have to worry anymore about being arrested. Life went on. The only people who had to worry were the Jews and the Gypsies and anyone reckless enough to resist."

Usually we sat alone at her small kitchen table, but not during that first visit when she began to offer her stories of Vilnis. I had brought my family along—as it turned out, the only time they would accompany me to Toronto. The folly of bringing the children slammed into us the moment we stepped into Mirdza's sparse, '60s-style apartment, decorated with oil paintings and handmade furniture wrought by the hands of her long-deceased, beloved husband. A cord of angst shot up my spine every time a child escaped parental grasp. "Don't touch!" can be said only so many times. No and no again and please come here to be clamped between the knees or tethered to the table leg. Please. My aunt is telling us a story.

This, in between her breaks from us, the trips to the four-by-six cement balcony for a cigarette. She was considerate in this way, in her own home, five floors up.

A black and white, miniscule snapshot of a young couple in '40s-style clothing was pushed toward me across the kitchen table with yellowed index and middle fingers, thready nails. "I said to them, either you can okay it now, or I'll just wait a few months and then there will be nothing you can do about it!" Said with a Canadian "ou" and two, hard little Latvian "t's" at the end. A glimmer of self-congratulation shone from her translucent blue eyes, so pale they verged on milky underneath the folds of slack lids.

That fog about her made me desperate to burn through it, to gather a complete picture of the love match, a chestnut-haired girl of nearly twenty-one and the inky-helmeted man of thirty-eight on their wedding day, standing vertical-legged in their best suits, the girl clutching a small bouquet of handpicked flowers, no money for anything more. Just beyond the lens perhaps my father, a mere nineteen, looked on with a smirk of disdain. Get over it, Papa. Your parents eventually did.

I was confused about the twenty-one business, wondering if it was just part of her anecdote, a made-up fact for family legend. "Was that German or Latvian law, there in the DP camp?" What a stupid question out of all the great questions that could have been asked and answered when there was still time. This one never was answered, inter-rupted by six-year-old Trina. "Mommy! I'm going to throw up!" I grabbed Trina for a frantic dash to the tidy little john, where we hovered, luckily, over a false alarm as I silently thanked my little one for sparing the grout between all those inch-square floor tiles in colors of salmon, pearl, and caramel.

When we returned, Marcus was down on a patch of open floor wrestling with little Ryan while I, very embar-rassed, apologized with the flushed girl in my lap, her head pushed up into the cozy cave under my chin. Mirdza gave a straight-backed smile and said with a sniff, "We never could have children." Of course I knew she was childless, but there was a certain awkwardness in that confession, delivered without a scrap of sorrow or regret.

It appeared then that she looked upon my children with a scientific, distant curiosity, those specimens of cell and gene descended from her brother. Not once did she touch them or attempt to engage them in conversation during that first visit or the single trip she made to my home, when the children were older and capable of human discourse. Against all reason it bothered me, her lack of grandmotherly ways, though I scolded myself for being so selfish.

On another visit, when we were alone, she explained, "I always thought it was because of the war. We were con-stantly hungry. Maybe it would surprise you what we thought about?"

Ears open, I awaited further nuance to her confession. The Childlessness of Mirdza and Vilnis.

"Not big juicy pork chops or cakes and cookies and whatnot. It was always bread. I thought and dreamt about bread, the smell and taste of it in my mouth." Her brow knit around the blight of hunger still engraved there. Finally she came to the point. "I lost my period for several years, you see, but I never did ask a doctor about it."

I didn't respond, not knowing quite how. "What a shame," should I have said? The enigma of her, everything about her, was neatly packaged within that rational, matter-of-fact delivery, at once suggesting and denying a cover-up or the possibility of deeper meaning.

"How wonderful!" should I have exclaimed? To be blessed with barrenness, given free rein in sexuality and art and nature in a dizzy time of political exile and personal liberation. To be a young girl defying her family to marry the man she loved, an artist, handyman, and craftsman. To be solitary lovers building a quiet, secluded life on that little farm in a clearing surrounded by woods and bordered by a crystal lake for summer swims in a rugged bit of Ontario. 1948 to 1967.

October 13, 1944: The Soviets Recapture Riga

"The Russians were advancing all summer from the east, pushing the German front toward the Baltic Sea. By October they were practically on our doorstep. We were all staying on the farm, thinking it was safer there. But then the Germans started to dig in."

"Dig in?"

"Making trenches in the garden, ready to fight. Then the shooting started. They were shooting left and right."

"There, on your land?"

"Yeah, in our garden. Nothing to it, I mean, you're so busy doing things you don't have time to be scared. You don't think about the future because you have to pack. We packed all kinds of stupid things. There were no trains naturally, so we drove the horses with two wagon loads.

"There was just one thing that really, really impressed me from the war, not the shooting, not any bombings. The Germans were withdrawing, their tanks and army vehicles taking up the whole highway and the refugees on horseback and in wagons, one after another, on the gravel shoulder. I was driving one of our wagons. There was a boy, maybe seven or eight years old on a huge horse, riding bareback. I don't know whether the horse shied or what happened, but the boy fell off and the horse stepped on his leg. I could hear the bones crunch. And of course he screamed and nobody stopped. You couldn't stop. You couldn't do anything, because the traffic was one by one. I can still see that boy on the horse.

"When we got to Riga we reorganized, made some backpacks from potato sacks and packed whatever we could carry. We gave everything else away, our horses and wagons, our apartment. I don't know who got them. And then we pushed onto a little boat headed for Germany.

"That night a Russian plane went over quite low, sort of limping back home. I was on deck sitting right beside the soldier manning the machine gun, shooting at the plane. And you know, if you have a weapon right there you're not the least bit scared! All that shining ammunition—you can see where it goes and it was fascinating."

* * *

One of my inherited treasures is an index-card sized plastic box containing Ektachrome 35mm slides and a teal and black colored plastic viewer that fits snugly in the palm of my hand. Unfold it, insert a slide against the translucent backdrop, press an eye to the crude magnifying glass, and magically they emerge in 3-D, Mirdza and Vilnis, their moments on this earth forever mine.

1952, 1956, 1961, in the woods, the clearing, Mirdza with the pig, Vilnis chopping firewood, slabs of bacon in the smokehouse, their new Ford, summer together on the shore of the lake. Cigarettes between their fingers in almost every picture, relishing the taste of tobacco in the brisk outdoors and in the yellow light of a close, wood-paneled bedroom. Mirdza, propped up against the headboard, is fully clothed in a dull, rust-colored sweater and plaid skirt, hands fisted together in her lap, knuckled around a jutting, burning cigarette as her soft, young, still round face, thirty-one years old, pushes up a shy, contented smile for her lover Vilnis, camera in hand. Just the two of them in that dim room with the single light, and there it is, on the nightstand! The little teak lamp that now graces my living room! "Vilnis G." is etched in cursive on the underside of the base, an imprint he left on all his woodwork and paintings with its assumption that anyone interested enough should already know the last name, Galdiņš.

They would have liked to live entirely from the land but needed to supplement their income. They both contributed. Vilnis was the relentless creator, most of it for Mirdza and himself, but reluctantly for money, designing wood furniture with distinctive hand-cut dovetail joints in woods of different hues, planed so perfectly smooth that the hand still wants to linger, caress, and stroke the living warmth that resides in these children of the soil.

His paintings, singular and disturbing, are composed of veneer shapes under oils in startling colors textured with a putty knife, deliberate, nothing haphazard or impulsive. The viewer, inexorably drawn, is the intended target of his images. Barren trees grope for the sun, a naked sliver of chartreuse moon floats in a dark-night spray of stars, an abandoned city of blue-gray skyscrapers thrusts heavenward. Empty and searching.

Mirdza's apartment was furnished with the smaller pieces of furniture and decorated with half a dozen paintings, each ingeniously hung with a jury-rig of string, paper clips, rug tacks, and double-sided tape. These methods were exposed after her death.

During their Ontario farm years, her monetary contribution was a part-time job she held for more than a decade as records keeper for their rural township. "It was the '50s and of course there were no computers and everything was on paper and done by hand. The real big deal was when we got a microfiche in '58 or '59 and began to store all the documents and certificates this way.

"Still, all the papers had to go through me. Every birth and death in our township."

In the first minutes of the visit when we discussed birth and death records, she asked me, as she usually did, "How are the children?" I responded, as I usually did, with the current list of their strengths and weaknesses in school, extracurricular interests, and recent illnesses. Follow-up questions were few to none. I didn't volunteer extended psychological insights or obsessive motherly gushing. They were my children. It was understood that I loved them boundlessly and achingly, spent my days and nights with them, had given up my career for them. Temporarily. She kept one ear open, would smile distantly and nod at each bit of imparted information.

"Will you be going back to the office one day?"

"Sure, I think so. My brain could use the exercise, and Marcus says," I laughed, "he says I'm really dying to get back. Anyway, the kids won't need me forever."

"Less than you think, perhaps."

I found this odd, almost offensive. "Yes, well..."

"At least, not when they get older," she put in, and my heart, a biased judge, took this as a calculated attempt to soften a blow which had been every bit as calculated.

May 7, 1945: German Unconditional Surrender
Leaves 150,000 Displaced Latvians

"It was only about seven months until the war ended, most of that winter. Luckily, my godmother took us in, somewhere in the middle of Germany. I had a job in a glass blowing factory and Karlis was in school. It snowed so much there were mornings I had to leave the house through the window on skis."

"Through the window!"

"No, really! The snow got that high! It was a tiny village, I can't remember the name. When the Germans surrendered, the Russians took over the town and we had the darndest time convincing the Americans we didn't want to stay. We had just run from the Russians! We had no country.

"That summer the Americans dumped us somewhere in Bavaria on a big farm, about twenty Latvians, mostly well-educated engineers and lawyers and mathematicians and whatnot. They all had to work in the potato fields in the summer heat, and I was the house Negro, the only one who could milk a cow, so there you are! I had it easy.

"And then we heard of the DP camps, so we went to Würzburg. That's where I met Vilnis. That's where we stayed, until 1948."

Each visit with Mirdza, after getting through the domestic small talk, I would leap time to emerge reincarnated as a fly on the cow's flank in 1942, or the tabby mouser on her lap in 1955. As yet unborn were Ry and Trina, my daily joy or leg iron, depending. Marcus was generous about my yearly solo treks, not wanting to repeat that disastrous family visit in 1995, happy to take three or four days off from work to be with the kids, using the excuse that we had no relatives or babysitters at the ready. Our relationship was built on this kind of cooperation, none of it a problem or a source of stress, although the limits were tested when it came to all my trips after Mirdza's death.

By then, the children were thirteen and fifteen, not really in need of a babysitter. But my return to Toronto, again and again, long after my aunt's body had been reduced to ash, might have been seen as a bit off. Marcus pretended not to notice. I see that now. To me, there was no question of the necessity.

Mirdza's friends arranged her funeral. She used to

speak of them now and then. There were a few from her childhood in Riga, others she'd known in the DP camp, and newer acquaintances who were members of the Latvian Lutheran Church in Toronto. The most prominent names were Ruta and Osvalds, but there were others, Ilze and Janis and Darta and Imants. I'd never met any of them, an amorphous subset of graying displaced persons labeled "Mirdza's Friends."

Ruta was the one who called me. Her voice, with its pitch and accent so similar to Mirdza's, startled me almost as much as the news. "Mirdza's niece?" she confirmed after she'd asked my name twice. "Your aunt died yesterday, in the hospital." I hadn't known she was in the hospital. "They said it was pneumonia." The endgame to undiagnosed emphysema, I thought, or more likely, a diagnosis known to Mirdza and never mentioned. Her breathing had become progressively labored over the years, and there'd been a previous bout of pneumonia only the year before.

Ruta told me more than enough without the need to ask questions. I listened quietly, allowing my chest slowly to clog. Mirdza and a neighbor in her building were in the habit of checking on one another—something I hadn't known, additional evidence of my dereliction. The neighbor discovered her in bed, limp and feverish, and called an ambulance. She died two days later.

"I stayed with her the whole night through until the end," said Ruta.

The belated, once-yearly niece exhaled a "God bless you" with real gratitude.

"In the last few hours she couldn't talk at all. She was drenched in sweat, her breathing was nearly impossible, a big rattling sound, and she was curled up in a fetal position. I wiped the sweat from her forehead and told her that everything would be all right. Her eyes flew back and forth, searching my face and the room. I don't know what she could see."

"Vilnis, I hope," emerged without thinking.

Ruta paused and I dreaded her response, even worse, her silence for what it would tell me about her thoughts. "Yes," she said finally. "I think you may be right." Ruta would know—she'd been Mirdza's friend since Germany—but her voice was unreadable.

"How did you know where to reach me?" I asked.

"How? But she gave me your number some years ago, after Karlis died. She said to call you if anything happened."

I was dumbstruck.

"Perhaps you didn't know." She'd analyzed my silence. "Mirdza spoke of you often. And your little ones, Ryan and Trina, her great nephew and great niece. She showed me pictures. The school pictures you sent every year."

Yes, I had sent them, hadn't I? Weeks later I would see all the snapshots again, organized by year in a disintegrating, multi-sleeved plastic photo holder in her wallet, some sleeves fat with more than one, the most recent on top. It was then that I cried for the first time.

May 10, 2004: Treasure Hunters Discover
WWII Artifacts in the Baltics

"We buried anything valuable we couldn't carry. Most people did this. We weren't going to give the Russians any more than we had to, and of course we thought we were coming back. Anyway, we were hoping to come back."

I became the harvester of the personal effects, a responsibility willingly relinquished by my sister, who lived a world away in Hawaii. We were the only living relatives, and Mirdza died intestate, a surprise to us. The last time I'd seen her, shortly after her recovery from the previous bout of pneumonia, she'd made one of her dry little jokes that it was time to rewrite her will. She was so organized that this seemed likely.

But there was no will to be found in the apartment, no correspondence from a lawyer or evidence of a safe deposit box. I combed every inch, the desk, the bureau, even the kitchen drawers, warding off the sentry from the Public Guardian's Office, a square block of a man in a plaid sport coat with distrust smeared on his face, dutifully protecting an old lady's meager possessions from theft.

My first shock was to see him instead of Mirdza, opening her apartment door under my knock, his dangling hand clutching my affidavit and birth certificate, faxed to him the day before. These documents should have been legally enough to convince him of my entitlement, but he clung to doubt with a benign, official sternness, standing briefly in front of each drawer I wished to open before stepping away.

When I reached up to grasp the frame of the chartreuse moon, he stopped me with a suggestion that the paintings and furniture could go to public auction. This was just too much, and I'm afraid I lost it. "These are family treasures!" I choked, teary eyed. He melted then and became a believer in me and perhaps the nicest man ever born, helping to load as much as we could fit into the rented van I had driven up from New York.

A few things I had to let go. Her desk. A hi-fi. Hand-crafted bits of Vilnis I couldn't keep. A list was made and a receipt with my signature under the Public Guardian's disclaimer, sealing my liability to any surprise distant relation who might materialize, looking for a chartreuse moon.

Back home, after Marcus helped me find places for the three small pieces of furniture, I took up residence in the basement with my boxes of Mirdza, surrounded by the mental landscape of Vilnis, propped up against the walls. My family didn't see me for days, possibly I didn't eat, much anyway. Nights I spent on the musty couch the kids used for sleepovers, peering into the dark void with tears in my eyes, wondering what I felt about this woman who had spoken so unthinkingly of Jews and Gypsies and house Negroes, who'd inquired politely after my children like a stranger while treasuring the bragging photos in her wallet. This woman who'd been put aside by her own brother yet dearly loved by Vilnis and a nucleus of survivors.

It had hit me hard, the specter of perpetual obscurity, the regret of unasked questions, facts lost forever as I dug through the personal effects, jewelry, scribbles in Latvian, photos and slides, fascinated, angry. Why hadn't she told me about this person or that place? Why hadn't I asked her to describe Vilnis at work, paintbrush in hand, the expression he wore when imagining these bleak landscapes and lonely heavens?

Hordes of ghosts, the undiscovered works, were scattered throughout Ontario, I was sure of it, never to be found. For twenty years with Mirdza on that little farm by the lake, Vilnis relentlessly created, the first decade in good health, the second in gradual decline. In 1958, an unnoticed cluster of mutant cells invaded his left lung, multiplied, obstructed, were carved away by the scalpel in 1963, and reemerged to multiply again, slowly eroding the mass into black soup.

Six paintings, a coffee table, a side table, a credenza with sliding doors. Smaller wood crafts, a tea tray, a traditional Latvian three-branched candelabra, an office wastebasket, the teak lamp. These were what I had, the desk and hi-fi left behind.

On the day of the funeral, before going to the church, my sister and I had spent an hour with Ruta and Osvalds in their spacious living room, drinking coffee. Centered on a wall under the two-story, cathedral ceiling was an enormous painting, a rectangle perhaps five feet high and three feet wide, its style and subject immediately recognizable. In this one, the barren arms of the trees reached beseechingly toward a pale, cold sun, the branches hollow and dead, like driftwood. The sight of it spurred my incipient confusion, precursor to an insatiable need. Discreetly, I inquired. Yes, they supposed, many more of his paintings must be out in the world, but they couldn't say where.

In my basement retreat, cross-legged on the floor, I inserted one slide after another into the little 3-D viewer and angled it up to the light, searching for clues. Melded into the images of their life together were his paintings and pieces of woodcraft, each of them known and recognized until—sharp inhale, beating heart—a sparkling blue image struck me with the thrill of an archeological find.

Vilnis sat on the couch, a burning cigarette clamped between thumb and two fingers in a masculine custom of old, looking cool and masterful as if to say, "This is my work." The large painting filled much of the wall behind him, caught with a sheen from the light of the flash bulb. A happy scene! He had painted six elongated V-shapes suggesting birds, each one rounded on top like the upper edge of a woman's evening gown. Individual yet social, they flew at angles in a careful hodgepodge, the most prominent among them painted in pure white, the others in graduated shades through a spectrum of blues—powder, periwinkle, cornflower, azure, iceberg—against a royal sky, indigo sun at center. Simple, this, the only truly happy image.

Letters and e-mails were written, photos enclosed and attached, phone calls made. My actions were automatic, necessary, unassailable. The inquiries concerned an artist by the name of Vilnis Galdiņš and his creations, the intricate wood crafts and oil paintings of naked trees, lonely heavens, abandoned cities, and most important, the happy birds. I'd found a new focus to my search for more of her, my Latvian aunt.

Time and again, Marcus said, "Go." I drove, I flew, I drove again. Gallery owners, artists, curators, art aficionados, all looked at my photos with interest before lifting their eyes to gaze at me blankly. A million and one cups of tea were sipped with my aunt's friends as they treated me to stories of war, exile, renewal, admiration for Mirdza's strength and her husband's artistry, but offering scant insight into their private lives which had remained locked up and inaccessible even to their closest, longest allies.

Among these people I made but a single discovery, a small painting of the familiar trees hanging in the dining room of a modest home inhabited by a skin-and-bones old woman, her accent stronger than the rest, her voice slurred with stroke. Lidija she was called, perhaps—I thought she said—a cousin of Vilnis. They shared the same last name.

Back home from this trip I asked Marcus, "Why are you letting me do this?" Mirdza had been gone eight months.

Never in his life had he experienced an ethnic urge, the pull of ancestry. An "American mutt" is what he called himself if anyone asked. His eyes bore deeply into mine with tragedy, benevolence, resignation. I hid from them, turning my head to press a cheek into the soft material covering his muscled shoulder like a cloth habit, awaiting the sermon I deserved, a tug of the rein.

My priest said nothing, a strong, silent pillar of support to my madness as thoughts raced in my head, a vision of Lidija's face, her eyes, the droning playback of her words, the puzzling congeries. A shudder had gone through her, almost a shake of the head, signaling a barely suppressed recognition as I showed her the photograph I had made from the slide so that I could keep the precious original locked up at home. The happy birds.

"Do you know this painting?"

"Yes, maybe," she said while giving off another kind of look. How did I see it? The deception hidden in her ninety-year-old eyes. There a secret she wanted to tell but knew she shouldn't. "Mukenzking house" it sounded like, but then she refused to say anything more about the "Mukenzking" family.

A click of connection. I broke away from Marcus and ran down to the dungeon where, amidst the scraps and scribbles was the one I sought, its significance previously unknown and ignored for its seeming irrelevance to anything Latvian. On an index card in Mirdza's hand was written "Mackenzie King House," an address, a phone number and another name, Francesca Veil-Cugina. Immediately I was on the phone with her, this Francesca, the woman who must know.

"My goodness!" she exclaimed. "Mirdza never said she had a niece! And you know, we only just heard! Poor thing. She stopped coming and we wondered what had happened but couldn't reach her or anyone else for the longest time."

"She was a friend of yours?"

"No, but yes, certainly we were friendly. A wonderful person she was. Her goddaughter V. lives here, and well, how about that! Here I am, talking to another V.!"

"I didn't know—"

"She's been so distraught, you can imagine. First, not knowing, and then, when she learned the news."

"May I speak with her please?"

"To V.?" Something caught in her throat. "I'm afraid she can't come to the phone."

I turned to see Marcus at the bottom of the stairs. Wilting slowly, he had the dejected look of a man left behind, his eyes a mirror for the intrigue that gleamed in mine. Even then, I knew that this story would be written, that the names would be changed to protect the living and the dead alike, that the goddaughter's name would have to be V., like Kafka.

"It's all right," I said to him, my hand trembling over

the mouthpiece, but already I was plotting, my suitcase packed, my mind on the next plane, in the air, stepping onto the Canadian soil I had left only a week before, driving my rental car through Toronto, its streets by now so familiar, and into the outskirts on a street that was new to me. The long number in the address took me to the very end toward which I hurled at a dangerous speed, up a slight incline, leaving other houses behind, arriving at the threshold of a driveway identified by a drab brown plaque with its announcement in white lettering, "Mackenzie King House." Entering the drive, I snaked in among the trees and shrubs to find the sprawling apartment building hidden from the road, something that looked oddly like an elementary school.

There was a front desk where a doorman sat, looking more like a watchman in charge of the inner door, apparently locked.

I stated my name and asked, "Would you please ring the apartment of Francesca Veil-Cugina? If she's not in, I'll speak to V.—I'm sorry, I don't know her last name."

The servant gave a doubtful look but complied, using a phone at the desk to make the call, and soon a little woman emerged, her features of Mediterranean origin, a smile open and warm. I was greeted and ushered inside with a buzz, the watchman's hand under the desk.

The portal closed behind us with an irreversible sucking noise, giving rise to a suffocating claustrophobia as we traversed a long hallway. Francesca prattled on through the shock of new details coming into my perception: a food stain on the upper sleeve of her pastel-print smock, the squish of rubber-soled shoes on linoleum, a man at the far end of the hall gently tugging on the hand of a childlike woman and the animal sound coming from her throat, echoing toward us.

"V. will be so excited to see you! She desperately misses your aunt. Mirdza always made sure she was well taken care of, you know." The tunnel narrowed, walls squeezing in. "Of course, I didn't know V. until she came here; she was in another home when she was young. I understand her parents died when she was just a baby."

"Who were the parents?"

"I could look that up for you. I believe the birth certificate is in the file."

A matter for the township records keeper, I could have thought. But by then we'd arrived at the door, all my assumptions shed like items of soiled clothing along the length of the corridor behind us, leaving me naked, quivering, and vulnerable, wanting but unable to run. Francesca knocked, flashed a card key, and pushed the door open a sliver, calling ahead in a soft, bright voice, "V.? You have a visitor!"

A low, rumbling human hum escaped the crack, and Francesca pushed the door wide to reveal, with a sudden burst, the glory of blue adorning the wall straight ahead of us, so close, on the opposite side of the small room. "The birds!" flew off my tongue in awe before I noticed her sitting—rocking—on the fully-made twin bed against the wall to our right.

"Birds!" she mimicked with an aimless swing of her head toward the painting and back to me, a momentary display of the wide-set, almond eyes. She stood and dropped her vacant gaze to the floor while shifting her weight from one foot to the other and back again in an endless, comforting, flat-footed rhythm, then laughed and raised her head, unashamed of the drop of spittle glistening on her chin.

There's a Baltic look that sets in particularly hard from middle age on. She displayed it in mild distortion, this V., a woman my age. Her face wore the mark of her parentage in a strange alchemic brew of juxtaposed images born from my little 3-D viewer, altered by an errant gene, and transformed by fifty years of time-lapse photography to become the incarnation standing before me.

I knew her instantly.

And, in the next instant, I knew just as surely that, to honor the secrets of the dead, I would not say a word.

Rosemary and Reuben

ANDERSON IS SINGLE by choice and always has been. True to his one love, he treats himself to an epicurean delight every Saturday night. At this stage of his life, he's indifferent to money and mortality and gladly indulges to excess. Only the finest restaurants in Manhattan will do.

Before stepping out, Anderson trims the goatee and puts on his evening best. Invariably he dines alone, although he isn't without a list of possible companions, female and male. Still, there's no wish for a lover to dine with. On his evenings out, he indulges a craving of a different sort, the sensual experience of taste, texture, and aroma, the heft of silver and gleam of crystal, the lengthening and savoring of time. For a few hours he forgets his life—everything it is and is not. A full belly and a buzz from the grape will do that.

On this particular Saturday, Anderson is fortunate to have a reservation at the celebrated Ole Factory in the Village. Competition is high. It's rumored that, after thirty-five years in business, Rosemary and Reuben Blandrigard will soon be retiring.

At seven o'clock, Anderson alights from a taxicab,

27

braves an icy blast, and darts over the frozen pavement into the restaurant. The small foyer is square, dim, and hushed like a confessional, with a single, warm light directed from the ceiling toward the opposite wall. Anderson is drawn to the sepia-toned photograph of the owners, framed in a simple mahogany rectangle, displayed on the eggshell wall. Rosemary lovingly gazes at Reuben, and Reuben gazes at Anderson with a look of glazed contentment.

Past the foyer and over the threshold, a young hostess looks up. Anderson squares his shoulders and announces his name. She seems to know him. "How are you this evening, Mr. Anderson?"

"Fine. Just fine, thank you." He strokes the goatee and drops his eyes to her neck.

"Is this your first time at the Ole Factory?"

"Yes, indeed it is," he informs her neck. "I've run the gauntlet successfully it seems."

"And you've earned your reward."

"I look forward to it."

He senses her amusement, feigned or real, from the tension in her neck.

"Right this way, please." She turns, sending her long skirt into a gentle swirl, and guides him at a leisurely pace through the well-spaced dining room of about twenty tables. The décor is spare but pleasing. In the far corner, a small, round table awaits him. The single chair is backed into the corner, allowing him a view outward into the room—a thoughtful arrangement. At some establishments he's made to face the wall, and at others, an empty, second chair stands in silent rebuke of his social failings.

Anderson sits and orders an aperitif. Glancing at the

menu, he senses, in the periphery, the sexual murmurings of a young, starry-eyed couple at the next table. Against his will, he's aroused by a fleeting emotional stirring. The moment passes, giving way to the pleasing texture in his hand—the single sheet of cardstock. This is the message printed on the front:

"Welcome to the Ole Factory. We've created a unique menu for tonight's meal. Let your server know if your pleasure is One or The Other. Your hosts, Rosemary and Reuben."

Always a surprise, always superb. (The critics agree.) Each meal at the Ole Factory is specially created for the clientele, a process that begins with a telephone interview to vet personal aversions and food allergies. Simpatico tastes of prospective patrons are carefully matched, and a guest list is compiled for each sitting before any reservation is confirmed. It can take a year to get on a list.

As a successful applicant, Anderson has won the right to ponder his two options for the evening. Without much thought, he selects "The Other" before flipping the card over. Printed on the back is a short paragraph entitled "The Story of Rosemary and Reuben." *Legend* might be the more descriptive term. Everything about them is legend, including their habit of circulating through the dining room during coffee and dessert. They appear at the kitchen door, wrench apart like cloven chopsticks, and weave different routes through the tables, separately greeting their guests.

As he sips his aperitif and reads The Story a second time, Anderson silently hopes that Rosemary will be the one to visit him at the end of his meal.

Two and a half hours later, he gets his wish. At nine

thirty, she emerges from the kitchen with Reuben. Nearly touching, they suspend all movement for barely an eye blink. Reluctantly they part. With a quick, light step, Rosemary toes a straight line along the wall to Anderson's table. She's a roundish, dwarflike woman of about Anderson's age, with silvery-gray hair pulled tightly back into a doughnut at the nape of her neck, exposing delicately lobed, naked ears. Coming to a halt in dramatic proximity, she's not much taller than Anderson as he sits. With a familiar air, she regards him from beneath jet-black eyebrows. *Hold still please*, says the creator of that sepia-toned photograph.

"Mr. Anderson. We're very glad you could come this evening."

His heart races in confusion. Her visit to his table fulfills his dearest wish, but everything else has been less than expected, troublingly so. He doesn't understand the meaning of the past two and a half hours. He wants to tell her, but the words are bottled under a well-aged cork.

Before Anderson can speak, Rosemary lifts a bent index finger and rests the knuckle on the tip of her sharply pointed nose. The finger covers her nostrils, the fisted hand covers her mouth.

Anderson searches for polite words but finds only the single, obvious truth. "The service was excellent, thank you."

With a nod, she removes her hand. "It's been our pleasure. Is there anything else we can get for you? Anything at all?" Pausing after the last word, the silence that follows announces her omission. She hasn't inquired whether he enjoyed his dinner.

*   *   *

In the middle of the night, Anderson lies awake, puzzled and unsettled. He remembers eating but feels hollow and unsatisfied. More than anything, he's deeply ashamed. The words of The Story march relentlessly across his brain like sturdy, soldier ants. Between the permanent black bits, the holes wait to be filled.

Staring into the lightless room, he mourns the passage of time. In 1975, the three of them shared this city, unaware of each other. For Rosemary, it was the year The Story began. For Anderson, it was the middle of the sameness of his life. In the inky stillness, he conjures her in the predawn streets of Midtown, January of 1975. Where was he, and what was he doing at that hour?

It's six forty, still dark. Rosemary scurries along the pavement on her way to work. She's a girl of twenty-five but looks older in her nappy wool overcoat and sensible, rubber-soled shoes. Winter is her friend, a time when outdoor offenders are put on ice. She avoids any close, overheated indoor space. She avoids the subway with its coffee spills, underarms, garlic, perfume, earwax, intestinal gasses, hair, breath, mothballs, greasy take-out, and aftershave.

Rosemary walks a mile to the forty-six-story office building of her employer, a monstrous insurance under-writer. Her cubicle on the thirty-third floor is stacked with claim forms. Check, check, check. She's the first employee ever to be granted flextime—a special medical dispensation for a disability of an indeterminate nature. In by seven, hungry by eleven, Rosemary takes her lunch every day at that early hour, avoiding the crowd. Food is not permitted in her cubicle, but the company offers more than one option for dining in the building.

On the second floor, a cafeteria exudes tumultuous, clashing odors. Spaghetti and meatballs. Fried chicken. French fries. Pizza. Turkey, gravy, and mashed potatoes. Hot and sour pork. Tacos and enchiladas. Rosemary avoids the second floor. On the third floor, the options are less fragrant. There's a lunchroom for brown baggers, offering a perfume of burnt crusts from the toaster oven, and an automat, where the food is pre-packaged in cellophane bags, neatly slotted into machines. Sterile, odorless, chrome, glass, plastic. Refrigerated. Rosemary always eats lunch in the automat, where her usual choice is American cheese on white and a bottle of sparkling water.

On the first day of The Story, another early lunch taker sits alone at a small table on the other side of the room. Rosemary has seen him before and feels embarrassed by her interest in him. She lowers her head and nibbles one corner of the white sponge in her hand, barely able to swallow the marble. Surrendering to an irresistible urge, her eyelids flutter upward, but he's gone. Disappointed, fighting tears, she drops her eyes to the table, unable to eat. Her nostrils prickle. There's a shift in the atmosphere, a softening of the air, and her nose relaxes. When she looks up, he's suddenly there.

"Hello," he says in a pleasing voice, clearly nervous. He's gaunt and pale, a sign of ill health, but his eyes burn with the desire to overcome his frailty. She smiles at him as she clutches a napkin in her lap. If he were someone else, that napkin would instantly be pressed to her nose in her usual pretense of needing to stop a drip. But something about him elicits the opposite need. She wants him to come closer.

"Hello," she replies.

He glances at the half-eaten sandwich while the fingertips of his right hand stroke the tabletop in round movements. "I had the same one today. American. I'm also okay with cream cheese."

In this, she hears a confession more exciting than any pickup line, but she holds back, not wanting to assume. "You're fond of milder cheeses then?"

"Fond?" He laughs heartily, revealing his true nature. "Those are the things I can barely eat!"

She laughs along with him, suddenly sure of his meaning. When silence falls again, their eyes meet in a sustained, intuitive gaze. It makes her feel daring, and she invites him to sit.

"My name is Rosemary," she says.

"I'm Reuben."

They shake hands across the table. "Forgive me," she says, "but, just now, I couldn't help wondering. Do you suffer from hyperosmia?"

He shakes his head, but his eyes sparkle. "No. Hypergeusia."

Sudden joy! Their teeth have never been so whitely exposed to the world.

Late at night, Rosemary lies awake at Reuben's side, thinking of Anderson sitting alone at the corner table with shame written on his face. Framed by his two forearms, the cranberry sorbet melts into the tuile cup on his plate, barely tasted. He's a curious character with a precisely crafted goatee, cherry-apple cheeks, and alarming intensity.

The Ole Factory has seen many solo diners over the years. Every sitting includes at least one, despite the lost revenue from an empty seat that easily could be filled. It's a tradition rooted in kindness. Recalling their many lonely sojourns in the automat before they met, Rosemary and Reuben feel an especial fondness for those who, by choice or necessity, must dine alone. These people, more than any others, are deserving of a sumptuous meal, or at least, the effort to deliver such a meal to them.

Anderson's ill-concealed torment haunts her. She feels no fondness or affinity for this man. She blinks him away and recalls other faces of single diners from times long past. A gallery of aging lonely hearts. Kindness? Is that truly her motivation? For the first time, she suspects something else. Arrogance. Maybe even cruelty.

A teardrop descends, carving a path along her cheekbone, making a final plunge into her ear.

In his coal black room, suffering from reflux, Anderson pulls the covers up to his chin and welcomes the chilly air on his cheeks. The Story is momentarily interrupted by a recurring image. He sees that dark-haired young man at the next table, depositing lascivious whisperings into the ear of his tawny-skinned lover. His lips touch the outer curve of cartilage, moving warmly and moistly against the opening of the auditory canal.

In his youth, Anderson had a handful of failed affairs. He was naturally timid with the opposite sex and moved slowly, afraid of rejection. Women usually left him even before he contemplated a move. Analyzing his failures, he resolved, in one instance, to move faster. That, too, resulted in a stinging rejection. *How dare you!* Her face is still vivid in his mind. She's the marching majorette with the thrusting baton at the head of his lifelong parade of humiliations.

His gratitude for the carefully placed corner table is fading. To be sure, that sexy couple was deliberately placed in close proximity. Why should Rosemary be entitled to make such arrangements? Shame might have been her fate too, if not for the fortuitous arrival of Reuben in 1975. Everything about her today might have been the same—the roundness, the tight bun at the nape of her neck, the skin translucent like filo dough—except for her brow, which might have been crimped and hard as a rim of crust instead of smooth like the uncooked pie shell that it is. It could have been.

But no, Rosemary meets Reuben a second time in the automat, and a third, and then it's on to greater things. A sexual conquest isn't on their minds, or even possible in light of their disabilities. Not immediately. They set foot on a cautious path toward healing.

Rosemary refrigerates all her food to mask the smell, but the ingredients are not always flavorless. The first night that Reuben visits her apartment, she serves a chilled pasta salad. What could be blander? White shells barely greased in the lightest virgin olive oil with green peas and a tiny shaving of red vegetable for flavor. It's cold and odorless, but Reuben nearly gags on the pimento.

"Dear Reuben! I'm so sorry."

Tears fill his eyes, and his fingertips race hectically along the tabletop. "Please don't be sorry. Let me try it again."

He clutches the fork in his right hand while touching her forearm with his left, girding for the excruciating hyper-sensitivity of his taste buds. But something magical happens. With the next bite he relaxes, and the magnificence of tang hits him in all its glory. "Pimento! So *that's* what it is!" He takes another bite. "Excellent. Give me more."

For dessert, they have vanilla ice cream. He encourages her to let it melt a bit, releasing the sweet fragrance. She leans toward the bowl and sniffs at the vanilla, cream, and sugar, but immediately she turns away. His heart goes out to her. Reaching across the table, he takes her delicate earlobe between thumb and index finger. She turns her head toward him, bringing her nose closer to the hand on her ear.

"Your skin is very soft," he says, like whispering in a closet.

She's intoxicated by the smell of his skin and the sound of his voice. How can it be? "Say that again," she says.

"Your skin…"

"Wait until I get a spoonful."

"No, *you* wait!" He drops his hand. "We'll do it together. Just… You'll have to, I mean, will you let me touch you?"

"Yes, please." She blushes.

They each scoop up a spoonful of ice cream. He waits while she holds her spoon under her nose, and he takes her earlobe again with his free hand. "Your skin is very soft." Her head clears and the nausea vanishes. With their eyes locked, they open their mouths to receive the cool sweet at the same time, each knowing the pleasure of every sense in perfect balance and proportion.

* * *

Standing at the edge of Anderson's table, Rosemary is suddenly in the grip of a revulsion she hasn't felt in years. The pong he emits is foul indeed, despite the cardamom in his coffee, a bad-breath neutralizer. His cup still holds most of the liquid, growing cold. She's compelled to cover her nose and mouth. He sees and understands. If this is kindness, it's the cruelest sort. She exerts the willpower she once needed so desperately, and her hand falls away.

"It's been our pleasure. Is there anything else we can get for you? Anything at all?"

She pauses, hoping he'll say no. She'd rather move on to that young couple at the next table. Their juicy bodies telegraph their enjoyment of each other and their complete satisfaction with the culinary masterpiece they've just consumed.

At Reuben's apartment, the food is bland and spiceless but warm, releasing its aroma. On her first visit, when he opens the front door, the smell hits her. Something is cooking in the kitchen. Later, she'll confront it on her plate: the boned and skinned chicken breast, no grease, no salt, no pepper, no herbs. But first, all she knows is an overpowering smell of gamey flesh. Her head tightens in pain and her stomach does backflips. She covers her nose with one hand while the other hand clutches the string of a boxed apple pie she's brought for dessert. It's still cold, and she's anxious to get it into the refrigerator.

"Rosemary," he says, moving toward her, touching the hand that covers her nose. It's enough. The smell of his skin replaces everything. In this way, she's leaping ahead of him. She has the scent and sound of him, but he doesn't have the taste of her. Only touch.

That evening, they take new baby steps. For Reuben, the chemistry of touch starts to regulate the pain and pleasure of taste. During the meal, he holds Rosemary's forearm with his left hand while eating. "It's as if I've never touched the skin of another human being before," he muses.

Batting her eyelashes mockingly she says, "You expect me to believe that?" She's acting the coquette, wanting to provoke a response so that his words will diffuse the molecules of cooked bird invading her nose. The mellifluence of his voice regulates the pain and pleasure of scent.

"If I've touched anyone before, it's never been like this. My fingers are melting into your skin. I have a feeling I could eat *anything!*" He sprinkles a bite-sized piece of chicken with salt and pepper, forks it into his mouth, chews and swallows, all the while holding onto Rosemary's forearm. His taste buds are calmed by the touch. "Almost too easy. Maybe even a little bland."

After dinner, in their anxiety about the pie, he insists on heating it because he loves the bouquet, a mixture of warm apple, cinnamon, and butter. She's able to tolerate it only because he's near. She no longer needs his hand next to her nose because his pheromone is released into the air, traces of his skin and everything it oozes—the oil, perspiration, and foods he's eaten. His thoughts and desires.

They sit down to their dessert. "What a delicious aroma," he says. But she notices his hesitance in taking a bite. He distracts her with a question. "Have you ever made a pie before?"

"I'm afraid not. I purchased this one because I've heard it's the best." She glances at the box, which bears the logo of a famous pie shop. Fearing a seizure if she set foot in the shop, she ordered it by phone for delivery to her apartment. "I'd like to be able to bake a dessert, but I'm sure it's impossible. Maybe I could handle the dough if it's cold enough. But it would get warm in my hands, wouldn't it?"

"Warm or cold, I think you could do it. You're surviving this heavenly scent right now, aren't you?"

"But you're here with me."

"Then, maybe we should cook together."

Briefly, her eyes reflect disbelief, and in the next instant, her face lights up. "Yes. I'd love it!" No one is more surprised than Rosemary to be excited at the thought of baking with all of its sensory consequences. Reuben makes anything possible. She notices then that her mouth has started to salivate heavily. Her enjoyment of the apple-cinnamon smell is translating into an urgent desire for a mouth-stuffing bite. Eagerly, she chops off a hefty forkful and shoves it in, clumsily leaving a morsel of crust and apple goo on her lower lip. She lifts her napkin to wipe it away, but he stops her.

"Let me do it." With an index finger, Reuben gently wipes at the crumb, taking it up with a bit of saliva from her glistening lip. He sticks his finger in his mouth, and his eyes go wide.

He's discovered the taste of her.

At the end of their evening together, they stand awkwardly in the tight space near his front door. She hopes to have stored enough of his essence—inhaled and deposited on her skin and clothing—to last until the next time they meet. Tentatively, he takes her in his arms and gently touches his lips to hers. The kiss deepens and calms his throbbing taste buds as he sucks and drinks her taste. They each take enough of the other to last until morning when, at eleven o'clock, they will meet again in the automat.

Someday, the cafeteria? With Reuben, anything is possible.

Rosemary sees the artery throbbing in Anderson's throat, telling her that their conversation isn't over yet. He's working himself up to ask The Question. It's a predictable inquiry that many solo diners have posed, but tonight, she's not in the mood for it. Not from him.

The color rises in his cheeks. "I *am* curious," he begins. "I'm wondering, is it true?"

She knows exactly what he means. A thousand people have asked it, and she has never been annoyed—until now. The odor emanates from his mouth as he speaks, hovering in the space between them. She does her best to ignore it while she smiles and waits for him to explain, as if she didn't understand.

"The Story. On the back of that card, the menu. I'd like to know. Is it true?"

The Question is an insult. Why has it taken her so long to know this? From the point of view of the inquisitor, two answers are possible: yes or no. Even odds. Anderson is suggesting a fifty-fifty chance that, for thirty-five years, she and Reuben have promulgated a lie on the back of their menu.

Perhaps no one else has ever seemed as earnest as this

Mr. Anderson. Her answer to everyone else is always the same, cheerfully given, maybe with a little laugh. *Yes, every word is true. Life is stranger than fiction, wouldn't you agree?*

This man requires something else. She echoes, "Is it true?" in a musing tone. "Let me put it like this. We've distilled our Story into about fifty words on the back of that card. The words decorate the page like the garnish on your plate—they're indispensable to the presentation, but only a small part of the meal."

As soon as the answer leaves her mouth, she's unsure if she actually said it. At any rate, it's what she wanted to say.

Only a small part of the meal. By three in the morning, The Story is well underway, and Anderson doesn't have much difficulty completing it.

After the exciting apple pie night, Rosemary and Reuben are inseparable. The symbiotic lovers are on their way to achieving the complete synthesis and perfect harmony of taste, touch, smell, and sound.

Every afternoon, at the end of their workday, they walk out of the building together, headed for his apartment or hers. "What shall we cook tonight?" They discuss the contents of their refrigerators, the ingredients they desire, and whether a trip to the market is necessary.

At first they keep it easy, nothing pungent or biting, piquant, sharp, or spicy to burn the tongue or sting the nostrils. Mashed potatoes are safe. Gradually, they start to add things: garlic or fresh grated parmesan, mushrooms or onions, sour cream and butter, lots of it. Chicken is safe. Later they add sage and start to experiment with paprika, green chili, shallots and white wine, stewed tomatoes and oregano. Fish is not safe, but eventually it makes the list. Filet of sole, unseasoned. On to salmon, broiled with Dijon and dill. Whiting with capers and lemon. Lobster with jalapeño and lime.

One evening, in the sixth month of their union, Reuben takes a cold shrimp by the tail, scoops up the tangy cocktail sauce they've crafted, and inserts the curled body into Rosemary's mouth. The offering is cold, but the horseradish penetrates the nasal membranes. Her nose, with its sharply pointed tip, has changed in the past months. The nostrils, which once appeared painfully sucked in, white rimmed, and narrow, have relaxed to their full, round circumference.

She chews, luxuriating in the zesty taste, and scolds him, "Didn't I tell you, Rube?" She scrunches her nose for emphasis. "Only a dash. You're trying to kill me with this stench." Her eyes shine, more from loving him and kidding around than from the odor of the horseradish.

"I didn't add any more than a soupçon, my love."

"Let's see about that."

"Testing me, are you?"

She takes up a firm piece of succulent white flesh with its painted coral stripes and applies a liberal layer of sauce. "Open your mouth." It hovers near his opening. Reuben has also changed. His lips are still slender, but the inside of his mouth has emerged from its shriveled constriction, pushing his lips out to their maximum fullness. A sexy mouth, Rosemary would say.

He pulls back, like the old days. They like to tease each other this way. All a prelude.

"Come on, now," she says.

Like a dutiful little boy, he opens his mouth to receive the acerbic treat. "Ouch! It does have a kick, doesn't it? I need a kiss." His favorite excuse. Their kiss turns into unbridled passion, and they make love for an hour before serving the entrée.

Indispensable to the presentation, but only a small part of the meal.

Rosemary doesn't follow the usual script with this man. She doesn't ask him, "Did you enjoy your dinner?" because she knows he wouldn't follow the usual script either.

Most of her solo guests are circumspect in their compliments. They tell her that the food is "just fine" or "very nice." Everyone else uses adjectives that range from "superb" to "heavenly" to "delectable." Because of this difference, Rosemary has every right to impart a bit of advice to the singles: "If you return, bring a companion next time. I guarantee, the experience will be improved."

But, no, she doesn't ask this man whether he enjoyed his dinner. In the aftermath of her statement about The Story, Anderson perks up and shows his indignation. "I've read some things about this restaurant that I don't find to be true."

"Oh? And what are the untrue things?"

"'Always a surprise, always superb.'"

"Well, you can't say it wasn't a surprise."

"Yes, certainly a surprise, but very far from superb."

"I'm sorry to hear that. Perhaps, Mr. Anderson...," and she's about to impart the usual advice to dine with a companion, when she realizes it would be wasted on him. "I can see that you expected more."

"I expected something with flavor, that's for sure. Taste. Aroma. Texture."

"And you got none?"

He screws up his nose and shakes his head in disgust. "Your server told me that the thing on my plate was a duck confit of sorts with *pommes de terre sarladaises*. Is that true?"

Again, with the "true." She says nothing.

"Indigestible grease. And the vegetables. Carrots, of all things. I know. You're going to say that the oyster mushrooms and onions make it special." He's working himself up into a lather. "I *did* taste the peppercorns, but in theory only. Actually, those little pebbles were like the grit on unwashed asparagus. And the thyme. Stuck in my teeth like shards of crabgrass."

Is this man saying these things? He looks as if he's unable to speak, yet Rosemary hears it all, feeling the heat of that sexy couple on her back.

He continues. "You call this a treat, a delight, a savory meal? You call yourselves chefs, master cooks?"

These are his last words. He gets up, steps away from her, and stumbles over his chair. The single chair at his table.

"Rube." It's three in the morning. She gives him a little squeeze on a fleshy love handle. "Reuben."

He rolls over to face her. "Wha...?"

"I can't sleep."

His eyes pop open in the dark. They're lying on their sides, his right, her left. The gauzy curtain filters the light from the street. Searching for his eyes, she discerns only a spectral gleam. He takes in a deep breath, puts a hand on her shoulder, and asks, "Why not?"

"We're getting old."

"Hmm. Old people sleep very well, thank you."

"No, I mean it's bothering me. That we're getting old."

"We're sixty-five. That isn't old."

"We're getting there."

"Like everyone else."

"And something else is bothering me. I don't want to retire."

"We don't have to. No one says we must."

"Okay. But we haven't talked about what happens to the person left behind when the other one dies. I can't bear the thought of it."

"Aren't you jumping the gun a little bit?"

"We have to think about it."

"Then we won't."

"I can't stop thinking about it."

"I mean we won't die one at a time. We'll go together."

"That's impossible."

"Suicide pact maybe?" He's been stroking the top of her head, and now he's running his hand along the side of her face and down to her neck.

"Not that. Not now."

"You need to forget."

"I can't."

"It's that man again, isn't it? The one you told me about earlier."

"Maybe it is."

"Why does he upset you so much?"

Rosemary visualizes the face with its need and dismay and accusation. "Why do we keep inviting the singles?"

"We always have."

"It seems terribly wrong to me."

"You've never thought like this before."

"Are we gloating over ourselves?"

"Not in the least."

"Maybe I just didn't like him. He isn't like the other single patrons. They're all a little sad maybe, but appreciative and accepting."

"You're wrong, my dear. I remember another one like him. At least one, maybe more."

"I don't remember."

"Maybe five years ago. A woman."

"The woman who wrote to us afterward?"

"Exactly her. She was just as confused and jealous."

"I don't think this man is jealous."

"If not jealous, he's in pain, so he took it out on you. It's the kind of pain that comes when…" Reuben stops to think a moment, "…when you've just been given a hard pill to swallow."

"You're saying he's starting to understand."

"That's my guess."

"Well." She stops to think. "I suppose that's the good of it, but we're still responsible for what happened to him."

"You analyze too much, my dear."

"But we're responsible, and I'm worried."

"About him?"

"No. About my lack of love or caring for him."

"Pity isn't a good foundation for love, or for any kind of good feeling."

She ponders this, and the room becomes darker in its silence.

Finally, Reuben says, "Even though you're *not* worried about him"—he's mocking her—"there's no need for worry anyway. That woman turned out all right."

"How so?"

"Her letter of apology. She explained what happened to her, and how her life became better. This man is like her in some ways. You'll see."

"He'll never write us a letter."

"It doesn't matter. I could see it in his eyes and that little self-righteous swagger. Maybe he'll keep his little protections, but he'll get over us. It's only a matter of time. He'll taste and smell again. And maybe more."

"You're sure of that?"

"Very sure."

"But it won't be at *our* restaurant that his taste returns."

"And why not?"

"He won't be asking for a return visit."

"That's true," says Reuben. "It will be somewhere else then. At a senior social, when a blue-haired lady offers him a stale cookie. The taste will be like heaven."

She laughs softly, cheered by the image.

"Come here now." Reuben pulls her close and blocks out everything in the world but him.

§○

Gray Zone

I DIDN'T NOTICE what went on between them until that September, a couple of months after *Proffitt v. Florida*, when death was again possible, intensely upon us. It was 1976. William Douglas Jones had just been sentenced under Florida's capital punishment law, found constitutional in *Proffitt*, and we were searching for mitigation, anything to convince an appellate court that Jones had been wrongly condemned to death.

The case weighed heavier than its two-thousand-page transcript, which Emma and I slogged through in chunks, the tissue-thin paper clinging to our sweaty fingertips. The heat was moist and the air thick with emerging personality—those secrets kept from me all the previous year.

Several recent setbacks for the Poverty Law Center added to our discomfort. My buffers, the older, more experienced attorneys, had left, Betty to care for her ailing father, and Keith to join a law firm. In the heat of August, our single, battered air conditioner in the communal office went down, and then, after Labor Day, our three summer interns in the anteroom went back to law school. A little money could have fixed these shortcomings, but the federal grant had been cut and private contributions were down as the popular sentiment swung slightly in favor of public execution, now that the Supreme Court had called an end to the moratorium.

Keith and Betty's absence should have given us more air to breathe in our shared space, but oddly enough, the extra room closed us in on one another. Emma and I, our tension, expanded into the vacancy, and what little remained was filled by increasing visits from Blake Adamson, our executive director. Wearing such an impressive title at the tender age of thirty-four, Blake worked at fostering a dual image of colleague and authority figure to Emma and me, both twenty-seven and only a few years out of law school. The mixture was imprecise and fed my transient bouts of insecurity despite the congenial looseness of our tight-knit group.

Blake would spring unexpectedly from his tiny private office, the door opening directly into our room, just poking his nose in or staying a while, mostly to hover over Emma. At first, I took these extra visits as a sign of his anxiety about the diminishing ranks and our inability to move through the stacks of waiting appeals. We were forced to concentrate on one case at a time, whichever presented the most compelling crisis. That September it was William Douglas Jones.

Our office, Emma's and mine, was a square room not much bigger than my Park Avenue office is today, crammed with four child-size desks. Each of three walls held a desk, and the fourth wall was cut in half by Blake's door, sandwiched by file cabinets. The fourth desk, mine, was plunked exactly in the middle of the room. No other place for it.

Emma was on the wall to my left.

At the time, I never paused to consider why I didn't switch to one of the vacant desks when our two colleagues resigned. Now I understand. Emma, Keith, and Betty all sat facing their respective walls, but I sat in the middle, facing Blake's door. I wanted to see him coming, to face him head on. And because I wanted that, I must have sensed Emma's need for protection, although it could never be said that her behavior lent a clue to her need.

Decades have passed, but some things I still miss. Not very many. Certainly not Blake, although I can't seem to erase the memory of him. Emma. Certainly Emma, when I get past a personal sense of betrayal and remind myself that it wasn't a socially conditioned covetousness that drew me to her. It was, quite simply, just Emma.

Whatever her external form, the remarkable qualities would have shone through. Openness, vibrancy, resilience. She defied and resisted categorization. She was not female, white, brunette, or middle-class Protestant; she was not a Georgetown graduate, a Florida native, a holdover '60s idealist, or a Poverty Law Center attorney. My act of conceiving this list, its blackness on whiteness, mirrors our faces, and probably says more about me than about her. In my mind's eye she reacts—incredulous, without disdain.

Some other things I miss: pulling on a pair of khakis and a polo shirt, walking to the office in that perpetual Florida sunshine, eating a messy sandwich for lunch at the park across the street. Sometimes with Emma, sometimes the three of us. The camaraderie of a shared purpose, the downtrodden holding hands against the world. The excitement of youth, intelligence, and idealism—my belief in idealism, until it faded. Transformed is a better word, for the only thing I've discarded is Blake's type of altruism, his establishment idealism.

He would laugh to hear me say that. *"Establishment* idealism? Who's the real establishment figure here, Verne?" Today, so many years later, he would still call me Verne, although I never invited him to shorten my full name, Vernon.

Just like PLC days, I want to see what's coming. I've positioned my desk so that I face the door when seated. Every once in a while, I visualize Blake, frozen in my memory at age thirty-four, entering my office, this time knocking first. He steps in with his flaxen curls of the '70s and elbow-patch jacket, allowing his blue eyes to sweep the room before he speaks.

"Cushy. Pretty cushy," he says with a grin, afraid to articulate his true thoughts out of concern for political correctness. This is a gray zone for him. Am I a sellout or a role model? What he really thinks, I see in his eyes: Look at you, so well scrubbed and benign in your hand-tailored suit, behind your mahogany desk. Litigating expensive cases for millionaires. Have you forgotten where you came from? Have forgotten who you are—your people?

I always have the perfect response: Yes, I'm an expensive lawyer, but I do my share of *pro bono* cases, working free for the poor. My practice is scrupulously ethical. But none of this really matters to you. There were things about me you never took the time to learn.

And I say: No, I haven't forgotten where I came from.

We didn't have material things, but I had enough to eat, a stable home, a mother and father who loved each other, worked hard and cared. I suffered my share of nasty looks and closed doors but was spared my share of violence.

And I haven't forgotten who I am. Not merely a dark brown face within a smudged sea of bronze to black. I'm Vernon Thomas Sotherland Jr., husband of Ruby Lynn, father of Leora, Amity, and Reginald. These are my people, and the hundreds of others their lives will touch, a spectrum of color and individuality. How I treat them and what I teach them will spread and grow. Stability, respect, commitment, and love.

Of course, Blake always listens to me and nods his agreement. Something he never did back then.

Goosenecked over our transcripts, Emma and I would tilt up at the sound of the door, anticipating Blake's voice. "What's happening at Willie's trial?" he would ask day after day, as if we'd just returned from court. The defendant, Jones, had become "Willie," just as Emma was "Emmie," and I was "Verne." Lucky for me, Verne was an easy stopping place between Vernon and Vernie.

When he assigned the trial record, Blake disassembled it like a sandwich, two slices of bread for me, ham and cheese for Emma. My top slice was the beginning section, the part with the pretrial hearings and jury selection, and the bottom slice was the sentencing hearing at the end, after Jones had been convicted. Emma got the guts of the trial: the opening statements, the witnesses' testimony, the summations, and the court's instructions to the jury.

Slowly, I came to understand Blake's motivation for this division of labor. From Emma he wanted a legal technician, someone to spot the technical procedural issues that arise at trial. But from me, Blake was looking for something more, a social and political ally. My part of the transcript contained most of the juicy issues he thrived on. Were the cops just looking to hassle another black man when they searched the defendant's car? Were blacks selectively excluded from the jury in favor of closet racists? When the judge chose death, did he ignore Willie's disadvantaged background, his victimization, all those social forces that molded him, quite involuntarily, into a killer?

I looked for the answers to these questions, the answers I knew Blake wanted to hear, but day after day, I failed to find them. They just weren't there. William Douglas Jones, serial killer, was important to the police and prosecutors, and they'd been very, very careful every step of the way, building an airtight case and trying Jones on the one murder with the most compelling evidence.

Emma, too, wasn't giving Blake the answers he needed. "There's really nothing here," Emma told him one Friday morning when she'd nearly finished reading her portion of the trial. It was the day I began to see things. "This is the cleanest transcript I've ever read."

Blake smiled. "In your long career."

"In my very long and distinguished tenure with this esteemed organization."

"Such as it is, Emmie."

"Yes."

Emma had turned in her chair to face Blake, and her profile was visible to me. She smiled wanly, her repartee falling flat. Blake took the four steps from his doorway to the space between Emma's desk and mine and stood behind her chair, peering down at the open transcript on her desk. All but a sliver of Emma disappeared from my view, behind Blake. He seemed to be standing very close to her, his beltline even with the top of Emma's head, and he touched her shoulder—that much I could see. Not so unusual for Blake, a person who touched frequently as proof of his warmth and connection to humankind.

"What am I going to do with you two?" asked Blake, his back to me, massaging Emma's shoulder. He lifted his hand, pointed a finger at Emma's head, and buzzed an imitation of a ray gun. "The thought police have sucked out your brains! You've metamorphosed into fledgling Assistant County Attorneys! Give me that transcript! Just give it to me!" He leaned over her head and lifted the huge binder of onion skin a few inches from the desk, then let it fall, as if it were too heavy for him.

All of this was a joke of course. There was a lot of joking. Blake had a way about him, and I could sense Emma's smile without seeing her face. He hooked a strand of her waist-length dark hair and stroked it between finger and thumb. This seemed too intimate, even for Blake, but Emma didn't react.

"There is one thing," she said.

"Oh, she's found *one* thing. The trial is almost over and there's *one* thing!" Blake looked backward over his shoulder, not at me exactly, but as if to remember me, and he replaced Emma's strand of hair.

"A little rhetorical flourish by the prosecutor during the summation."

"A flourish," Blake said with a French accent.

"Here's what the prosecutor said." She started to read: "'Just imagine it, ladies and gentlemen. Mary Griffin coming home from work, just two blocks to go, almost home, and this defendant waiting in the shadows, a snake in the grass, viper's fangs dripping, coiled up for the strike.'"

"Animalistic metaphors. Reversible error. New trial." Blake whirled around to gauge my reaction, looking for a sting on personal sensibilities. Emma's big find bordered on my area of "expertise"—the thing that Blake needed me for—and he was testing me.

Unimpressed, I said nothing, just shrugged my shoulders. I doubted that the jurors had convicted Jones out of a mistaken belief that he was a poisonous snake in need of extermination.

Blake wouldn't take a shrug for an answer. He needed dialogue, and his blue eyes bore into me, looking for a response. "Maybe snakes don't offend you? What if the prosecutor called Willie a chimp or gorilla? One of those nasty ape metaphors?"

The blood rose to my face, a reaction invisible to Blake's eyes, which only saw the surface. There was nothing I could hope to say that wouldn't be sapped of credibility in the heat of Blake's intensity and conviction.

"That's the trouble, Verne," he went on. "You need to put yourself in Willie's shoes, sit at the defense table next to your sweaty, inept, underpaid court-appointed attorney and see how it feels to be called a dripping-fanged viper, knowing you're innocent of this heinous crime."

"Innocent?" I managed.

"You, Verne. We're talking about you. Did *you* kill

Mary Griffin? The cops are circling the ghetto one night and they spot you in your rusty Cadillac and say, 'well, he fits the description.' Five-ten, one-sixty, dark-skinned Negro. It's all so scientific, Verne. You know you're innocent. You know you're the type of guy who brakes for squirrels. But it doesn't matter to them. The cops know they're right, and even if they're wrong, to them you look like the kind who could rape and mutilate their white daughters and sisters, so they search your car, maybe plant a few of Mary's hairs from the crime scene. They give you this sorry mistake of a defense lawyer, put you on trial for murder, and to top it off, they call you a venomous reptile, coiled for the strike. How does it feel now, Verne? How does it feel?"

I couldn't speak, and I hated myself for it, as much as I hated Blake in that moment. I kept my eyes on him, knowing that I needed to show this small kernel of strength while I grappled with the decency (or timidity) that prevented me from expressing my rage at his insult and his obliviousness to it. I groped for Emma with invisible touch and sensed the quality of her energy. There was a change in her. The awe and delight she often expressed for Blake's little expositions had been replaced with a tired sort of annoyance.

"I, I have trouble with that," I said finally.

"Trouble with what?"

"With the concept of the defendant's—*this* defendant's, innocence." I caught myself before the nickname "Willie" slipped from my mouth, sure that Blake's habit of using diminutives was just as objectionable when applied to a serial killer.

Blake took a single step toward his door, swiveled to face me once again, and laughed like a father would laugh at an erring child, sure of his superior knowledge and experience, but good-natured, without malice. "Then why are you here? Why are you helping this son of a bitch?"

Feeling the hot seat, I couldn't prevent a glance at Emma, hoping my desperation didn't show. In that glance we shared the knowledge of Blake's ploy. He couldn't possibly believe in Jones's innocence, although he never would admit it.

"The death penalty is unfairly applied to some and not others," I said. "Besides, the Constitution guarantees a fair trial for everyone. We're defending all our rights here, not just this defendant's."

In Blake's smile I saw recognition of his philosophy — the part I still believed and had successfully mimicked — before his face changed to that look of inviolable sincerity, a familiar, convincing expression. "A nice thing, Verne. A nice side benefit. But your client isn't the Constitution. Your client is Willie Jones. And how can you be so sure of his guilt? Who's God here? How do you know that, ten years after Willie fries in the chair, you won't hear about the new evidence that proves this was all a big mistake?"

Leaden silence hung between us, and then, instantly, I was invisible again. Blake had turned his eyes on Emma, and he stared hard at her for seconds that ticked with inevitability. She was frozen in her chair, boldly returning his stare while he stood above us with arms crossed, evaluating the extent of her resistance.

"Life," he said like a preacher, his voice scratchy with emotion. He paused before continuing, still looking at Emma. "Life is here and gone in an instant. Think about it, Verne." An invisible Verne.

Blake didn't want my answer and he didn't wait for Emma's but turned to go. At his office door, before closing it behind him, he remembered me and aimed the ray gun. "Find something," he said.

Emma turned away from Blake's door and sat with her back to me, hunched over her transcript. Stillness. For a long time, I waited to hear the crackle of turning pages.

Later that day, Emma did another new thing. She recruited me as her ally in a lunchtime escape from the office. I'd had lunch with Emma many times, but never in a sneaky way, always very open. Informally, but in compliance with an unspoken rule, we would tell Blake we were stepping out, giving him the opportunity to join us or not, as he pleased. A yell through the door was enough.

An hour or so after Blake's retreat, while his door was still closed, Emma turned to me and whispered, "I have to get out of here. Come on."

The command confused then overwhelmed me in the moment it took to understand its significance. Without hesitation, I stood to join her. Neither of us yelled at Blake through the door.

Outside, the immense sunshine and diffuse heat were a relief from our sweltering box. On the way to the park she said, "Do we need to stop at the deli? I'm not very hungry, are you?"

"No," I lied.

"Look, there's some shade."

We were lucky enough to find a bench under the mimosa tree, and she offered an apple she'd been carrying in her handbag. I accepted it gratefully, uttering a few words that diminished my need for it. The important thing was to be alone with her, to be favored with her request for my exclusive company, out from under the imminent presence of Blake.

"I didn't know you had a rusty Cadillac."

"Neither did I." Our eyes met, and we both smiled before she looked away, gazing into the distance.

A moment later, "He can be a bit much sometimes, can't he?" She turned to me again, this time her eyes wide with sadness. So beautiful in her sadness.

"More than a bit," I said.

"I used to find that attractive. I saw only the good intentions, and his belief in his good intentions. But he's blind to a few things about himself, isn't he?" She didn't expect me to answer. Her mouth turned up into a little smile that told me she could imagine being inside darker skin and could feel what it was like being me, listening to Blake, but would never presume her entitlement to frame that feeling in words and demand my agreement. I thanked her silently for that and knew then that I loved her.

The moment was soon gone. "I won't be at work on Monday," she said. "Maybe Tuesday too, depending. I know it's a bad time to take off, but there's something I've got to do. I can't get out of it. Sorry to leave you alone with Blake."

"I'll survive. But what's—"

"How's Nadine doing?"

"Nadine," I echoed. My girlfriend at the time, a law student, a woman I liked very much but did not love. Early on, when I'd begun to doubt that I had a chance with Emma—or that I should risk the consequences even if she had some interest—I may have verbally puffed Nadine's significance, just to let Emma know I wasn't a sorry fellow. "She's doing just fine," I said.

"This is her last year?"

"Yes. Studying hard already. Toward finals, she'll vanish completely." Not such a sorry fellow, but maybe left alone at times. That was the implication, something for Emma to pick up on, if she wished.

Emma smiled again, still low. "You're a lucky man."

"Lucky?"

"To have a big love. Some of us just have mistakes. Mistakes that breed other mistakes."

At that moment I didn't understand. Not many days later, I would discover Emma's "mistake" in my memory of the countless little things I'd failed to evaluate. But for then, my discovery not yet made, her mistake took the form of a ponderous, nameless thing, a tragedy for her, and the messenger of my failed opportunity.

Inside, I cried out to her. *Emma, my big love.* She leaned toward me and put her head on my shoulder, and we sat that way in silence for a long time, people walking by, wondering.

That Monday, Emma gone, Blake proposed we do our field work, and we set off early for the penitentiary. This would be my first visit with a convicted murderer. Keith had always been the one to accompany Blake on these interviews with our clients, but now it was my turn.

The car trip took a good two hours. I'd spent a lot of time with Blake but never such a long time alone with him, no one and nothing else to distract us. No possibility of escape.

Early into the trip, its dual purpose became apparent to me. Blake's anger sought an outlet, and I became his target, the recipient of biting remarks and petty sarcasm that soon developed into bigger issues. Confused more than threatened, I did little to defend myself. I'd done nothing to deserve his ire, except, perhaps, to be the unfortunate, daily reminder to him of something beyond our control: we hadn't a prayer of helping Jones.

We'd found no surprise evidence of his innocence, no illegal police conduct, no unfair trial tactics. There were a few small complaints about the proceedings—the "viper" comment one of them—enough to fill an appellate brief, but nothing momentous enough to require reversal of his conviction. Still, we maintained a small hope of winning a reduction in his sentence from death to life imprisonment, and for that, we were looking for mitigating circumstances, anything from Jones's background or personality to arouse the court's sympathy and speak for clemency.

Blake, of course, sensed that I wasn't as passionately committed as he to saving Jones from the electric chair. In the course of reading the proof against Jones, I'd developed a visceral hatred of the man, an emotion that didn't easily lie low. An eye for an eye was not a difficult concept for me where William Douglas Jones was concerned, and by the time we neared the end of our trip to the pen, I came to believe that this was the source of Blake's anger: his frustration at being unable to mold my views to his own.

"You ever fried a living snake, Verne?"

From the passenger side of the front seat I glanced at

Blake, hoping that his casual manner of steering the car—right wrist atop the steering wheel, left elbow out the open window—was a disguise for innate attentiveness and dexterity. "No," I said.

"Probably not something you'd enjoy watching."

"Doubt it."

"I never fried one either, but I bet it would jump and squirm and pop for a long time before it died. A long time." He let that one rest for a couple of miles before he continued. "It's easy to sit in the office and smell Emmie's perfume and read a transcript. Easy at a distance to pass judgment and let someone else do the killing. But today you're going to see the flesh on Willie's bones. Flesh just like your own." He momentarily took his eyes off the road and flicked them at my face and hair, recording my features for easy reference and comparison later on. "When you see Willie, think of that flesh jumping and sizzling."

"Blake, you know I've been working on this case. Working hard on it."

"Blacks who kill whites get death five times more than whites who kill blacks. Think about it when you're talking to Willie."

"Don't you think I know that? Don't you think that's why I'm here?"

"But I know damn well you won't lose a night of sleep if Willie fries! You or Emmie."

"You can't say that about Emma."

He turned and looked at me longer than safety allowed. Icy blue. "Our hypocritical little Emmie, out taking care of business today!" He laughed and turned his eyes back on the road. "So she really wants to save Willie, but other little people aren't worth the bother? Maybe there's some distinction here I'm not getting. Maybe you know more about the way she thinks than I do. All that time together in your office, all those lunches in the park. So what did she tell you? She's done her own study on the condemned, his identity, his traits, and his lineage. Who is he, Verne? Where did he come from? Who's responsible for him? We know the mother, but do we ever know the father? Sometimes the color of his face can't hide his identity and society scorns him, so why not make it easier? Let's execute him and prevent another life of pain. Isn't that what Emmie really thinks? *Isn't it?*"

The emotion showed, and he was aware of it. He held back then, and we didn't speak again until we reached our destination, while I silently evaluated my memories—the looks, the touches, the times they'd been together alone. My heart sank low.

The prison was just as I'd imagined it. Two guards led us down an echoing linoleum corridor, the air stale with antiseptic and body odor. Death row might have been worse than death, something easier to lose sleep over than the finality of the electric chair.

But when I saw Jones, there wasn't much about his flesh to arouse my sympathy. Never having laid eyes on us before, he had difficulty understanding that we were there to help him. Physically and verbally he expressed his distrust. Before letting us near him, the guards made much of shackling Jones by his wrists and ankles to a chair bolted into the floor.

"We're your lawyers, man," said Blake, over and over.

"Ain't no lawyers," spat Jones, looking at me alone. He was missing half his teeth, and the remaining ones were large and yellow. I thought of the medical examiner's testimony: the bite marks in distinctive patterns.

Blake was louder than Jones and thoroughly convinced of his beliefs, giving him the ability to tranquilize the irrational with his own form of reasoned zealousness. Our client eventually understood and quieted enough to be interviewed. For the next half hour, we—mostly Blake—peppered him with questions, hoping to learn something encouraging that couldn't be gleaned from the court papers and written psychiatric reviews in our possession.

The chains rattled, shoes scuffed linoleum, and desperate laughter burst from Jones's lips between his two favorite sentences: "I'm innocent," and "Ask Mama." Blake failed to chip anything else loose, and we eventually surrendered to the prisoner's recalcitrance. Not having much else to go on, we decided to take Jones's advice and visit his mother, who lived a short distance from the penitentiary.

We didn't speak during the next leg of our journey, or later, on our way back to the office. Knowing what we suspected about one another, we couldn't possibly talk about the case or pretend an interest in our work. Under the hum of engine and traffic noise, I thought of a time, a year ago, when I was so taken with Blake I would have asked every naïve question about what he thought and knew, his psychological profile of our client and how it might help us in our fight for his life.

Briefly, I longed for that time, but my thoughts kept returning to Emma and the hideousness of Blake's confusion of thought, his mixture of victims, condemned murderers, and executioners, the lines smudged, individual colors and circumstances indistinguishable through the narrow reference of his jealousy and personal need, the emotions and biases facilely disguised as political platforms.

But my judgment of Blake caught up with me the moment we arrived in "Mama's" neighborhood, a row of houses not unlike the block I grew up on, very poor but neat. I was surprised that Jones had grown up in a house like mine, and I was reminded how easy it was to fall into the comfort of categories. Blake was guilty of this need for comfort, but weren't we all? And maybe Blake felt more keenly about others and distinguished more exactly than I gave him credit. He loved Emma, that much was clear. Loved her so deeply he was sick over it.

We knocked at the front door and were allowed entry. Jones's mother was a wisp of a woman, apparently stick thin under her shapeless cotton dress. Three or four adolescents wandered in and out of the living room as we talked, Blake and I on a lumpy couch, Mrs. Jones in a rocking recliner. The room was sparse, the surfaces rubbed to inner layers with age. A thick green glass ashtray sat on the low coffee table in front of us, a brass Jesus sagged on a cross affixed to the wall.

She offered us nothing and glanced upon us infrequently. Her eyes were vacant, devoid even of indifference. Trying to warm things up, Blake made small talk. "How many brothers and sisters does Willie have?"

"How many it say there?" She glanced at the folder in Blake's hand.

Caught in his knowing omission, Blake laughed and

said, "Was it eight?"

"Could be it."

He went on to other subjects, asking how Willie had done in school as a child, what his interests were. Each time, her answer was about "them," her children, apparently one and the same. "They always be doin" this, or "they always talkin like" that. She seemed unaware of her son's murder conviction and incarceration, although Blake and I knew the opposite; she had been interviewed more than once by probation authorities who must have told her, even if she'd been oblivious to the extensive news coverage at the time of Jones's arrest and trial.

Perhaps hoping to provoke a response, Blake hinted at a few details of Willie's crimes, the torture and mutilation. "Allegations," Blake still called the facts. It was then that her expression changed for the first time, a slight turning of the mouth that, for her, could be called a smile.

"Finga'n'toe," she said. "They used to call it."

Blake probed until she explained.

"Pigs feet. I make a stew and that what they always call it: 'finga'n'toe pot.'"

Emma only needed the Monday off. She was back on Tuesday, looking pale and tired. We arrived before Blake, and when he came in, he said "good morning" and barked our assignments as he walked through our office on the way to his own, then closed the door behind him.

After some time, alarmed at Emma's pallor, I asked how she was, thinking I hadn't revealed anything in the way I asked. But she gave me a searching look, leaned forward in her chair, and whispered, "Blake told you, didn't he?"

Her eyes made it impossible for me to hide, and so I told the truth. "Yes, but not in so many words." Should I go the next step? "He also—" I couldn't finish the sentence, but it was too late.

"What Vernon? He also what?"

"He also... He suspects me as the father. *Me*."

Her eyes widened. I couldn't stand to see her shock, and I glanced at Blake's closed door. "What did you say?" she whispered.

I kept my voice low. "Nothing. I didn't get it at first. He was talking about our lunches in the park—he must have seen us on Friday—and about Jones's mother and father and executions and...and then I got it."

She turned away from me, put her elbows on the desk, and buried her head in her hands. "I don't think I can see this case through, Vernon. I have to leave."

At that moment, Blake stepped in with an accusing look as if he'd heard us, although I knew he couldn't have. "You finished, Verne?"

"Not yet," I said, only two sentences on the yellow pad in front of me.

He looked at Emma. "Maybe you want to help Verne write up the summary of the mitigating circumstances. I'm sure you have some good ideas. Maybe this was a justified murder. Have we probed that angle yet? Did Mary Griffin deserve to die? Maybe Willie did us all a favor when he killed her. Or maybe he just *thought* she was someone who deserved to die. A case of mistaken identity. But that's okay, as long as he believed the world would be a better place without her. Right, Emmie? Some people shouldn't even be born, so why should Willie be electrocuted for that?"

"Stop it, Blake," said Emma.

"How about the psychological profile of a serial killer? All those women, one after another, it didn't much matter to him *who* he killed. Nothing personal against Mary Griffin, so what's so terrible about that? He was indiscriminate, unbiased. He picked up whoever was convenient, had a good time, tossed her away and picked up the next one. Not such offensive behavior, no bad feelings, no real malice involved. No love either—but so what? I could tell you about some people. Should we send someone to the chair for that?"

"Stop this! There wasn't anyone else! You're way off—" Emma's lips trembled.

"We know someone like that, don't we, Verne?"

I jumped from my seat. Blake stepped backward, his eyes popping open with alarm, then narrowing defensively. He knew he'd gone too far.

"I've been thinking about this hard," I said.

"Oh?" His sarcasm sounded like a parody of himself.

"I have a mitigating circumstance. A new one, not one of those you mentioned. It's one you haven't considered."

Blake and Emma kept their silence, as if they were relieved, my interruption saving them from each other.

"It came to me when we visited Mrs. Jones and I saw the way she regarded her own son, no more than one of her nine children, just another head in a swarm of heads. If there'd been anything unique about him when he was growing up, any small talent or interesting trait or special feature, she didn't notice or acknowledge it. His individuality was wasted and became emptiness. And whatever the reason, maybe it was a predisposition, Jones filled that emptiness with every bad impulse and desire. He wasn't seen, and he's angry. He may not know it, but he wanted to be seen, because that's what each one of us really wants. We want to be seen and heard apart from everyone else."

Emma stood then, and we were all standing, our eyes darting from one to the other, shame and pride dividing us. Emma picked up her handbag, I picked up my briefcase, and we walked out the door.

My final words to Blake may have been my finest, but I felt no righteousness or glory in them. For once, I had spoken my mind, but it was a small piece of a much larger map leading to so many thoughts and ideas left unsaid.

He had the decency, at least, to avoid retribution. He could have punished us for leaving him high and dry, alone with Willie, but he gave us only the most glowing recommendations when future employers called to inquire about our performance at PLC. And from what I heard, within a few weeks, he was fortunate enough to hire two decent attorneys to replace his wayward fledglings.

Emma and I kept in touch for a short time. She moved to D.C., joined a law firm, and soon after that stopped writing or calling. I moved to New York where I restarted my career, found my true "big love," and had a family.

And Blake, despite what I'm sure was a wholehearted effort, was unable to save William Douglas Jones. From afar, I kept abreast of the case, following it through a series of appeals and habeas corpus petitions until, ten years after I left PLC, Jones sat in the chair.

Just as Blake predicted, I didn't lose any sleep the night

I learned of the execution, but I'd lost so much sleep during my PLC days and in the years since that I've never become a proponent of the death penalty. I maintain a tenacious belief in the statistical and ethical objections to government execution, arguments that are easy to conceive and embrace when sitting in an office, reading transcripts, remembering the smell of Emma's perfume.

॰॰

The Missing and Uninvited

"SO, TRENT UNINVITED his girlfriend. Is that it?"

"In a nutshell, yes."

One of Justin's annoying words. "Nutshell." A lawyer-sounding word, his favorite, often following one of his lengthy, methodical, monotone orations. Blah, blah, blah, blah. In a nutshell, blah.

"Have you ever met this girlfriend?" Mallory asked him.

"Charlotte? No. Never."

"They've had a fight? What did Trent say?" How inconsiderate, Mallory was thinking. Four around table was intimate, cozy, barely enough. Three was impossibly embarrassing, even though Mallory was enthralled with Trent, found him stimulating and wonderfully new after just a brief encounter, that quick exchange of words in Justin's office. Trent popping his head in, flashing that smile: "So, you're the wife?" in a sexy tone, mocking the chauvinists.

Still, it would be awkward to look at him, sitting alone at her table, while questions about the girlfriend lurked beneath the lilt of polite conversation. To ask, or not to ask?

she would be thinking. To delve or not to delve? Knowing herself, she would likely probe deeply, ending in Trent's embarrassment or not, as the case might be, depending upon the strength of his character.

"Just said she couldn't make it. He was sorry. She couldn't come after all."

"Just like that? No explanation?"

"No. But it's not important anyway."

"How could it not be important?"

Justin paused before responding, his expression indicating mild resistance to her question. "Well, I doubt they're a solid couple. She doesn't meet Trent at the firm — you know, for lunch or after work — and she doesn't come to any of the office social functions. So, I get the sense they're somewhat on again, off again, that sort of thing. In a nut-shell, nothing serious."

Lunch and social functions, the proof of solidity? Mallory did little of that.

"But he says he's free and would like to come," continued Justin. "We'll have him over on his own. Nothing wrong with that, is there?" He looked at her with a face devoid of social understanding. Most men were like that, Mallory had found. Something she'd learned in her profession. They failed to understand the error in forgotten introductions or poorly timed eye contact or sitting with an ankle propped on opposite knee while wearing too-short socks under business suits. Or inviting a single individual, male or female, to dine at the home of a married couple.

"No, nothing wrong. We certainly won't cancel. It's only a picnic on the deck, after all," Mallory said, making noise while she thought. On again, off again. A man like that couldn't be averse to filling in the fourth side of the square, another female to tighten the gap. Benita came to mind. Benita Vanderlyn, Mallory's new friend, a classy looker albeit with a past, that interesting, quirky, and sad story. Another topic of conversation Mallory would strive to avoid, if she could, while sitting between two terribly interesting newish people with intriguing secrets behind their faces. Trent's on-again-off-again and Benita's—well, what would you call *that?* Something so tragic and titillating it begged disinterment.

Mallory didn't stop to analyze the plan or her motivations behind it. Perhaps it came naturally. She wasn't a social matchmaker, never had been, but her daily existence revolved around plugging holes, filling business needs with appropriate skills, linking people with complementary personalities and backgrounds. So, without once considering whether to seek Justin's approval, she called Benita straightaway. With her usual dose of self-confidence, Mallory conveyed the invitation as a sort of gentle demand, slipping in a word or two about Trent—a small hint at the significance of the event. The suggestion of matchmaking was there, oblique but unmistakable.

Benita hesitated in her shy and simple way before responding. "I, I'd love to come." A little stutter rarely evident in her speech. "Just the four of us? This man—Trent—he's single I suppose?"

"Did I mention a wife?"

"I—how can I put this? I appreciate the thought, but I don't think I'm ready for this."

"Oh, I'm not asking you to be *ready* for anything! It's just a casual barbecue, and Trent is a fun, *fun* person, you'll see. Justin *too* of course—remember you said you'd like to meet him? We'll just be a merry bunch, nothing stressful." Mallory wondered at her cheerleading. Fun, fun, rah, rah. Trent would be entertaining, but Justin? Mr. Even-Keeled, Mr. Rationality? Still, the cheery falsehoods spouted forth, something she'd done before with Benita, whose sweet sadness always seemed to inspire it. What a sad, sad girl, but a girl with such potential! It was Mallory's gift to recognize the potential in others and develop it. She'd built her reputation on that premise and the proof lay in her results, always true to her initial vision—well, almost always.

On the eve of the barbecue, Mallory informed Justin of her plan. He responded with his characteristic nod of the head, brow crunched into concentration: that intellectual mystique Mallory had once found attractive. Now, after six years of marriage, she knew it only too well. An ineffectual intellectualism—mental prowess without results. He exuded these little signs constantly, these needling reminders of her flawed vision. "Benita, sure, fine, we'll have her," he said absentmindedly in response to Mallory's belated declaration of intent.

But Justin's lack of interest didn't really matter. The plans were laid. And what could be more relaxing and sensual than a summer afternoon on the deck, shaded by heavy, big-leafed trees? Mallory couldn't deny that suburban living had its charms (even if she *did* always begin to long for the city the moment her train pulled out of Grand Central on weekday evenings).

Their home, Justin's and Mallory's, was picture perfect, straight from a magazine. "Great for entertaining" said the real estate listing when they were looking. A large, elegant dining room and a modern, well-mapped kitchen. French doors opening onto a spacious wood deck in a private yard. If Mallory had to live all the way north like this—her one concession to Justin—then it had to be in *this* house, something way beyond their means at the time they bought it five years ago and only marginally within their means now. And perhaps forever after only marginally within their means, a constant source of strain and worry, never to be taken for granted—if recent events were any indication.

Hours before the guests were to arrive, Justin was into his routine, measuring and mixing. These were his creations, but nothing was ad-libbed, every recipe mentally recorded in perfect three-quarter teaspoons of this and one-eighth cups of that, ingredients planed straight as ice at the top of measuring implements with the sharp edge of a knife. It was Mallory's job to wash, chop, and assemble—tasks she performed in a slapdash way but well enough, relying on Justin's sauces, dressings, and garnishes to make these very ordinary picnicky dishes into culinary masterpieces.

What a shame I've no accounts with gourmet French restaurants, Mallory often mused on occasions like this, watching Justin cook with precision, exhibiting his own quiet version of zeal. He really did enjoy it. Perhaps had missed his true calling, she thought with a bitter laugh bubbling up internally under the influence of her pre-company, pre-dinner glass of chilled white wine.

They were both outside on the deck when Trent arrived, Mallory finishing the table, Justin at the barbecue setting up his utensils and that silly little plastic timer. Mallory heard the car on the driveway, heard the door close solidly, went to the deck railing, and saw a brand-new black

Mercedes convertible, top down, and the man next to it, tanned, dark glasses, khaki shorts. Sun glinting off car and hair, both gleaming black, matching in color.

Mallory leaned over the deck railing at her waist, causing the fabric of her V-necked cotton shirt to pull down tight across her chest. "Hello, you!" she called. "Come around back!"

Trent looked up, removed his sunglasses. Smiled. Walked into the backyard toward the steps up to the deck. Mallory noticed his legs, muscular, pleasingly haired. Not apish, nor embarrassingly bald and shiny like Justin's. Eighty-four degrees, and she couldn't very well ask Justin to wear long pants, so there they were, all three of them bare-legged, the men cloned in khaki and polos (Trent's shirt a deep lavender, Justin's a drab olive), Mallory in her vibrant turquoise cotton tee and white shorts—dangerous with barbecue sauce, but would she really be eating anything anyway? Still, it was a crisp, sporty look that did her well and something that Benita would unlikely copy, at least that much Mallory could predict based on her knowledge of Benita's wardrobe, those loose, chiffony things she liked to wear. Benita, always a bit different, but somehow entirely proper looking—and prepared for every possibility. (Well, not *that* one, but how could she have ever predicted?)

In fact, it was Benita's preparedness that had led to their meeting, six months ago, in the locker room at the health club. Mallory had forgotten to bring her socks and was muttering something to that effect under her breath when Benita, quietly but firmly, had offered hers. "Here," she said, handing them to Mallory, "I have an extra pair." Clean, not just clean, but brand new, Mallory was sure of it.

Never before worn. She accepted.

And what could Mallory do, failing to wash and return them by the next Zumba class (and the next and the next) but drag Benita into the club's sportswear shop and buy her a new pair? "No, please don't," Benita protested while Mallory stubbornly repeated, "I insist." This awkward interlude was followed by an hour-long chat in the juice bar, Benita's sad history emerging over grapefruit juice. Mallory subtly elicited the details, absorbing them in silent triumph.

An interesting girl, that Benita. Too interesting for Trent? Mallory watched him ascend the five steps to the deck, his tan very rich against the deep lavender shirt. Dashing and handsome, but still quite conventional. Justin extended his hand, Trent's sprang out to greet it. A snapshot of that handshake might have passed in a poster touting racial harmony. At one time, Mallory had admired her husband's gentle, dusty good looks, but now, in the summer, and especially next to Trent, he simply looked dustier, pasty, and shorn.

Retrieving her glass of wine from the table, Mallory sauntered forth noncommittally, as if the dinner party had been entirely Justin's idea. Trent leaned slightly forward, touched her upper arm, and kissed her cheek, natural as can be. A hint of musk on his face, not overdone. He was taller than Justin. Mallory noticed that.

"So, you found us," declared Justin.

"Sure, but my *God*, what a hike!" complained Trent with a grin. "That Mountain Ridge Road—"

"I guess we're used to it."

"*Jesus*. I should've brought my shotgun. A herd of deer ran me down."

Laughter.

"At least our wildlife is prettier than yours down in the city," said Justin with a little smile that said he was attempting a joke, his voice remaining even and colorless. Mallory and Trent looked at him, not quite sure.

"How long does it take you to get to the office?" asked Trent.

"Entirely too long," said Mallory.

"An hour and fifteen," offered Justin.

"Hour and forty-five."

"Hour and a half max."

"For you maybe."

"Mallory is all the way downtown," explained Justin.

Trent emitted a single, musing laugh and folded his arms while the married couple exchanged looks of regret. Mallory jumped into the silence. "What can we get you to drink?"

"Anything cold."

"Wine, beer, something softer, something harder?"

Trent's eyes briefly roamed, spotting Justin's frosty tumbler of cola on the deck railing and Mallory's half-empty wineglass in her hand. Evaluating. "Wine would be great." He nodded toward Mallory's glass.

"Sure now? Maybe a gin and tonic? I also make a mean margarita." She had done her own evaluating and knew he would enjoy a drink.

"No thanks. What you're having is fine."

Tactful. Still too early for anything but tactfulness.

Mallory smiled at Trent before turning, retreating, passing through the French doors into the kitchen. She breathed in deeply, quieting a flutter in her chest. Cooler inside with the central air on, but still not so sticky outside as to justify abandoning the barbecue-on-the-deck plan. She took the wine bottle from the refrigerator, topped off her own glass, took a few sips, topped it off again, then filled a clean glass for Trent. By the time she returned to the deck, Benita had arrived and was extending a timid hand toward Justin.

"Benita!" exclaimed Mallory. "So, you've all met one another?" She handed Trent his glass of wine and eyed Benita's outfit. Just as she'd predicted. Slightly overdressed in a loose blouse and lightweight, flowery skirt to mid-calf, but still cool enough and not inappropriate. Mallory was grateful for Benita's unique fashion, something that masked her ample curves, a contrast to Mallory's style which always did the most to expose and amplify her own athletic line.

"I made the introductions," testified Justin.

"Yes." Benita gave an affirmative shake of her small oval head, sending a shudder through her thick black hair from crown to mid-back. Mallory looked at Benita, then Trent, then Benita. The same, exactly and precisely the same color and consistency of hair. Benita and Trent—and that Mercedes. It seemed embarrassingly wrong, even though Mallory's two guests were so different in other ways. How could a man and a woman with identical hair (except in length of course) possibly be right for each other? One thing so obviously the same, and another so obviously different: Trent all square-edged and self-assured next to Benita, retiring and ill at ease. How hard for her this must be! After everything she's been through, getting out socially again!

Mallory offered a drink; Benita requested a cola. After Mallory filled the order, the foursome remained ensconced around the barbecue, sipping drinks, exchanging pleasantly inane chitchat, Benita mostly quiet, Justin professorial and correct, Trent and Mallory high spirited and growing ever more so, trading comments about Justin's detailed preparations and exacting method of grilling the meat. Tongs, sauce brush, cooking mitts lined up on the left; platter of chicken and Justin's special sauce on the right; lid closed for preheating until the thermometer reached 400; timer set for ten minutes; bare chicken on the middle rack, placed with a sizzle; sauce brushed on after the second ten-minute side; timer reset for five minutes. Justin took the barbs good-naturedly, attempting his own flat-sounding repartee. "Laugh all you like. You won't be laughing when you taste it!"

"No, we'll be enshrining the barbeque!"

"And worshiping that little timer!"

Benita remained silent, her eyes dark and compassionate.

Noticing Benita's maturely distant look, Mallory began to wonder how a thirty-something group could sound like a bunch of seven-year-olds. She left for the kitchen, returning with the bottle of wine for the table, a couple of extra cans of soda for Justin and Benita. They were about to start serving.

"I have to admit, this is delicious," said Trent when they were all seated, taking their first bites. Trent across from Mallory, bottle between them, Justin across from Benita.

"The chicken's great," said Benita. "And the salads are wonderful too, Mallory. You'll have to share your recipes."

"Thanks," said Mallory, glass to lips. She glanced to the side at Justin over the top of her glass but said nothing to correct Benita. Justin didn't look at his wife, keeping his eyes cast down at his plate.

"I feel like I'm on vacation at a country resort," said Trent. "A sort of mom-and-pop operation."

"Mom and pop?" Mallory gave Trent the evil eye.

"You know what I mean. This is a very…married sort of thing. It's great for you two of course." He waved his fork at Justin and Mallory. "You have a great house, a wonderful yard. Just not for me at this point in my life."

"You ought to go for it, Trent," said Justin. "The life is good." He patted the top of Mallory's left hand where it rested on the table. "Green trees and fresh air to come home to."

"And a *lovely* wife, isn't that right, dear?" Mallory inadvertently bumped the table, sending plates and forks jumping as she leaned toward her husband with an upturned, kittenish face. Justin maintained his straight-spined posture and smiled. "But I suppose," said Mallory, pulling away from her husband and regarding Trent, "that you aren't any closer to marriage after recent events."

"How do you mean?"

"Well, this girlfriend we've been dying to meet. Charlotte."

"Oh. Charlene. I had thought of bringing her, but it just didn't work out. You're right, though, I'm nowhere near marriage. Not that I don't envy you, it's just not for me right now. I'm enjoying the city too much. It's the place to be when you're single." Trent took a large swallow, finishing his glass, and reached for the bottle. "But I guess you wouldn't agree, would you, Benita?" he continued, looking at the bottle as he poured.

"Agree?" she repeated, fork halfway to mouth, her dark lashes fluttering briefly.

"I mean, you're single, but you live all the way up here in the sticks, right?"

"Well, yes..."

"She's just a few streets over from us," chattered Mallory, "but like everyone else she got married before moving up here, right Ben?"

Benita flushed.

"So, you're married?" asked Trent in a dull voice.

"When she *first* came up here, sure, but now they're separated of course." Mallory reached for Benita and squeezed her forearm reassuringly. "But you're right, Trent, this is a very married sort of a place. As for me, I was always more of a city girl. I *love* the city and feel a little isolated up here with all these mommies and their toddlers." Another slip. She glanced obliquely at Benita but continued without hesitation. "Justin, dear, would you get us another bottle? There's one in the fridge. You'd like some more wine, wouldn't you, Trent?"

"Thanks, I'm fine." He leveled a hand over his glass despite the want that showed in his eyes, Mallory was certain she saw it there.

"No, really, we could use a little more. Benita, sure you don't want to join us? Please, Justin."

Her husband, grim faced, obeyed without comment.

In his absence: "That was all part of the plan when we came up here," continued Mallory, picking up the thread she had left dangling. "Move to the suburbs and have kids. Change my name to Melrose so the child won't have identity confusion. Can you imagine? 'Mallory Melrose.' I've told

Justin it's nothing personal and not even women's-libbish but I'll keep my own name, thanks, Mallory Boyd. It just goes together, and there's no need to change it, especially since we have no little ones to confuse. We've been here five years now, and I could still move back to the city in an instant. Just pack my bags and go. Leave all this behind!"

She was looking into Trent's eyes, imagining a shining ray of approval in them. He was certainly returning the gaze with the hint of a thought underneath his grin: *My kind of girl*, it seemed to say.

The sound of Benita's voice cut through. "That's too bad."

"Too bad?"

"Well, that you've had trouble having kids."

"Oh! No trouble! We just haven't gotten around to it. Ah, here he comes now. Justin, I'm about empty." She lifted her glass. He poured just a third of the way up. "It was all sort of more Justin's idea anyway, wasn't it, dear? You see, having kids would ruin my career right now." Justin paused, bottle in mid-air, then moved his arm mechanically toward Trent's glass, poured. Trent did not refuse. Justin resumed his seat behind a dirty dish, empty except for a few bones and the traces of his secret sauces.

"What is this career you'd be ruining?" inquired Trent. "You haven't mentioned where you work."

A giggle bubbled up into Mallory's mouth and threatened to burst forth. How absurdly funny! Her own Justin, never mentioning a word about her job to Trent! Of course he must be embarrassed. Had to be. The idea was inexplicably hilarious.

But Mallory suppressed the bubble, allowing its

effervescence to emerge in the form of a little smile. "I'm a headhunter," she said.

"I always thought that was such an interesting word," offered Benita. "Headhunter."

Mallory turned to Benita and voiced her immediate thought. "Interesting maybe because the word almost seems to fit your situation, doesn't it?" She lifted her glass, swilled a bit more.

"But I have a job," replied Benita with polite insistence.

"Oh, sure, of course, but Trent, did we tell you that Benita is a graphic artist? She does layouts for magazines and book covers and such. It's all very creative."

Justin sat up taller and leaned toward Benita, incipient language on his lips. But Trent was too quick. "Is that so?" he said, throwing Benita the shortest of glances before turning to gaze at Mallory. "And what kind of headhunting do you do?"

"Corporate, executive, upper management, and law. In fact, law is my biggest area." She looked at Justin, then back at Trent. "I have a very large account with your firm."

"The way we've been growing it isn't any wonder."

"Listen to *him!*" exclaimed Mallory, feeling very familiar. "'The way we've been growing,' like he owns the place now that he's made partner. My congratulations, by the way."

Justin stood and raised his tumbler with an inch of melted ice and liquid the color of weak tea. "Yes, our congratulations. Here's to your continued success at Belknap and Stone." They all lifted their glasses.

"That's very big of you, man," said Trent as Justin sat down again.

Big is right, thought Mallory. Justin was never one to begrudge anyone anything. So big, magnanimous, and self-less. Too good for his own good.

"I suppose being a lateral hire didn't hurt your bid for partnership," she said. "And you did it in just a year's time!"

"I made it clear that my six years at Gersen Finch had to count for something. We didn't use the word 'partner,' but Steve implied it would be mine as long as I didn't commit any major screwups."

"Steve Belknap? You already knew him?"

"A friend of my folks."

Benita's eyes jumped from Mallory to Trent to Justin, her expression mildly befuddled.

Mallory patted Justin's hand while sending Trent an admiring look. "Ah, yes. Those with connections are never in need of my services." She and Trent shared a sparkling gaze. "Maybe Justin should have transferred before it was too late," she said as if he weren't there. "They strung him along for seven years, and then—"

"It's a tough call," broke in Trent diplomatically. "We have three hundred lawyers and just a few openings for partner. Why do you think we have the Senior Associate position? To hang onto the good ones, and Justin's one of the best."

Justin fidgeted, remained silent.

"Of course, I said as much to the hiring committee when I sent his name over, seven years ago," said Mallory.

"You?"

"Yup."

"You got him into Belknap?"

A moment of awkward silence.

Benita broke in. "What a lovely way to meet! Such good luck to get a job and a future wife at the same time." She was looking at Justin, her skin soft and dewy.

"Yes, well, I thought it was great luck," said Justin. "Listen, why don't we get up and take a walk before dessert? I'd like to show you the neighborhood." He stood.

"Still trying to sell me on the life, old man?" asked Trent with a grin.

Benita stood. "That's a wonderful idea. It's so much cooler now." She started to pick up her plate.

"No, leave it," said Mallory, waving a hand at Benita and pushing herself up from the table. "A walk? A walk he says."

"Just to the end of the street."

"It's almost dark," and "Such a lovely time of evening"—a cacophonous blend from Mallory and Benita.

Justin led the way to the deck steps, followed by the guests and finally Mallory, whose complaints evaporated once she realized that she was more or less floating, her head miles above the contact point between feet and ground. Down the back steps, out to the driveway, to the street, then four across, Justin, Benita, Trent, Mallory, then somehow Benita and Justin ahead, Mallory and Trent behind. The sun had set, and it was cooler but a bit more humid, the thick atmosphere a straitjacket against Mallory's tendency to drift, while moisture sprang to the surface of her skin, making her simultaneously hot and cold like a sweating glass of iced liquid in the sun.

Mallory did her best to ignore Justin, who immediately launched into his "tour guide" persona, directing their attention to one side of the road then the other: those two giant sycamores in front of the Morgensterns' house, the spectacular spray of dianthus at the Caronellis'. But soon, shortly after they'd broken into pairs, the commentary stopped, along with the obligatory, noncommittal responses from their guests.

With the other two ahead, Trent and Mallory fell silent—a condition rarely experienced by either one—an unspoken something inside the decent column of space between them. The silence wasn't uncomfortable for Mallory, her sensibility dulled. But she did feel Trent next to her, sensed his height and weight and breadth, all slightly more than her husband's.

They slowed, watching their feet. Mallory looked up. Benita and Justin seemed miles ahead, their faces alternately turning toward each other and away. Lips moving. A lot from Benita's lips. So shy all evening, now a chattering doll. What could they be talking about? Impossible that she could be telling him about *that*.

"So, what's the big secret?" asked Trent with such familiarity that she knew him, saw herself in him.

"What secret?" Coy.

Trent laughed. "All this stuff you were covering up about your friend's marriage. You're not very good at keeping a straight face." She looked at his grin, the glint in his obsidian eyes. He turned his face forward, glanced at Benita's backside, and nodded his head by way of indication. Interested? Not that kind of interest. Mere curiosity.

"Oh, *that*." She giggled. "Poor Benita's had such a hard time of it. Really something." Her tongue was loosening, a surge of speech ready to spill with the relief she felt to be talking about someone else.

She began the story in a raised, hoarse whisper simply to add suspense, for the other two were so far ahead there was no chance they could overhear. "She was married a few years ago to a wonderful, wonderful fellow. You know, hardworking, good looking, upstanding, Mr. Nice to everyone, fun loving, generous, you name it—of course this is the description Benita gives. I never met the man. Corey Vanderlyn—she's kept his name. They moved into their house up here right after the honeymoon, and about a year and a half later Benita is two months pregnant with their first baby, and, and then, unbe*liev*able. He just disappears. Corey is gone. Drives off to work one morning and no one sees him again. He could be in China or at the bottom of the river or wandering around with amnesia for all we know. And poor Benita was so heartbroken she had a miscarriage, a very bloody and painful one. She's been in shock for almost a year now and tries to feel like a widow, but she has *no* way to be sure and keeps hoping that..."

A big laugh from Trent. "Sorry," he sputtered in his mirth. Mallory caught his laugh and felt a smile curl her lips. "Sorry," he said again. "It's not a funny story. So sad maybe it's funny. She's just killing herself with this widow fantasy."

"Oh, no, no. It's *not* a fantasy. He adored Benita and wasn't the kind of man to just run off, so there's every reason to assume the worst. His parents and friends haven't seen him since. I mean, there's no proof, his body hasn't shown up and he didn't seem to have a single enemy in the world, but anything could have happened, an accident, a carjacking."

"He'll show up. It's been, what, less than a year? Can't hide forever. It's nearly impossible to cover your tracks."

"Hide?"

"Come on, Mallory. A wrecked car and a body don't disappear so easily. The guy has no enemies but all at once he has a mortgage, a wife, and a baby on the way. Maybe even a job he doesn't like." Trent shook his head. "Most men in that situation would at least think of cutting out."

"On Benita? Who would ever cut out on her? Someone as sweet as Benita?"

Mallory noticed the way Trent eyed Benita up ahead, for the first time regarding her as a woman. The attraction was there. But a moment later, he averted his gaze, seeking freedom. "Yeah," he said. "Someone as sweet as Benita." Then he looked at Mallory, the attraction harder. "After all, don't women always complain there aren't enough men like Justin in the world?" Trent's eyes were taunting, teasing, urging her to shed the last bit of decency.

She returned his smile, feeling dizzy and drowning, caught her breath and looked away. Regarded her husband. Maybe Justin was abnormal. Too good. But what good was goodness if it didn't make people happy?

The distance between the pairs had diminished as they approached the dead end, the two in front pausing in the turnaround before heading back. Still talking, Justin and Benita seemed engrossed in their conversation, oblivious of Mallory and Trent, who slowed their pace to gain a few extra moments of privacy. "Maybe I understand what you're saying about Benita's husband," said Mallory.

"I thought you would." He paused and turned to her. Their eyes met. "You're dying up here, aren't you?" His voice a sultry whisper.

She returned his gaze, not shrinking this time, her eyes

saying *yes*.

Justin and Benita, sensing the others nearby, cut off their conversation and looked back. "So this is the end?" Trent called out as they closed the gap. "What a great neighborhood!" He was square and forthright, using a voice that Justin and Benita would find sincere. Mallory, and perhaps only Mallory, could detect the sarcasm.

"Nice, isn't it?" said Justin, a proud look on his face. Benita at his side, face serene, nodded approval in slow motion with a languid, heavy-lidded blink.

They turned and started back, this time careful to remain a group, four across, the suggestion of their private conversations lingering underneath the pleasantness of superficial observation. The gradual descent of evening had left them near the end of a long summer dusk, still light enough to see. Justin, the tour guide again. Benita demure and correct. Trent diplomatic and witty. Mallory quieter than before, with an urgent need to pee.

They rounded a bend, the Melrose-Boyd house coming into view. The outdoor lights had come on automatically in their absence—another one of Justin's timers. Mallory noticed a strange car in the driveway, parked behind Benita's which was parked behind Trent's. A tattered, aging luxury car of a forgotten decade, a big rusty boat. Something that didn't belong here.

At her side, Mallory felt Trent reacting, growing tense. "How in the world...?" he muttered, shaking his head. A woman emerged from the driver's side. Tottering on high-heeled mules, she clicked around to the back of the car. Tight miniskirt, tube top.

"Must have peeked in my address book. Sorry about

this, old man…," Trent apologized to the man of the house.

"Charlene," whispered Mallory under her breath.

"…it may get a little ugly."

The forgotten girlfriend was not looking happy, blonde hair standing in shock waves around her puckered face.

"Hello," said Justin, when they were close enough. "Hi," from Charlene, glaring at Trent, then glaring at Mallory.

"Meet Charlene, everyone," said Trent. "Justin, Mallory, and Benita." Realization of her mistake crossed Charlene's face. She switched her glare to Benita. "If you could just give us a minute?" Trent said to Justin, eyebrows raised.

"Sure, no problem."

Charlene exploded well before the others were out of hearing distance. Who was that woman, and I'm not good enough for your friends, and I embarrass you, and the like, all in hysterical outer-borough tones, while Trent, remaining the diplomat, offered deep-voiced phrases of reason and control.

Inside, Justin and Benita went into the living room while Mallory headed for the powder room and spent a long time peeing and thinking. She thought of the absurdity of Charlene with Trent. The incongruity. Trent's messy little secret. She thought of Charlene's eyes on her when she first walked up and laughed at Charlene's perception and choice. The perception of threat had been correct, but the perception of affinity incorrect. After all, it was Benita who'd been loved and left, just like Charlene. No one had ever left Mallory. But maybe that was because Mallory had always done the leaving first.

Mallory spent a moment in front of the mirror, noticing pink in the whites of her eyes, feeling the beginnings of a headache. She heard Trent come in the front door. Impressive. He'd gotten rid of Charlene in just a few minutes.

When she stepped out of the powder room, everyone was congregated in the foyer near the open front door, the guests in the preliminary stage of taking their leave.

"I apologize for the scene, old man. Charlene wasn't too happy when I called it quits last week."

"It's okay. Understandable," said Justin.

"A bad way to end a great evening!" Trent looked at Mallory, a hint of guilt under his smile.

"The dinner was fabulous," said Benita. "Thanks so much for having me." She looked up at Justin gratefully. He returned the look, lingered, his glance filled with something Mallory had never seen.

Benita and Trent inched toward the door. Mallory thought of protesting, reminding them of the forgotten dessert, the after-dinner drinks, the possibility of intimate conversation in the living room. But those possibilities were gone, no one wanted them now, at least not the four of them together, all at once, in the same room.

Trent shook Justin's hand, then turned to Mallory, touched her shoulder and bussed her lightly on the cheek. He caught her eyes on the way up from his kiss, sending a spark meant to inflame earlier intimations. She was reminded, knew she wouldn't forget, and knew this wouldn't be the last time. But for now, her head throbbed, obliterating everything else.

Justin's eyes followed Benita and Trent as they traversed the front walk to the driveway, parted with a polite handshake, and got into their cars. Mallory, standing behind her husband, turned and walked away from the front door.

"Too bad," she heard at her back. Justin's voice came out heavy and slow—from fatigue or emotion?

She hesitated before taking another step.

"It's just too bad," he echoed. They remained frozen, back-to-back with a yard of distance between them.

When he spoke again, his voice was barely more than a whisper. "It's a shame you're so disappointed in me."

Justin closed the front door quietly and went off to collect the dirty dishes.

Mallory headed upstairs to bed.

ॐ

Dust of the Universe

ON A COOL October night, Kip is balled up in the middle of the king-size bed, covers pulled over his head. This is Leila's way of sleeping when she gets in first and waits for him, but the position is not natural to Kip. He is thirty-eight, still hard muscled from workouts in the gym. Stretched out, his length of six feet, two inches, places his head at the top and his heels at the very bottom of the bed. Now, curled up inside his soft, dark cavern, he tries to feel his bigness and strength. They are lost to him.

The hour is still early, yet he must sleep. Tomorrow will be his first day back at the office. He lies on his left side, making a tight "S." In the quiet under the down comforter, he can hear his own breathing, not much else. The enclosed space gives each breath a bellows-like whooshing sound to complement the whooshing of blood in his veins. He becomes aware of his shallow breathing and endeavors to deepen it, but the changes in rhythm and effort make him doubly aware of his beating heart. Its power reverberates throughout his body.

The effort to keep his mind blank is exhausting but does

not lead him into sleep. He opens his eyes. The absence of light is complete under the thick, tightly drawn covers, but there's always something to be seen. He looks into the dark. Thousands of tiny white specks dance about like atoms at boiling point. Intermittently, in the middle of their bright dance, pulsing flows shove them aside, like muddy disgorgements from sewage pipes, rushing rhythmically with every beat of his heart.

In time, his breath and blood warm the air inside his self-made tent. He rolls onto his back and throws the covers off his face, escaping the pitch black with its boiling atomic particles and flowing phantoms of blood. The moonlight casts the room in grainy relief, a surprising amount of natural light. The bedroom is on the second floor and has two large windows, bordered only with decorative swags — Leila's touches. They've always left the windows uncovered because they live in a wooded suburb, very private. Quiet.

He knows he will not be going to sleep. He gets up.

At the window on the front of the house, he stops to look out. Near the mailbox, a glimmer catches his eye, a single gentle swing in a sudden breeze. The realtor came by that morning to post the "For Sale" sign. The outdoor lights are off, but everything can be seen in the moonlight: the driveway, the rock garden, a patch of lawn, the outlines of branches, and in the distance, the porch light of their nearest neighbor. The sky is shot with stars but lacking the moon.

He goes to the back of the house, to the master bath. It has a small bay window with a ledge to rest his elbows upon while gazing out. Low in the sky, the enormous moon bathes the large backyard in a silver shimmer, bright enough to cast shadows from the surrounding trees. The realtor told him to leave the swing set up, it will help to make the sale. He turns. He needs to tell Leila what the realtor said today.

Kip moves back to the bedroom. On the bed is a lump of covers, head invisible. He draws and releases the next breath without noticing it, and the corners of his mouth turn upward. She's climbed in while he was in the bathroom, and now, maybe, he can go to sleep.

"Leila," he whispers when he's pushed up behind her, his head still outside, hers inside. There's not a sound, but the bed is warm. "Are you asleep already?"

Always, Leila has been nearly soundless in the way she sleeps, a kitten without the purr.

"Are you all right, Leila?"

"Fine. Just fine." The voice is barely audible under the covers yet so familiar in the dark. The tone is gentle and sweet, full of contentment. At rest.

But he must know. "You're sure?"

"Yes, don't worry."

"And the kids?"

"I checked on them."

"I'm sorry."

"Don't be sorry."

"I can't sleep."

"You need your rest."

"Tomorrow... How can I...?"

"You'll get through it. They just want to help."

Leila has always believed in the goodness of people, and he tries to be more like her.

He lapses into silence. They both lie on their left sides but her head is still covered, and he tries to hear her breathing, to gain a complete image of her buried under the covers without lifting them. An edge of the pillow she sleeps on is sticking out and he pushes his face into it, smelling her hair, her skin, drawing up the warmth. Her power should be enough to pull him down into her deep well, a dreamless limbo, an obliteration of consciousness.

Minutes or hours pass. He may have fallen when he senses something behind him, a sound or a movement near the bedroom door. They're in the habit of leaving the door open in case one of the children calls out.

Kip turns onto his back and props himself up on his elbows. The small silhouette in the doorframe belongs to Jonathan, their six-year-old.

"What's doin', buddy?"

The silhouette takes a single step in, then another.

"Come here. Come on!" Kip pats the bed on his right. Leila is on his left.

The small figure is up beside the bed now. A fist rubs an eye. "I can't sleep."

"You've been asleep. Your mom saw you."

"I don't want to sleep."

A choking sound jars the stillness. "Come here, bud." It came from Kip's throat.

He holds the covers up, and the boy climbs into the bed. Kip slides his right arm under the small, bony shoulders and pulls him in tight. They snuggle close.

"Did you see the moon Jon-o?" The boy's room has a window on the backyard.

"It's huge. I touched it."

Kip gently places his lips on top of the head, feeling the silky softness, smelling the snips and snails. His lips move across his son's hair as he talks. "It seems close enough to touch, but it's thousands of miles away."

"Closer than Zorq?"

"Way closer."

"How far away is Zorq?"

"Oh, at least a million light years."

Jon thinks a while, imagining life on Zorq, the fascinating aliens his father has conjured so many evenings at bedtime.

"I forget, Dad."

"What?"

"Do the Zorquians have cars?"

Kip falters.

"Shh, now Jonathan," says Leila, thinking of Kip.

She always uses their son's full name when she's serious. Kip takes in a deep breath and says, "They don't need cars. They dematerialize and rematerialize at their destination."

"Oh yeah, I remember."

"They just have to think of where they want to go."

"They blink, and when they open their eyes, they're somewhere else."

"Right. Like magic."

"We did that."

"Now, now," says Leila. She rolls over onto her back and exposes her face.

"Well, we did," insists Jon-o.

It was instantaneous, the man said. Others agreed.

Kip turns his head to the left and brings Leila's profile into view. He can feel the length of her right leg along the length of his left leg and his left hand reaches for her right. The fingers are slender and cool, and they intertwine with his and press in restrained urgency. He turns his face up, and the three of them lie on their backs, looking into the invisible ceiling.

Minutes pass. "Why is it so light?" says another voice at the door.

In the frame now is a taller silhouette, the outline of their eight-year-old, Isabelle.

"You can't sleep?" Kip asks.

"You're so dark over there. It's like I'm on the stage again."

Her words take him back to springtime, the recital, her pale pink tights and pure white tutu, her long, dark hair pulled tight and slick into the bun that Leila made. "Come here, sweetheart," he says.

She doesn't move. "Not really the stage," she muses. "It's that other light. The light that came for us!"

"No," says Kip. "Come here if you can't sleep."

"But Daddy. I don't want to sleep."

There it is, that choking sound again, coming from a body not his own. "Come here." He feels it in his throat. "There's plenty of room! Isn't there, Leila?"

"Plenty," she says.

They've done this before and like to joke about it. "This is why we stopped at two—there's no more room in the bed!" On nights like this.

Isabelle is at the bedside.

"Izza lizard," says the boy.

"Jon wonton," says the girl, and they both giggle. Their sweet sounds play together, bubbling like fresh, clear water.

"Here," says Kip, scooping the boy up. "Get between me and Mom. Leila, scoot a little. Here, Izza." Jon's bony knees dig into his chest on the way over, but the rearrangement is accomplished, and Isabelle climbs in beside him on the right, her long hair brushing his face before she lies down. Jon is on his left, and then Leila. Each of Kip's arms is under the pajama-clad shoulders of a child, his left fingers cupping Leila's shoulder.

They, four, stare into the invisible ceiling with no beginning or end. Kip tries to slow his breathing, but the wetness on his cheeks turns into trembling that quickly becomes shaking.

"You're not going to ask us again, are you, Daddy?" says Izza.

"I'm sorry," says Kip. He wants to know about their day. Over and over again.

"I love the summer," says Jon. "I never want summer to end."

"There's nothing to be sorry about." Leila speaks over Jonathan in her comforting voice, because she wants so much for Kip to feel better. If he could feel better he would, just for her, not for himself.

"I don't have to ask you again. Ella told me all about your day." Ella is the mother of Ben and Riley. The friends.

"They were late," says Jon. "We had to wait for them in the parking lot."

"Only a few minutes," says Leila. "Patience does not come easily."

Patience, waiting, stages, change, little people. They want their day to begin sooner than now, yet they have their whole lives to look forward to. Impatient. Their whole lives ahead.

"I wish you could've come," says Izza. "We had so

much fun! I made a sandcastle with Riley."

I wish... "I'm sorry, I had to work."

"Don't be sorry." The comforting.

"The waves were gi-normous!" says the boy, using his favorite new word. "Me and Ben ran in, but Mom called us back."

"On the way home...," the girl begins.

"We just blinked, Dad. That's all."

"Jon was being annoying, Daddy." Her favorite grownup word.

"But you didn't look, you didn't see—"

"They didn't, Kip! They were playing and arguing and laughing in the back. Only me."

"What about the light, Mommy?"

"I just blinked anyway."

"It was a light, wonton."

"But you, Leila."

"Don't worry, darling. I'm sure they didn't see a thing."

"But you—"

"Just for a flash of a second when it jumped the median."

"The rig."

"Jumped and it was too late, but so fast, so fast."

Instantaneous they said.

"Did you...?"

"No, Kip. No pain."

"A blink."

"A light."

Kip's heart is racing again, and his eyes are closed tight against it. He's heard their answers countless times in a blur of endless nights. He wants to know.

He knows.

Now he doesn't.

He's ashamed for asking again because it does nothing to ease his mind. Always the tears come, the choking, the shaking, and afterward, a blank exhaustion that can never be blank enough.

After a time, the night becomes still once more. He closes his eyes to look for the bright, dancing specks of light, the dust of the universe. If he looks hard enough into his closed eyelids he can pass right through the frantic specks and out to the other side.

He keeps trying.

Minutes pass, hours, days, and nights pass.

A voice emerges from the void, steady and deep with truth.

"I miss you." His.

Followed by three others.

"I miss you too, Dad."

"I miss you, Daddy."

"I miss you, Kip, my darling."

Lying on his back, he gathers up the Isabelle pillow and the Jonathan pillow and the Leila pillow and squeezes them tight against his chest and face, breathing his family deeply into his lungs to capture their dwindling particles of skin and hair, sucking in the tear-drenched linens. Maybe he can suffocate.

But then Leila says, "No, Kip," like she always does.

"Why not?"

"Because I love you."

"But you're gone."

"I'm here with you."

This is not the truth. She is not here, but he can go there.

He starts to tell her this again, but she interrupts. "You can't, because you know what I would want." It is the voice she uses when she is very sure, and none of them, not Jonathan, not Isabelle, not even Kip, can contradict.

Her words, theirs, have found him out. He opens his eyes and the dancing specks rush in, condense, and explode.

This is the truth.

He allows for some air, still resisting.

"I can't. Tomorrow, and the next day. How can I?"

"You will," says Leila.

"For you, I will."

"For yourself." She waits a moment to let him know this before adding, in her comforting voice, "Now get some sleep."

And it becomes like any other night in the time when they had nothing but any other nights.

"I love you so much," he says. A new stream of tears is flowing, but his chest is calm.

"Daddy, don't cry! I love you."

"I love you, Dad."

He holds them tighter because the hours grow short, and the light has changed in the way that signals the other side of the dead of night. In the morning, he will have to let them go.

"Goodnight, darling," says Leila.

"Goodnight."

"Goodnight."

"Sleep tight."

℘

Reckoning

THE LITTLE MAN, as crisp as the fall morning, arrives at Arthur Creaton's office. He's punctual, eight exact, the clock marking a third of the pie.

His name is Thomas Henry or Henry Thomas—first and last impossible to put straight and keep in order. Somehow, this small blip in memory doesn't bug Arthur. It's easy enough to think of him as "Henry," sometimes with a "Mr.," sometimes not.

Henry is gray-business clad, about thirty-two or thirty-three, slight and trim, no more than five-seven, multi-American-racial, closely cropped, unimaginative, staid, but also carefully manufactured, rehearsed, and aware of his presentation. By contrast, Arthur is a WASP of fifty-seven, worn and rumpled, unassuming and ostensibly timid, although he knows more than this about himself. He surpasses Henry's erect stature by at least four inches despite his stooped shoulders under the oxford button-down and a well-worn tweed jacket, his standard ensemble while in the office.

There's been a progression to things. First, in the mail, Arthur received a photocopy of the front page of his 2007 tax return, black-ink stamped "NRP," with Henry's business card attached. A week later, Henry phoned. Arrangements were made. "Have all your bank statements, income and expense records available. Business and personal." Thoroughness was implied. *I will find it, yes, I will.* Finally, the day arrives for the big event, the audit.

On the phone, Henry had avoided that term. It was to be "an examination" as part of the National Research Program. A statistical study of compliance. A random selection of small businesses. Of course, any necessary adjustments to the taxpayer's return would not be left uncorrected.

"Make sure you have all records available. For *both* of your Schedule C's." A vaguely sinister tone.

Henry's exacting voice foreshadowed the outer package arriving today. Tidy and precise. His eyes are a scrim over the suggestion of wheels turning inside, the well-oiled machinery of the many lessons learned in agent school. His mission is to extract proof of his preconceptions, to detect what he judges to be the carefully guarded flaw in the record of the older man, the taxpayer, his target.

Arthur might simply tell him there isn't a flaw to be found, at least not where his tax affairs are concerned. His business, a sole proprietorship, is an insignificant bit of nothing from a federal standpoint, merely enough to keep him alive while he pursues his passion, dreams his dreams, and massages his concept of reality onto the canvas of life. His balance sheet for the business is clean and complete. His honesty is embarrassingly meticulous down to the penny. Such virtue surely beams from the figures on his tax return. How dare this stranger imply otherwise! Yet, these are not the kinds of things one should say to an IRS agent.

Arthur's place of business for the last many years occupies a barren landscape off a lonely stretch of the interstate, and its vivid orange and black sign is visible from it. Easy enough for Henry to spot. On the driveway in, the first building has a glass door looking out onto the world, bearing the black vinyl press-on logo "Store-All." Directly inside is the office, a shell on the clam of Arthur's studio, moist and wiggling behind a door in the back marked "Private." Past this building runs a long drive with four slender, parallel lanes shot straight out from it like the tines of a comb, each with a neat row of connected boxlike sheds.

Orderly and symmetrical and pedestrian as this layout appears, the studio bears witness to the other.

Arthur is behind the counter, looking out the glass door, when Henry, Mr. or not, pulls up in his sage-colored government sedan. Henry gathers his things and takes the walkway briskly, carrying a cardboard, plastic-lidded deli cup and a small laptop case. Cup in left hand, case handle in right. Even then he's plotting his entry, the need to free up his right hand to open the door, and moments later, to feel the skin of the man he's about to deconstruct. In a swift move, clutching the large deli cup in the left hand, he shoves the laptop case firmly under his left arm and squeezes it tight against his ribcage to avoid dropping it. The door is opened efficiently, a whoosh inside, three paces neatly taken, a deliberate grip offered. "Mr. Creaton?" A brief flash of teeth.

Arthur nods and extends a diffident hand. The counter is between them. As they physically disengage, an inch-square piece of paper at the end of a slender string flutters and comes to rest at the side of the deli cup.

"Excuse me," Arthur says. "I'll lock the door." He rounds the end of the counter.

"Yes, of course," Henry responds, stepping aside to avoid further physical contact.

Privacy is ordained, one of Henry's implicit demands. To accommodate, Arthur reluctantly granted him a Monday, the official "closed" day, although Arthur is always around, hidden from view in the back. Monday is *his* day. Paid-up renters are free to come and go to their units at any time, but the office door is locked on Mondays and Arthur enjoys his freedom from the needs of the public during daylight hours.

Now, a Mr. Public of a sort has come to take a precious Monday away. Arthur's blood simmers even as he maintains the studied, blanched exterior of the innocent. He can play along—he will have to.

Without invitation, Henry has made his way to the nook in the office. The small waiting area has four moderately uncomfortable chairs, a low synthetic wood coffee table, a square stand for the Mr. Coffee and Styrofoam cups, a vending machine packed with junk food, and a rack of sales brochures and rental forms. Henry takes a seat, unbuttons his suit jacket, places his teacup on the coffee table, his laptop next to it, and powers up. Arthur notices this with a glance over his shoulder as he locks the door.

Henry's cache of niceties was exhausted with that initial flash of teeth. Now he's down to business in a peculiarly awkward way, bent forward from the waist to reach the low coffee table, elbows resting on knees, and fingers just below them, pattering at the keys. "We'll start with the ten-forty and the first Schedule C, the one for...this." Henry looks up from the screen and slides a withering look around the office.

Arthur is walking back to the counter when he catches the look. Instantly, he forms judgments of his own but holds his tongue. He's learned to remain quiet. Honesty doesn't require more, and self-explanation is useless when the recipient will never really understand. Arthur learned this hard lesson years ago, when his youthful exuberance fell on deaf ears and his colors met blindness and his ideas were received with blank smiles and speechlessness. Gradually, over time, he's been shaped on the outside to resemble anyone else, a creeping crumble into grayness, while he continues to live on the inside, sending out tendrils of hope.

Wishing to maintain a distance, Arthur takes up a place on his stool behind the counter. Except for a phone and computer at the far end, the countertop is empty. Underneath the counter, on a shelf out of Henry's view, Arthur has placed an expanding file folder containing all the documents he might possibly need, assembled in advance. Black figures on paper—the concrete proof to supplant his unacceptable word. The tax year in question is now ancient history, its financial transactions long forgotten, but Arthur's conviction as to the accuracy of his tax return holds steady.

Henry does not remove his eyes from the screen of his laptop as he starts the inquisition. "Your full name is Arthur, middle initial F, Creaton?"

"Yes."

"Date of birth is May 24, 1953?"

"Yes."

"Social security number 826-13-4198?"

"Yes."

Henry pauses to move his unusually small hand, sliding the tip of his slender index finger around the mouse pad of his laptop. The hard tip jabs a click. Arthur's dignity is already wilting under the subtle heat of Henry's test questions, the baseline against which the answers to the really tough questions will be measured. Henry absently picks up the deli cup and slurps through the hole in the top. A messy sound, somewhat out of character. He carefully returns the cup to its exact position on the table.

"Your filing status is single?"

"Yes."

"You claim no exemptions other than yourself?"

"Yes. I mean, no."

"You have no dependents."

"Yes. No family."

"No dependents."

Henry looks up and aims his surprising kiwi-colored irises. In a small moment of truth, Arthur's imagination is awakened. He lives for these moments, but this one disturbs him. That eye color is the only remarkable feature of the little government agent, a fleck of beauty completely wasted on his tasteless and banal task. Arthur's kaleidoscopic lenses shift and close. He responds to Henry's question with a trancelike nod which becomes, in the next moment, an affirmative shake.

His examiner is absolutely right. There are no dependents. Arthur left home at a young age, never started a family of his own, and has lived alone these forty years. He rarely sees his aging mother and older sister, who live a thousand miles away within blocks of each other. His father always refused to see him, but his mother pretended otherwise. Up until a few years ago, in every conversation, she would say things like this: "Your father says hello." "Your father sends his love." "Your father is asking after you."

Artie is the frozen baby boy, at best grown to age seventeen, wearing his navy blazer with the school insignia. Mom calls him on holidays and birthdays, but his sister, Elise, calls more frequently, their conversations going deeper, especially now that her two children, Arthur's niece and nephew, are fully grown and independent. She lives with her husband in a cavernous house with nothing to want but food for the imagination.

In the early years, Artie quite looked up to Elise. She was one of the few to come close, and she still tries, but he resists, preferring the rare, pleasant surprise of an insightful stranger. If a sister should try, and fail, the disappointment will cut deeper. "I'd so like to see them, Art," she says every now and then on the telephone. She remembers the early, childish works, and now, well, he senses it would be too much for her. He never gets around to arranging a viewing, even today, when distance is a dimension so easily erased yet queerly maintained on the Internet, by virtual tour.

Henry is already on to the next topic, something more important to him. Line 7 of the 1040.

"Income, wages, salaries, tips," says Henry. "You've listed zero."

"Zero, because, of course, you look farther down…"

"Yes, I know, I know. Your two Schedule C's. But wages, salaries, and tips must take into account income from all sources."

"I understand."

"You received no income in 2007 from any source other

than the two," he searches for a word, "businesses?"

Arthur shakes his head. *No.*

"I'll just need to confirm."

Their eyes meet again, but this isn't enough. Henry seeks the precision and comfort of documentary evidence.

"I suppose you want…"

"All checking, savings, and money market accounts. I'll start with the first three months of 2007."

Arthur's hands shake as he rummages around under the counter.

"Personal and business, whether in your name or the d/b/a."

Surely this is another test: will Arthur disclose everything or attempt to hide? He well knows that the IRS has a record of every bank account linked to every social security number. He's unnerved by his sweaty fingers and slight tremor, a reaction he didn't anticipate, made worse by his fumbling under the counter. He decides to make an open show of it and hoists the entire expanding file folder up onto the counter. As he riffles through the compartments with eyes cast downward to the task, his ear picks up Henry's loud slurping from the sippy cup.

Arthur finally extracts the statements and looks up to see Henry's affected nonchalance, a half-lidded gaze at his screen while the material of his white business shirt stretches taut against an impatient expansion of chest. Arthur walks around the end of the counter and offers the statements from two banks, M &T for Store-All, Citi for himself.

Henry accepts the offering, drops the stack onto the table, and pulls a small, handheld calculator from his right jacket pocket. "I hate those damn calculators on the computer." He chuckles demurely, as if this is the most exquisite of accountant jokes.

It's now 8:20 by the digital wall clock. A painful hour follows, cut into four segments. Every quarter, Henry asks for the next three months of statements. He examines each batch of thirty pages or so, one page at a time, tracing down line by line with a fingertip, every once in a while reacting. He emits a small grunt, or raises his eyebrows slightly, or slurps audibly from the sippy cup—until it runs dry—followed by an intense computation on the handheld calculator and a computer entry.

Perhaps there's a worksheet of sorts on the screen. Arthur only guesses. He cannot see it. He faces Henry, or rather the top of Henry's thin-cushioned head, which is dipped downward to the screen or the handheld or the papers. The silver-colored cover of the laptop with its backlit apple, marred by a generous bite, stares back. After each little episode of discovery, Henry makes a delicate swerve of the fingertip and jabs a click.

Henry thus absorbed, Arthur periodically rises to stretch his legs and walk about. Standing near the front door, he folds his arms and rocks back and forth, heel to toe, looking down at his brown scuffed Hush Puppies. The left toe bears a noticeable vermillion splotch.

Gazing now through the door, he sees a van pull into the driveway and continue past the office, heading for one of the units in back. If he were to enter his studio and look through the northwest window, he would be able to see the van's course and determine its destination. Beyond that window, the symmetrical lines of units are laid out into the distance on a gentle slope. The last two units of the farthest line are filled with his own life works. Soon he will need a third.

On the other side of the studio, the southeast window faces a small clearing and a wooded area beyond. This is the window Arthur most often faces when he's at work, hugged by the clutter of easels and canvases and paint-spattered walls. The blood red, bile green, and pus yellow of a previous period are now partially overlaid with the sunset orange, aqua blue, and shining white of recent years as Arthur begins to feel his mortality. In the studio, he's completely alone in his universe, not wanting it any other way.

Edging near the fourth quarter of 2007, Arthur is back on the stool when Henry makes a discovery of significance. He sits upright in his chair and exclaims, "What's this?"

Arthur's heart stops.

"A deposit of $20,000 on November 29, 2007. $20,000 even."

"Twenty...?"

"The Citi account," adds Henry. "Your personal savings account."

Arthur is dumbfounded. The amount is completely foreign to him. $20,000! A staggering sum bearing no relation to the rental of a unit or the sale of a painting.

Henry leans forward, picks up the deli cup, then remembers it's empty and sets it down again. "I don't recall this figure. Will it show up on one of your Schedule C's?" His voice betrays mild annoyance.

A bead of sweat runs from the base of Arthur's right armpit down the length of his ribcage, rolling past an intestinal growl. The explanation is on the tip of his tongue but cannot be found. With an electric zing, this feeling of separation and mystification is replaced with something worse—gut recognition. This figure, this twenty thousand, twenty thousand, twenty thousand, is now so blaringly familiar he has no reason to doubt its veracity.

"Yes, I did receive it, but..." He is equally sure it does not appear on his tax return.

"The source?"

That is the question. Emotion rises from the depths of this new doubt about himself, his shame at being unprepared. He tries to rationalize. How could he have prepared for this question when the twenty thousand is not on his tax return? This thought, however, merely seems to confirm a subconscious act of concealment.

"The source," Arthur repeats, buying time. He knows he received this money. It's associated with a strange voice, an unexpected call from an attorney in a distant city, yes, that was it, and a day later, a call from his mother. "He was thinking of you, Artie," in the past tense, finally.

Arthur's cheeks grow hot and his eyes sting. The tears well and threaten to spill because now he remembers this "gift" from his father, the man made of millions who had forsaken him, convinced of Arthur's uselessness to the world of true men. His father's bequest was a business strategy, a token to thwart any possibility of a will contest. *Yes, he was thinking of me.*

Arthur chokes on a sob, angry at himself and supremely embarrassed. "It was an inheritance. From my father. He died in 2007." He swipes at the single drop of water under his eye and clears his voice, ashamed, profoundly disappointed in himself for succumbing to these mind games, acting as though he had something to hide. There was nothing to hide, not from himself, and certainly not from Henry.

The government agent is taken aback by this show of emotion, clearly mistaken as to its cause. Well, maybe not completely, thinks Arthur, doubtful as to his own feelings. Whether an expression of insight or not, Henry says, "I see." And Arthur now sees that the agent's clean edges are tarnished. When did he loosen the knot of his tie at the collar?

Henry rebounds quickly from his momentary empathy and shows a small twinge of disappointment. No big discovery after all. The recipient of a gift or bequest of that size does not pay income tax on it. "Do you have a legal document to back this up?"

"Yes, somewhere."

"I'll need to see it."

"All right. I have to look for it."

"Of course, you can forward it later. I'm sure there will be other documents as well."

"Then, we won't finish today?"

"We never do." Henry moves his eyes back to the screen, looking for what comes next. "Now…"

It's 9:30, and Henry is finally satisfied with line 7.

Coming up on one o'clock, Arthur has twice retreated to the back. Each time, he waited until Henry's nose was buried in paperwork, then opened the "Private" door just enough to duck inside and close it carefully behind him. There's a small washroom in the studio. He never allows his customers to use it. "No facilities," he says if anyone asks.

Henry, however, seems to have a bladder of steel. He has not asked once. In their silent, endless minutes together, Arthur has thought many times about that large cup of tea. The deli container still resides in the spot Henry made for it, undisturbed by any of the myriad documents absently laid alongside.

The agent has risen from his chair only once. At about 9:45, he inserted a power cord into his laptop and connected it to the outlet directly under the Mr. Coffee. Henry, the man, has more modest energy needs. There's been no hint of a lunch break, and Arthur's stomach is growling audibly.

"Utilities?" asks Henry, in a voice grown gentler over the hours. They've become automatons in a jointly crafted ritual. Henry says a word, and Arthur produces the needed documents.

Henry is nearing the end of the first Schedule C. All of the income and expenses of Store-All have been checked, and utilities are last on the list. The modest profit—Arthur's livelihood—has been accounted for. Finally, there is nothing else about Store-All to confirm.

Eight a.m. to one p.m. may be the longest period Arthur has spent in the same room with a single person in a very, very long time. Subtle discoveries have blossomed incrementally:

At about ten o'clock, Arthur noticed a slender gold band on the ring finger of Henry's caramel-colored left hand.

At a quarter past ten, a cell phone in Henry's jacket pocket musically sounded with a popular rap-like mantra, albeit on low volume. Henry quickly removed the cell, glanced at the screen, and pressed a button to silence it.

Several times, with a slight grimace, Henry has bent forward absently and inserted his right index finger between his sock and the opening of his black, oxford business shoe. Arthur wonders if the hard leather has caused a painful blister.

At about eleven, while handing over a stack of documents, Arthur was amazed to discover, in Henry's left earlobe, a tiny pinprick of a scar, an abandoned piercing. Perhaps not abandoned but involuntarily forfeited.

And for the past hour, Henry has been noticeably over warm—his forehead has an oily, glistening sheen. He periodically lifts the lapel of his suit jacket to let the air in but refuses to remove it. Arthur supposes that Uncle Sam's rules forbid it.

Time enough for other discoveries as well. The paper ritual, daily schedule, accounting, and planning that go into the storage business—Arthur now admits to himself that he takes pleasure in these activities. Not for the first time, he wonders what his life would have been like without the need to work for a living, if his father had given him a cool several million and a studio bursting with supplies—if he'd had unlimited time for himself. The fantasy is not new, but for the first time he emerges from it without the bitter after-taste of resentment.

They both know what is coming next. Arthur's second Schedule C. This one shows a loss, the expenses exceeding the income. Entries on the form are few and brief. In 2007, Arthur had two sales, totaling $250. Oils, brushes, and canvases, gallery fees, travel, and correspondence—these expenses have far exceeded the income. But Arthur can account for every penny.

Henry lifts his head from the screen. Their eyes meet and lock in the lengthiest sustained gaze they have yet shared, at least two seconds. Arthur quickly averts his eyes and becomes busy, moving the heavy expanding file folder from the countertop to the shelf underneath.

While so engaged, with his head ducked low, he hears this: "About your second Schedule C." There's a pause through which Arthur makes some noise with the papers in his file. Then the voice sounds again: "Is this your only hobby?"

Arthur is cut to the quick. All the breath goes out of him. For the second time, tears spring into his eyes. Anger and the old humiliation. He looks up, ready to fight or to cave in, he doesn't know which, but he sees—what's this? A most astonishing sight! Henry's face is lit up with a full-toothed smile, friendly and companionable without conde-scension or any trace of sinister accusation. What on earth does this mean? A backward sort of recognition? A joke meant to convey the opposite? Arthur discerns a nub of understanding in Henry's eyes, those unusual, dreamy irises.

"You mean, my work," Arthur says quietly.

"Reported on this Schedule C, 'profit or loss from a business.' In this case, a loss."

"What do you need to see?"

"Nothing."

"Nothing?"

"Nothing at all. I have it."

This doesn't seem possible.

But then, Arthur understands. Henry already saw the proof—he knew what to look for—when he examined

Arthur's personal bank statements and credit card purchases the first time. All expenses are confirmed, and the two deposits, the checks for $100 and $150, are there. But how would he know that the checks were in payment for works of art?

"Don't you need to see...?" Arthur's eyes flit to the studio door.

Henry glances at the door. Is he tempted?

But then, from Henry's pocket, the rapper bursts into the silence. Henry answers this time. "I'll be there in half an hour," he promises the caller. To Arthur he says, "That's it for today," and unplugs the cord from his laptop. "You'll just need to send me those items we discussed."

Arthur watches the drab sedan pull out of the driveway. Henry said he would be back—the NRP regs require the agents to discuss their results with the taxpayers personally.

Arthur forgets how hungry he felt a moment ago. There are two things he must do immediately.

First, he goes to the phone at the end of the counter and dials Elise. Some time ago, she extended an invitation for Thanksgiving, to join her and her husband and children, their mother. He's put it off, and it's time he accepted. Later on, he'll consider whether he wishes to bring a small gift. If so, it will have to be one of his more conventional works.

Second, he enters the studio, sets a new canvas on the easel, and starts to mix his paints. The toughest color will be the kiwi. Flecked with black seeds, this particular kiwi has been enjoyed—a generous bite is the evidence. It floats in a rectangular, gleaming silver backdrop, and in the far distance, another shade of green, the color of money, is fading from view.

In this moment, as he creates in his studio, Arthur doesn't know that, in a few weeks' time, Henry will telephone and say, "This is Tom Henry." Arthur doesn't know that, on the day Henry returns, he will be dressed casually in a stylish leather jacket. Whether it's Mr. Henry or Arthur's perception of him, he will be a different man, relaxed, warm, and jaunty. A large-toothed smile will be pushing out his cheeks, all to convey the genuine relief he feels to be confirming Arthur's meticulous honesty—there will be no adjustments to his 2007 tax return.

In this instant, Arthur does not know that Henry's transformation will be a continuation of the one they started this day, together. He is not yet fully aware of the lines they were drawing, Arthur's toward Henry, Henry's toward Arthur, in the resonance of five hours shared in the same room, on the other side of "Private."

Will he invite him in for a look?

∽

Malocclusion

"THE ODDEST PART of it is...," the patient looked down at her hands in search of an elusive synapse, "I don't remember his name."

Dr. Reckner took full advantage of her downward gaze to roam the contours of her face, the border of carefully misplaced, highlighted strands of brunette, evidence of her attempt at youth. He lingered along the periphery for now, studiously avoiding the mouth, the universal center of need and desire: sustenance, communication, gratification.

A strange habit for someone in his profession, but his first inclination—more of a trained practice—was to look everywhere but the mouth, to gather in the person, beginning his study of the problem from the endpoint of its consequences, tracing those outer layers of symptomatic adjustment backward to their source, to the malocclusion. A soft tendril graced her temple and tipped at the point of a faint crow's foot. Another one caught in a lash near the delicate bridge of her nose, sending shudders up to the hairline with every blink.

To remind himself of her name, he glanced quickly at the manila folder on his desk, its green-edged label color coded for the middle of the alphabet, L-M-N. Janine Lindstrom. Mrs. Lindstrom wasn't old, but neither was she young, and the haphazard bangs failed to conceal a three-quarter-inch crevice between her eyebrows, etched there, he knew, by her mouth. Everything came from the mouth.

He suspected that her age would come into stark relief once he escorted her away from the soothing, low wattage of his office into the adjoining room, where he would invite her to recline in the examination chair while directing the unforgiving high beam down into her core. He looked forward to that moment while enjoying these preliminaries, the easy foreplay to his ultimate, exacting handle on her problem.

"Try as I might, I can't remember!" Perhaps the doctor was God. She latched onto him with lost, pleading eyes. He quickly searched them, feeling the tug of a familiar cord — the first step toward his gradual descent. He also saw the pain in her eyes, had known he would find it there even before looking, but the beauty remained. What a waste! Years of waste, and all from the mouth. Still he avoided it, that shadowy maw lurking beneath the pretty nose.

"I was certainly old enough to remember something like that. A name. I was fourteen and fifteen. The treatment ended when I was almost sixteen. The whole experience was so painful I must have developed a mental block against it. The name that is." She issued a lusty sigh, surprising for its contrast to her bare murmur of a voice. "The rest of it I can't forget." Her head bobbed and fell to regard her wringing hands once more.

With the downward motion of her head, so went his, dropping below the neck, reaching forbidden territory, rebounding. He would have liked to remain there, exploring her unrealized corporal beauty—something he'd sensed (without looking) five minutes earlier when Mrs. Lindstrom had followed him into his office, heating his back with round suggestions under the puritan clothing. Her anxious gait was tense and bottled instead of free and easy the way nature would dictate if not for the influence of the mouth. That mouth.

At fourteen (before the damage had been done) the budding flower must have been irresistible. Dr. Reckner pushed the thought from his mind and averted his eyes, searching out the sterling-framed photograph on his desk, equidistant from doctor and patient, angled for the benefit of both. His wife Clarissa and their two teenagers, Bradford and Jake, displayed an abundance of dental glow, mouths he'd crafted to perfection.

"I remember my mother driving me there, and I have a vision of the street and the building and the waiting room— and the examining room. Recently, I went back to the place I thought it would be, but nothing looks the same. I have no other clues. Names in the phone book mean nothing to me. He would be quite old by now, and for all I know he's already dead. Believe me, I'd look him up if I could. I'd make him account for this! That man ruined my life!" Her eyes flashed at the doctor, and he swallowed hard on the wad of anxiety that always bubbled up at the suggestion of a lawsuit against one of his brethren.

A disgruntled neurotic, a person overly sensitive to pain and unrealistically convinced of entitlement, was a doctor's worst nightmare, could put the blight on career, reputation, and financial security. Mrs. Lindstrom seemed the type, but he hadn't yet completed his examination, and so, couldn't judge. Possibly her statements had real basis in fact. A mouth could ruin a life, he'd seen it before.

More from self-preservation than from a need to see the ancient x-rays of this woman's mouth, the doctor feigned interest: "Perhaps your family kept records," he suggested, "your parents—"

"Are dead."

"I'm sorry."

"Thank you, but they died many years ago. A horrible car accident. They were on their way to visit me at college."

"I'm so sorry."

"Yes, well, even then I was in some pain from this," she motioned to her mouth, "but didn't think to save my parents' old bills and records. After their death, my brother and I sifted through so much of their stuff. Why do we need to save this, we said? A bunch of old orthodontic records? I remember holding that file and looking at it, hesitating before I threw it in the trash. Who would have thought?"

"Yes, who would have?"

"I was in denial, you see. I'd been through treatment, I'd gone through all that pain and was supposed to have a perfect mouth as a result." Her small voice quavered. "And there I was, even then in college, only a few years after treatment, already with headaches, a pounding in my ears, clicking and jaw dislocation, lumps of food I couldn't chew, indigestion, and reflux."

"All from the mouth."

"Yes."

"The bite."

"Yes."

"And I'd venture to guess, it has gradually worsened over the years? The teeth, positioned badly, tend to shift."

"Yes!" She looked at her savior, the man who understood. "Yes, you know the problem exactly. My friend, the one who recommended you, said you were the only orthodontist to consult."

The doctor nodded modestly. He was, indeed, well regarded. Would go so far, in his own mind, as to say he was the best in the East Bay.

"I've waited a long time, I know."

The doctor nodded amiably.

"My dentist tells me, year after year, it's nearly impossible to correct, and it's risky to move my teeth. I may lose them. But I can't tolerate the pain any longer."

"No, and why should you?"

"Yes, why? But, Doctor—" She stopped on the edge of her words, a voice no more than a whisper and a gasp of air, pushing color into her cheeks. She hesitated, hovered, waiting for a response from him, waiting for a sign of irrepressible curiosity. All of it, a danger signal. Yes, why? What else could she be asking of him? He couldn't deny his need to know.

With a sage twist of the brow, he leveled his eyes on hers, fighting the growing urge to let them drop. "Yes, you'd like to know…?"

"Is it too late?"

His eyes went hard to the point of their intercourse. *Is it too late?* He saw her lips opening and closing in slow motion, words crawling through the tiny, withered, painted hole—*too*—a push and pucker—*late*—a pull and stretch. Her speech barely added shape to her mouth, what was visible of it on the surface, the greater part sunken deep inside her head without the support of teeth, a skinny dash with its sad attempt at enlargement: a thick layer of lipstick, a conservative mauve, extending above and below the lips into surrounding skin. It was the mouth of a gummy eighty-year-old, shrunken and lined, set within a rigid jaw marked with the unmistakable traces of clenching and gnashing, the flex of stressed muscles and tendons.

He straightened up against an involuntary shudder, successfully concealing it.

"Let's take a look at you," he said and stood, holding his hand out, motioning toward the open door into the examining room.

Dr. Reckner had seen many poorly aligned teeth, but none quite as bad as this. "Re-do's" and adult cases accounted for a large percentage of his practice, the middle-aged mothers and fathers of his preteen patients and their referrals, patients like Mrs. Lindstrom. Fairly immune to the sight of disfigured mouths, he'd shuddered not so much from the sight of hers as from the abominable thought of a doctor (someone who called himself a doctor, a member of his profession!) committing such a heinous act on the teeth of another human being.

From a long line of distinguished dentists, and as the second in his family to practice the specialty of orthodontics, David C. Reckner Jr., DDS, had maintained and built upon the legacy of David Sr. A solid reputation such as his wasn't seriously threatened by the butchers, hacks, and incompetents in his field, but still, his laurels moaned in outrage at any senseless deconstruction of a mouth.

Some consideration had to be taken, he knew, of the significant strides in the field of orthodontics since the days of Mrs. Lindstrom's first treatment. Even so, he couldn't pin her mouth on a competent dentist, one strapped by the ignorance of a science in its infancy. After all, hadn't his own father labored under the same state of incomplete knowledge—with excellent results?

Orthodontics was an art more than science, requiring that rare blend of muscular strength, precision, skill, vision, and sensitivity to gently prod the teeth into proper alignment, finding for the twenty-eight their ideal sixty-eight points of contact, a neat fit to the puzzle, all with an artist's intuitive eye on the natural contours of the mouth, cheeks, and jaw. A Michelangelo with hammer and chisel he was, chip-chip-chipping away at seemingly immovable, obtuse and resistant stone, rendering the ultimate aesthetic angle to a scrupulously smooth, mechanical, interlocking fit.

David Sr. had been a perfectionist, relieving thousands of malocclusions, and what better example than the mouth of his own son! David Jr. confirmed it every morning he awoke refreshed from a restful night of relaxed-jaw sleep, every time he bit into a carrot, every two years when he made yet another plaster impression of his own teeth (just to check!) and clacked the two beheaded jaws together in their perfect grooves. After all these years, each of the sixty-eight contact points remained perfectly aligned!

So, no, Mrs. Lindstrom's plight couldn't be blamed on an ancient age or a simpler time. A certain amount of common sense and humanity should have spared her from the butchery he found in her mouth. Pain was always involved—a criticism of his profession, that thoughtless question to which he was acutely sensitive: *Do you actually enjoy this infliction of pain?* But in her case, the pain must have exceeded the point of tolerance, for the best scenario he could fathom put her in the hands of a reckless dentistry school dropout—at worst, a downright sadist.

On the way to the examination chair, Dr. Reckner all but forgot that brief foreboding moment in his office. Mrs. Lindstrom was at once different. Relieved of her initial confession, she walked easier, allowing a show of life to the doctor, who followed closely enough to measure the greater breadth of his chest and shoulders on either side of hers while discretely consuming her backside from a pleasingly superior height. At the edge of the chair she lingered, touching it as if to remember, then hovered over it with her jutting, prudently covered tail, lowering herself familiarly into the curved joint of the seat before reclining fully, gently rotating the back of her head into the padded rest.

The doctor took his own stool, the round one on wheels. Moving in, sitting erect, he lowered Mrs. Lindstrom's torso with the foot control while adjusting the overhead light, extending and fully exposing her prone form, chest rising and falling with every needful breath. Tension remained in the hush before each breath, in the clutch of her hands on the armrests. A large diamond in the wedding set on her left ring finger attested to another man's discovery of her finer qualities, a man who hadn't been fooled by that mouth.

"Marjorie," the doctor said, looking down into the orifice, absently holding the patient's manila folder out to the side. His assistant, arranging instruments in the corner, abandoned her task and turned toward him, hand out-stretched for the folder. "Yes. Oh!" she said with a fleeting glance at the patient. Momentarily, her forward motion was arrested, and a tiny flush came into her apple cheeks before she took the folder and focused her full attention on it, pulling out the preprinted examination form with its black-on-white outlines of numbered teeth and lists of symptoms and diagnoses, all awaiting checkmarks and notations where appropriate.

Dr. Reckner didn't seem to notice the hesitation. Despite Marjorie's advancing years, she was quick and vital, an invaluable assistant. She put on her glasses and readied herself for the report, pulling a pen from jacket pocket.

With bare hands, warm, the doctor placed tips of index fingers, right and left, high into the symmetrical depressions of Mrs. Lindstrom's face, feeling for the hinges of her jaw, left and right. "Open and bite several times." She looked up at him and obeyed, deepening the crease between her eyes. Her skin went suddenly moist. "TMJ locking," said the doctor. Marjorie dashed off a checkmark. He looked down into the patient's eyes, now flitting along the ceiling. "TMJ locking and pain," he said. A notation in the margin.

With thumb and index finger of left hand, the doctor clamped her cheeks and rotated her head from side to side. "Bilateral mid-face retrusion." Check. Efficiently, he spun away from the patient, applied the prophylactics, and turned back to insert his smooth, latex-encased fingers into Mrs. Lindstrom's small opening, gently forcing it wider against taut skin. The lack of dental support had caused the mouth to sink inward, tightening the opening, making the lips resistant to stretching. Her self-conscious habit of speaking softly through motionless lips—an effort to avoid drawing attention to that horribly shrunken slit—had only accelerated the atrophy of muscles and further shrinkage.

The doctor's fingers explored inside the lips along the gum line while Marjorie looked on, pen in hand. "Bite." Gently, he peeled away the lips to get a better view of the teeth, running his rubbered digits up under the lips, stroking the gums. Mrs. Lindstrom's eyes watered from pain and longing. "Deep impinging overbite, over-retracted upper and lower incisor profile, upper anterior teeth inclined lingually." *Pushed halfway to the uvula. The butcher!* "Lower crowding." Check, check, notation. A haphazard sprouting of lower teeth stood like young shoots pushing up from the floor of the mouth, fighting for room under the shade of a very normal, long, and lovely tongue.

He pulled out, gloved fingers wet. "Marjorie," he said, still looking at the patient, this time into her eyes, which found his eyes briefly before her hand whisked up to push away a tear threatening to spill. "The lower ones," interrupted Mrs. Lindstrom, lips trembling. "They were straight once, when he finished the treatment."

Dr. Reckner intensified his gaze, lost everything around him but her. "I know," he started, unable to remove his eyes. *Was she out of her mind? Suddenly trying to defend the man who had "ruined" her life?* "But they've shifted over the last several years, haven't they?" She nodded in agreement. "The upper teeth have no support and they've sunk very deep. The lower teeth are pushed back, they're trapped, nowhere to go. Nowhere…," his voice trailed. Lost.

He turned away, needing a moment to find the room, his hands, his gloves. He removed them, limp and wet. He cleared his throat. "Marjorie. Do you have those x-rays from Dr. Broadhurst?" Marjorie's eyes darted up over rims of glasses. "There," she said, tipping her head toward the wall behind him. A stupid oversight! Of course, Marjorie had already pinned the x-rays on the back-lit display.

The doctor wheeled over to take a look and confirmed the suspected danger. "You see here," he pointed, becoming professorial. Mrs. Lindstrom, hair mussed and cheeks damp, pushed up awkwardly onto an elbow against the reclined back of the chair. Her eyes caught Marjorie's but quickly pulled away again, focusing on the x-ray at the end of the doctor's pointed finger, while Marjorie hastily stuffed the examination form into the folder. "There's evidence of root resorption on all four upper incisors," explained the doctor.

"Yes, Dr. Broadhurst mentioned something about that."

"The scars of orthodontia. You've lost a good third of the root structure."

"How?"

"Your teeth were moved too quickly, too..." violently, he wanted to say, "too far, too fast."

"But is it...?"

"No. It isn't. It's not too late." He was firm and adamant. A man. But on the inside, this is what the good doctor meant: *I'll help you! I'll help you, by God, I'll rectify this!*

As a very young boy, Davey loved to play with the plaster molds his father would give him from finished cases, the pre-treatment impressions. These disembodied teeth, white and crumbling, were fascinating in the seemingly infinite patterns that nature designed for a mouth. Crooked teeth, jutting teeth, crossed teeth, huge gaps, holes where teeth should have grown, pegs, all gums and no teeth, all teeth and no gums, lower jaws twice the size of uppers, cross bites, overbites, werewolf fangs, multiple rows like sharks. The most grotesque were the most exciting and awakened his need to fix them, but when he got a little older, they awakened other needs as well, giving him the idea to touch himself in their presence, doing it again and again—a memory he now liked to suppress, remembering instead the innocent games of a younger age.

He would line them up, rearrange them, mismatch a lower jaw with someone else's upper, and even break them into sections (using his own bare hands in the years before his father allowed him a knife for that purpose). Individuals, twos, and threes, patterns mapped out on the floor of his bedroom. A ten-foot, wall-to-wall line of twelve-year molars. A circle of upper central and lateral incisors belonging to a dozen faceless kids.

Most fascinating were Davey's own teeth. The ankylosed lower bicuspid had presented his father with a most challenging problem. There was surgery to remove it, and two years of braces to fill the gap and correct the bite. These were the years, ages twelve and thirteen, when Davey began to linger in the office after his treatments, peering over his father's shoulder. In high school, he'd often walk to the office after school, interspersing homework with informal future career education.

Dr. Reckner Sr. was a big, robust man, a commanding presence, the kind of father a son obeyed and sought to please. "David," he would say in a powerful voice (by high school, the boy was no longer "Davey"), "hand me a couple of separators. No, the posterior, not anterior." His assistant, Marjorie, easily could have helped, but she stepped out of the way, a benevolent angel overlooking the lesson, never coming between father and son.

This good, healthy curiosity about teeth seemed to run in the family, Sr. encouraging Jr.'s interest without demanding it, just as his own father had. He would talk at length about malocclusions, their many manifestations, the theory and practice of movement, torque, and union, the infinite positions on the way to a perfect fit, the means to the end. "It's an exciting process, isn't it, David?" he would say, absently tooling an elastics hemostat between index and middle fingers. "Yes, it's the process itself that's exciting."

His meaning came clear at the conclusion of every case. David saw it. The last brace was removed, and the doctor's hands would go slightly limp and spent, his mouth turned downward with sudden disinterest, not proud and beaming the way David thought it should look. Completion. A rolling over. Sleep. The next day, a virgin mouth and new interest.

At his father's office he often saw kids he knew from school, mostly girls, because even though boys' teeth were just as bad, parents were more likely to spend that kind of money on their daughters. It was there he got to know Clarissa. She began treatment her freshman year in high school, his sophomore year, but he didn't have the courage to ask her on a date until her teeth were finished, the second semester of his senior year. He made a point of knowing her schedule and never missed a visit, pretending he just happened to be around.

The doctor saw his son's interest in the girl and fully approved, maybe because the doctor himself responded well to her pleasantness and compliance, traits that reminded him of David's mother. He allowed his son to hover close behind while Clarissa was in the chair, and even made a second set of plaster impressions for David to play with early on, not waiting until the case was over.

Clarissa's God-given mouth had a buck, gap-toothed smile. Some would call it ugly, but her teen admirer kept his copy of it preserved in plaster, took care not to damage it, and stored it in a box, taking it out from time to time when he wanted to recreate that small thrill of excitement he felt the first time he'd laid eyes on her. At night, he would dream of his father's hands in her mouth, inserting instruments, twisting wires, tightening and adjusting, Clarissa's eyes darting in pain, searching for him just behind his father's shoulder, silent, rapt. He would awake in the middle of the night sweating, in a puddle of sticky wet.

Two and a half years of this, after she'd been weaned from the last retainer, David asked her out, and on their second date, worked up the courage to kiss her new mouth. It was a flawless mouth but surprisingly bland, nothing near what he'd dreamed. Pleasant, vanilla, comfortable, an immaculate fit with his, also perfect. Later that night, at home, he removed her original teeth from their box, set them on the bedside table under the blue glow of a nightlight, and stared at them until his eyelids grew heavy with sleep. He maintained this ritual for several years but was ashamed to tell Clarissa and hid the plaster teeth in the basement once they were married.

After Mrs. Lindstrom had gone, Dr. Reckner asked Marjorie

for her opinion. She wasn't a doctor and hadn't the schooling, but her years of experience—eighteen with his father and twenty with him—had given her uncanny wisdom and insight.

Not intentionally had Dr. Reckner courted this family institution. His employment of Marjorie had been quite unplanned. That first day, she'd simply shown up at the door of his new practice in Piedmont, the year he'd gotten his degree and board certification, five years after his father's shocking and untimely death at the age of fifty-three from a heart attack.

Her visit came as a surprise. His last vision of Marjorie had been from a distance, out the corner of his eye at the funeral as he huddled with his mother, supporting her by the elbow. His mother barely gave the woman a glance. Understandably, Mrs. Reckner was overcome with grief, but still it was odd that, as many years as Marjorie had served the doctor, she hadn't grown closer to his family. There was no animus between the two women, but neither was there much in the way of acknowledgment. Marjorie was always in the background, even then at the funeral where she stood ten feet apart from the rest, her black clothing blacker than theirs and her face tough but puckered from secret crying. Spinster, was the word that came to David's mind, knowing he shouldn't think it.

Explaining her unexpected presence in Jr.'s office that first day, Marjorie made an uncharacteristically intimate admission. She'd been despondent ever since Sr.'s death, living frugally off her savings and the profit-sharing plan, coming dangerously close to becoming destitute, unable to bring herself to apply for another job. "I'm aware, even before looking, that other dentists and orthodontists won't measure up," she told him. "You're the closest to him, and I'd like to work again. So, I'm asking you for a job." She was willing to commute the considerable distance from her apartment in San Francisco to the outlying East Bay suburb of Piedmont. Moving from the city—the place she'd lived and worked for so many years alongside his father—was out of the question.

He wasn't quite sure how to take her. As a boy he'd seen her work. He remembered his father speaking highly of her, knew she was a superlative assistant and someone he should hire in a minute, but her surprise visit with her admitted depression and neurotic show of loyalty placed her in a new light, somewhere on the fringe. And another thing, she was looking at him in a way that said she knew him completely, at once putting him on edge and convincing him of her place in his office.

Suddenly he was reminded of a time, or times, when she'd looked at his father the same way, times when he'd been excluded. A girl would walk in, chin tucked into her neck, eyes darting from side to side, needful and scared, and Marjorie would give his father that look. Their eyes would meet, and they would exchange a little smile just before the doctor discreetly placed a hand on David's shoulder and led him out of the examining room, whispering low, "There's only so much you can do for some of these patients," closing the door behind him while Marjorie, in the background, sought to make the girl comfortable in the chair. There'd been a few cases like this, ones that, young David assumed, were beyond his ability to comprehend, or perhaps too painful for a boy to watch.

Momentarily taken by this memory, he hastily blurted a response to Marjorie's job request. "Well, I'm flattered you've taken this trouble to look me up."

"Don't be," she said. "I'm not trying to flatter you. I would like to work for you." Her sincerity was apparent. The doctor was fascinated enough to give it a try, reminding himself he would be perfectly entitled to fire her if she couldn't meet his demands, if she got too kinky and showed some kind of morbid obsession with his father.

But she started right in, worked hard, needed no training, understood every wire, elastic, and retainer, never gave him a reason, personal or professional, to fire her. Even better, she was understanding and instinctively supportive of the Reckner male tradition whenever his fifteen-year-old son Bradford was around, in the same way she'd facilitated his own hands-on education in his father's office.

And so, with time, Marjorie had surpassed the position of subordinate and was now regarded as a colleague. The doctor's respect for her judgment was such that, on the day of Mrs. Lindstrom's first visit, he automatically turned to her after the patient had left and asked, "What did you think of that woman's teeth?"

Marjorie tipped her head in thought and took her time answering. "This one, I'm afraid, will be your most challenging case," she said. "A Class I+ malocclusion."

And she might have left it at that if the doctor had been satisfied and walked away. But her opinion clearly did not stop there. Dr. Reckner could see it in the way she wasn't looking at him. Marjorie was a woman who, while distant in some ways, never shrank from direct eye contact, and her difficulty in looking at him seemed to say something new—

just *what* he couldn't guess. Her eyes were examining every tool on the instrument tray, as if checking each one for cleanliness. He followed her gaze and a glint stabbed his eye, a line of white light glancing off the silvery sterile hue of the ligature pliers. He felt something unspoken like an impossible, baseless intuition, and he chose to ignore it.

"Yes, challenging," he agreed. "But not impossible?"

"No, not that." Still, she didn't look up. "In some ways it might appear that way. The root structure could fail us completely, so I know you'll want to move slowly with this one." She stretched the word "slowly," making the doctor catch his breath. "But for you, not impossible."

"You have great faith."

"I only say what's true. You are your father's son." She paused as if considering whether to go on, and when she did, her voice was quiet but measured and sure. "This was— would have been—his dream case."

He nodded. He knew this.

She looked up at him then, smiled fleetingly, and dropped her eyes again. "This is the case you've been waiting for."

He knew this too.

Mrs. Lindstrom returned the following week to begin her treatment on a day when Bradford happened to be visiting his father at the office. Behind Marjorie's lead, Mrs. Lindstrom walked in from the waiting room, chin self-consciously tucked into her neck, eyes darting and needful. Dr. Reckner, explaining the different functions of needle-nose and flat-tip pliers to his son, turned around to meet

Marjorie's eyes and suddenly felt a curious wave of fatherly protection and concern. No need to show Bradford just yet—such a grotesque mouth, such a difficult case, and what would be, necessarily, a painful treatment.

He glanced at Mrs. Lindstrom and his pulse quickened in the same way his own father's might have surged at the prospect of a challenging case. Had he been given the time to think, the chance to step back and observe from afar, he might have remembered this particular case. But how could he remain detached in the presence of Mrs. Lindstrom's mouth with that small tremor of fear it evoked, something the doctor instinctively defined as a proper concern for his son? Not good to let Bradford remain. No need to discourage the boy so soon from the high practice of orthodontics. He nodded to Marjorie, who escorted Mrs. Lindstrom to the chair while he put an arm around the boy's shoulder and gently steered him into his office, suggesting that he finish his homework.

He took the stool and wheeled up close. Mrs. Lindstrom was willing to go all the way, to do whatever the doctor wished, but still she had many questions. The doctor explained the need for full braces, upper and lower, to be worn for a lengthy period of time because he would have to proceed with caution, applying only the gentlest pressure to avoid further damage to the root system, to preserve teeth whose integrity was threatened by bone loss, receding gums, and blunted roots.

"How long?" she asked, already settled into the examination chair, looking as if she belonged there. She wore a dark, long-sleeved turtleneck dress of a soft knit fabric, something that clung to her body, outlining it against the beige upholstery of the chair. He looked down and saw he would have to cover it.

"Lift," said the doctor, indicating her head. She did as he said, jutting her head forward, ready for the paper bib for her upper body. Covering it. He affixed the clasp around her neck. "Hard to say," he replied to her question. "Usual treatment time is about eighteen months. In your case, it will be longer." His left hand lingered briefly on her shoulder. "At least two years, maybe two and a half or three." He would see how it went with her. He would see from month to month what he needed to do inside her mouth.

"Marjorie," said the doctor loudly to drown out the noise in his head, but his assistant was just behind him, looking down into Mrs. Lindstrom's hole. Fumbling with latex gloves, the doctor wasn't aware, but there was another look from Marjorie over his shoulder, away from that mouth, up into the patient's eyes, a look that was greeted and reciprocated and understood.

"It's been a long time," said Mrs. Lindstrom, still looking at Marjorie. The doctor, oblivious, slid inside, pushing her open.

"Yes, yes, just relax. Marjorie, I'll start with a 16."

His assistant found the requested item in her large plastic tray with dozens of inch-square compartments for metal bands of every size, for every tooth. The doctor took the one she handed him, positioned it on a back molar, pushed, found his rubber hammer on the table, tapped it down. A perfect fit. Later he would remove it, apply the cement, tap it down again for permanence.

"14."

Marjorie handed it, he positioned, pushed, pushed

again harder, tapped. He stopped to consider his next move, and the patient spoke. "Your hands are like his," she said, making him pull away, startled. "So sure," she explained. "At least, they seemed sure at the time, but they were doing the wrong thing, weren't they?"

"Yes, that doctor." He busied his hands again. "Marjorie, I need another 14. That nameless doctor in, where did you say?"

"San Francisco."

"Yes, a big town, many orthodontists. Don't worry, Mrs. Lindstrom. I'm doing the right thing here."

Blind and deaf, he ignored the clues, feeling only annoyance at this interruption of his work. He didn't want her to speak any more. He wouldn't give her the chance. He positioned each band, pushed and hammered and kept going, one tooth after another for an hour and a half, cemented each one, applied brackets on two uppers and two lowers, threaded the wire, pinched and tweaked it with the flat-tip pliers, inserted elastics with the grooved hemostat, and used the twist-on to place the elastic ligature ties. All the while, he glanced now and then at her eyes, closed and drawn tight against the pain, tears squeezed out the sides, nostrils flared and cheeks in high color from the pushing and pulling inside her mouth.

Was this the kind of pain he saw in every face, in all his patients? He'd always regretted it, or thought he had, but with her there was no regret, only necessity, certainty, drive. Every atom of her face was exposed under the light, the crease between her eyes deepening inside those delicate accordions of brows pushed up tight together over the bridge of her nose as she and the doctor came closer and closer, nearing completion. She couldn't speak, wasn't allowed to, couldn't possibly have uttered a word as he worked and worked on her, probed, pushed, and pulled deep inside that mouth.

But what was that coming from her throat? He heard it, a word grunted between needful breaths. *Tighter.* And again. *Tighter.*

At last, they reached the end. He wiped his brow, his hands trembling as he removed the gloves. He was aware at once of his breathing, his pulse, the quickness. But he was finished with Mrs. Lindstrom. For now. There would be many other times.

He rolled back from the patient on his stool and instinctively swiveled around to look up at Marjorie. This time, her eyes did not shy away from direct contact. Her face was content, filled with a maternal glow, the benevolent look of a proud guardian. The facilitator of something good, something exciting, something her son needed, especially now at this stage of his career, at this stage of middle life.

And all at once, Dr. Reckner saw it. He knew what her expression conveyed, and he accused her silently.

He did this, didn't he?

The glow of pride, the slightest of smiles.

My father! He destroyed this woman's mouth!

With his eyes he penetrated Marjorie, hoping to see something else in that unchanging countenance as a persistent thought played again and again in his mind. *He did this for me! He sent her to me!*

Stunned, he dropped his eyes to the floor. Marjorie's face, that single look, had shattered all his carefully laid images of his father. Still, in the midst of his profound shock, he felt the gradual swelling of enormous awe. What genius! The timing of it, so perfect, a glacial, twenty-five-year collapse of dental health.

He turned to look up again at Marjorie. "How could this…? When?" He searched her eyes for the answer.

Marjorie's face was at once transformed, becoming businesslike. "Would you say about four weeks, Doctor?" she asked, picking up the file and a pen to make a notation.

"Yes," interrupted Mrs. Lindstrom, pushing herself up, dazed and heavy-lidded from pain. "I can barely speak," she panted and smiled. "About every four weeks, isn't that it? The usual time between appointments?"

The doctor spun around to behold her, and she returned his stare, mouth pink and battered, lips slightly swollen from all the tugging and pulling. Fuller, almost pretty. Her eyes, so familiar, knew exactly what she was about, who he was and why she was here. Forgot the name! Mrs. Lindstrom had come looking for him, for what she needed, and what she needed she would be getting right here, in this chair. Instantly, the doctor lost any fear of consequence. He could see that his father had chosen the right one, had chosen well. A gift from father to son.

"Yes, four weeks," said Dr. Reckner. The days in between would be their time to recover, to envision, to anticipate.

She stood up, and with a small wobble, was on her heels and gone.

A sudden hush enveloped the examining room, now with only the doctor and Marjorie and the chair and the instruments. Other patients couldn't be seen, but they could be felt outside the door in the waiting room sitting restlessly, reading magazines. Bradford sat behind the closed door of the doctor's office, innocently doing his homework. Dr. Reckner walked to that door and stopped, hand on the knob, suddenly unable to face his son, not knowing what to say, unable to envision anything normal coming from his mouth.

"Doctor?"

It seemed now that he'd been standing immobile for quite some time. It was apparent in Marjorie's tone. At once, the certainty and strength he'd felt when looking down into the patient's eyes dissolved into nothingness.

"What am I to do with this woman?" he whispered, not turning to face his assistant.

"You will do what you do for every case, for every one of your patients."

Yes, this is what he did for his patients, for every one. Relied on his judgment, wisdom, and experience, used his best efforts, applied every tactical consideration, every innovative procedure, gave of himself one hundred percent toward one goal: to fix the malocclusion. He'd always been proud of that. With Mrs. Lindstrom, he would remind himself to indulge that professional pride, would convince himself of its legitimacy despite these other, messy things that were, after all, merely visceral and hidden.

His son waited. He started to turn the knob.

"There may be others," he heard at his back.

⁊

Journal Entry, Franklin DeWitt

January 24, 2015

GOD OR THE DEVIL awaits me. On March thirteenth I'll be eighty-nine, if the earth hasn't claimed me first. It's time to write about Maya.

Alexis encourages me. "Write, Grandpa. Write everything about your life. People want to know." My lively firebird, a promising ballerina. She says she wants to transcribe and publish *The Memoirs of a Ballet Critic*. I won't disappoint her, although I doubt that anyone is interested in the recollections of a teary-eyed man sitting alone in the dark, rapt and spellbound by the beauty he beholds on stage. People would rather know about the private lives of the dancers.

I've known many, but Maya soars above them all. I can't take her story with me and must release it to the world.

Alexis has delivered my lunch on a tray and I'm alone again, without much appetite except for thoughts of Maya.

On Monday, June 5, 1972, New York caught its first glimpse of Maya Volosova and Dmitri Guryev. In that era of

149

famous Soviet defectors—Nureyev (1961), Makarova (1970), Baryshnikov (1974)—Maya and Dmitri fascinated the public more than any others. They were striking and exquisite together. She, twenty-four, he, twenty-five. They were inseparable. They were lovers.

That first day, I was invited to observe the spectacle. We stood awkwardly in a wide semi-circle, fifty members of the press corps and theater critics, enthralled like children around a monkey cage at the zoo. Location: New York Ballet Theatre on Broadway, the grand rehearsal studio, wood floored, mirror lined. The defectors, Maya and Dmitri, were performing their tricks for the media. It was silly and beneath them. Their new ballet master had put them up to it. I was awestruck, pen and pad forgotten in my hand.

In moments of rest, the Russians glanced dazedly around the room, shell-shocked and disoriented. An irrevocable decision had placed them in this strange land, their proclaimed kingdom of artistic freedom, never to return home. They performed admirably under the circumstances. Maya took a few, quick running steps and was suddenly in the air with a light javelin thrust of her legs into a perfect split, torso arched backward. The gallant, muscular Dmitri effortlessly held her overhead. Cameras clicked and whirred. Gently, she alighted, executed a few *piqué* turns, found her lover's forearm, and held it to balance. *Sur la pointe* of one foot, she extended her free leg up behind her in *arabesque*.

Standard steps, nothing new, but Maya had a singular manner of execution, infused with nuance and the illusion of trifling ease, like breathing. Her countenance was relaxed in the sort of aloof loveliness that doesn't even know it exists.

Ballet master Colin Welby, the instigator of this pageant, stood on the sidelines. What great press for him! NYBT had signed the new stars within a day of their setting foot in New York, less than a week after their dramatic leap to freedom during a Kirov tour in Paris.

They finished their partnering stunts, and Colin got them each to improvise a few solo movements. Maya skimmed floatingly on her *pointes*, an ethereal being, waif-like, tiny as a child, a sprite one minute, a goddess the next. When it was Dmitri's turn, our impressions of him died fast. Of course, in 1972, we hadn't yet seen Baryshnikov—the moving picture of the dance—but even then, we knew the difference between greatness and mere competence.

"Did you see that?" I asked Laura Kensington, the arts columnist standing next to me.

"Four *pirouettes*."

"Only four. And a small stumble."

"Ever so slight. Give him a chance. We'll see..." Clearly, he was nothing special, but Laura was willing to wait!

I was already convinced that Maya couldn't be in love with Dmitri, a mere prop standing in the shadow of a ninety-five-pound *prima assoluta*. If anything, he was her ticket to the West. This was my hunch. This I would find out.

It's Saturday, my three-meal day with Alexis. Here for breakfast and lunch, she'll return at dinnertime, after another ballet class and rehearsal. Alexis is my son's greatest gift, a living angel who attends to me in every free moment. Last year, when it was easier to get out of bed, I sat once again in a darkened theater, this time beholding my lovely granddaughter. Only fourteen then, fifteen now. Already, she's a true artist.

Alexis pores over my scrawl, the only person who understands it. She's convinced that the old ballet critic is a personage of some importance. I won't dissuade her, but I don't kid myself. She wants to know about the famous dancers, not me. If my wife were here, she'd have better stories to tell, but she's been gone now these many years. Her life was harder on account of me, and she died of cancer when Alexis was only a toddler.

"Let me get your laptop, Grandpa," Alexis insists. "I'll set it up for you on the tray." She thinks this will get the words out of me faster. Not anymore, not with these eyes. Though my hand shakes, I can only put pen to paper. A keypad would be useless.

When she returned to pick up my lunch tray, she was surprised to see my plate nearly full. I'd been writing, as she wanted, not eating, as she also wanted. She gave up on feeding me and got me out of bed. A strong girl, she effortlessly supports her old grandpa as he shuffles around the house and back to the bedroom. Before she left she asked me: "I know you've been writing—may I see it?"

"Not yet, my dear girl."

"Are you writing about *her*?" Alexis urgently awaits the full story of Maya, but I won't show her these pages until I'm near the end.

I've had a moment of shut eye, when the vision of the first performance came vividly to mind. Friday, June 9, 1972, *Swan Lake*.

The timing of their defection was good for Dmitri and

Maya, not so good for others in the company. Colin signed them for the two weeks that remained in NYBT's spring season. Their lawyers (already the defectors had them!) advised against signing away any further rights, leaving them free to perform elsewhere if they wished. Among the several ballets on the daily schedule, three performances remained of the full-length classic, *Swan Lake*. Colin bounced the leads, Suzanne Violette and Timothy Jordan, and replaced them with his new darlings of the dance.

A few days of hurried rehearsals were enough to get the Soviets in shape. They intimately knew the choreography of Petipa and Ivanov, which had been their bread and butter growing up at the Kirov. This was not the artistic ideal that Maya and Dmitri had been dreaming of, the abstract, contemporary American ballets that were verboten behind the Iron Curtain. But there was no time for anything else, and it was only fair to make them pay their dues, if only briefly, before casting them in new roles.

That first night, there was a heavy police presence at Lincoln Center. The tension was palpable, a rumbling, wavy mix of ecstatic anticipation and intrigue. As I took my seat inside the Met, I spotted, scattered along the periphery, several unlikely ballet aficionados: single men, strong jawed and square shouldered. Each one scanned the wide hall as he stood with his arms crossed or hands clasped in front, fig-leaf style. I feared for Maya without understanding why. These were the good guys, right? Security guards. But I couldn't decide if they were all in the same camp, if their faces were foreign or domestic, if their occasional, telepathic eye contact with each other conveyed affinity or enmity. One of them stared me down briefly as he made his visual rounds—it was enough to turn my gaze unwaveringly to the stage.

I sat precisely in the middle of the orchestra section, my usual seat, far enough from the stage to appreciate the full panorama, close enough to see the dancers' feet and facial expressions. The defectors injected this classic with a life that Timothy and Suzanne had never achieved. They brought Russian drama to it, a passion and inflection that were so exciting.

Especially Maya, playing the dual role of white swan/black swan. In the second act, as Odette, she was chaste and alluring, trapped and desperate, fated to turn into a white swan by morning, under a spell cast by the evil sorcerer Von Rothbart. In the third act, as Von Rothbart's daughter Odile, she was fiery, devious, and seductive. A temptress in black, transformed by the sorcerer to appear identical to Odette. Maya's rendering of these opposites was astonishing.

Dmitri, the handsome coatrack, did admirably well supporting her as Prince Siegfried, but when the time came for his solo, the mediocre technique and dead eyes lacked the power to inspire. It was just as I'd thought.

Afterward, I joined the company at a private party to welcome the newcomers. You're right, Alexis, maybe I *was* important. Only certain people were allowed into these company events. Big money patrons were always invited along with a few "inside" reporters and critics. I'd paid *my* dues with two decades of cutting-edge reviews that could make or break careers. Over those years, I'd gotten to know the dance celebrities, and in a way, they included me in their set while I remained an island, authoritatively apart. I couldn't be bought. A good review had to be deserved.

At the party, Maya entered the room on Dmitri's arm. He wore a fashionable sort of dressed-down tux, and she wore a white, watery gown. The clothing was supplied by NYBT. The defectors had arrived in the country without anything except practice clothes.

I was drawn to Maya. I was already in love. Forgive me darling Zanni, but we weren't married yet. Still single, I was already an old man of forty-six. Far too old for the new object of my desire. She stood at a distance with Dmitri and Colin on either side of her. How was I to edge in between them?

Surprisingly, Timothy and Suzanne were also in attendance, stewing in a corner. Suzanne's redhead was difficult to ignore. Although my destination was Maya, I stopped along the way to converse with the outcasts.

"Did you watch the performance?" I asked Suzanne.

"What else was there to do?" With artistic delicacy, she flung a handful of her ample tresses over a bare shoulder. She was a beautiful, outgoing woman, almost too big and luscious to be a ballerina, about five foot seven, 115 pounds. I'd known Suzanne for sixteen years, from the time she joined the company at the age of eighteen and as she worked her way up from corps member to principal. Socially, her manner was tart but full of fun. That night, she was all acid.

"I thought you might have avoided it," I suggested.

"Colin wants me to 'learn from her.'"

"Hmm. He couldn't want my all-American girl to become a Russian hot-blood."

"Hah! You should see him lathering at the mouth over his new foundling. Artistically, of course." Suzanne's green eyes flashed. "She *is* an interesting little thing, though."

I turned to her ballet partner. "What say you, Tim? Anything to learn from Dmitri Guryev?"

"Not much that I can see," he retorted.

"I would have preferred to see *you* as the prince tonight," I told him.

Suzanne sputtered into the emptiness where I should have deposited a compliment for her.

"You know how he got here, don't you?" Timothy was on the verge of confirming the rumors then circulating in the media.

"Tell me." I already knew the story, but wanted to hear it from Tim.

He lowered both his brow and his voice, for my hearing only. "Guryev was the one with the connection. Volosova was the one everyone wanted."

"Not surprising."

"You heard about Claude Fournier?"

"The impresario who arranged their escape through the back alleys of Paris."

"*And* paid their way to New York. Don't worry. He got his kickback. A year ago, that Frenchman made a trip to Leningrad and became acquainted with Dmitri. They conversed quite easily in French. Dmitri doesn't know a word of English, by the way." Tim smirked. "Dmitri whispered his secret desire to defect, and Claude suggested he could help—he's a very close friend of Colin's. But Claude was no fool. He told Dmitri he needed a Kirov prima ballerina thrown into the deal to sweeten the pot."

"And how am I to believe you know all of this?"

"Claude was also…a friend."

"Of yours."

The male liaisons in the dance world were multi-layered. Colin and Tim, despite their age difference, were also rumored to be an occasional couple. To my credit, Tim must have perceived me as "safe," otherwise he wouldn't have confided such intimate details. Or, maybe he just needed to vent—he was noticeably incensed to have lost his starring role in *Swan Lake* to a second-rate Russian.

"You must be angry at your old friend Claude for making this casting switcheroo possible."

"Let's just say that Claude and I didn't part so nicely. He and Colin are better friends."

"Unlucky for you." But I was already bored with Tim's grumblings and wanted to hear about Maya. It was clear that the Soviet "lovers" were less than that, or something else. Each was the passport for the other. Dmitri needed someone with real talent, and Maya needed a connection. My heart began to pound the seconds until their inevitable break up. "So, you're saying that Dmitri started up his affair with Maya..."

"...to offer Claude a prize in exchange for his help. But Dmitri didn't need to do much coaxing. It was obvious that Maya was also looking for a window to the West."

At my side, Suzanne was sniffing for attention. "Now that the Kirov has lost their Odette," she said prettily, "maybe I should defect to the Soviet Union."

I laughed. "Yes, darling, you do that. Just like Lee Harvey Oswald." But I stroked her head to show it was all in fun. She had such luxurious hair, I can feel it now.

With a few words of condolence, I quickly parted from the disgruntled stars. An opportunity presented itself. Just then, I glimpsed Maya stepping away from Colin and Dmitri, making her way along one of two intersecting lines. I took up the second line and met her about twenty yards away from her male escorts.

"Miss Volosova, let me introduce myself. Franklin DeWitt, columnist. You may have seen my reviews."

"Yes, yes, of course, I read all the time." What a lovely sound! Her voice was rich and deep for such a petite woman. I expressed my admiration for her command of the English language, and this was her reply: "Many years study. In private. Secret. I know I must come, you see."

"To the United States."

"Yes, this is the home for my art."

"Your art is everything to you?"

"Everything." *Effrytink.*

"You danced beautifully tonight."

Her head dipped slightly. Trite expressions of praise wouldn't impress her; she'd heard these words often enough. If I didn't act quickly, the opportunity would be lost. Behind her, Colin was exuding fatherly anxiety, casting a protective shadow. "When can we meet again? I'd like to interview you."

She looked up at me for what seemed a long time. In her very high heels, she came only to my shoulder. Almond brown hair, an aristocratic face like a czarina's, unafraid, naked, washed clean of stage makeup. Her eyes were gray with flecks of yellow.

Before she answered, her gaze darted to the side in a little show of terror at what might be lurking at her back. Both Dmitri and Colin were behind her, but so were a lot of other people.

"Yes," she said after a long pause. And then—how can I forget?—she put her hand on my arm. "We should meet." She was looking into my eyes when Colin came up alongside.

I smiled at him and staked my claim. "Miss Volosova has graciously consented to an interview."

"Really now?" Colin threw back his head with those artistically longish locks, everlastingly salon blond to cover the gray. I was forced to look up his nose for an instant before he lowered his head and directed his eyes at Maya, then me. Having demonstrated his authority to withhold consent, he granted it. "I suppose I can arrange that."

My hand threatens to spasm. The pen is laid to rest.

That Sunday, my review appeared in the *Times* on a full page of the arts section devoted to the defectors. Laura Kensington was a contributor. Nestled inside her prose were photographs, including a close-up of Volosova's face in the role of Odette, full stage makeup and white-feathered headdress. The caption beneath it read: "The lovely Soviet defector prepares to go on stage at the Met." So, Laura and her photographer had gotten to Maya first! Or was this a mock-up with fabricated content, embellished with a smuggled file photo from the Kirov? I examined Maya's image for details. The photo could have been taken anywhere.

The next day, I had my interview. Colin gave us the use of a small office at the NYBT studios. I arrived early and was nervously reviewing my questions when Colin's young boy assistant escorted the ballerina into the room. Maya was dramatically attired in layers of dance sweaters and leg warmers, a long scarf wound multiple times around her neck. "A cold," she said.

For the first ten minutes, while we talked about Maya's training at the Vaganova Ballet Academy, Colin's assistant examined and picked at a hangnail, refusing to budge from his seat. Eventually he left us alone.

I tested the waters obliquely: "That article in the *Times* yesterday, I imagine it was distracting to be interviewed right before going on stage."

"That woman, she arrive in my dressing room. I don't know how."

"Did she say her name?"

"Laura Kenzingk. And a photographer. They bring me some letters."

"Letters?"

She leveled an intense look. "*This* is why we must talk."

We? My love for her swelled magnificently—she'd chosen me for a secret! The subject was obviously delicate. Her eyes grew moist with emotion, although it could have been a symptom of her cold virus.

"That woman give me letters from my mother and my brother! 'Heartbroken,' they say. Why did I leave them? Why this...this 'betrayal' of my teachers at the Kirov, my family and the motherland?"

"Did she say where she'd gotten those letters?"

"She didn't!"

"Do you suppose—?" I stopped myself. A KGB connection to Laura Kensington? Unthinkable. But there'd been stories like this about other defectors. Attempts to sabotage their performances, backstage "accidents" with falling props, faked or coerced emotional letters from family members. The object was to crush any chance of success in the West, or to instill enough guilt that the defector would return home and be charged with treason, stripped of any further life as an artist. Defection was an intolerable insult to the Soviet delusion of cultural supremacy.

"It was their handwriting, but it was not them."

"How was it 'not them'?"

"My mother and brother — they want for me what is the best. They never write these things. Oh, Franklin," the tears started to fall, "tell this woman to stay away!"

"You want me to tell Laura..."

"You know her, yes?"

"I do."

"Tell her do not come! Never try to see me again!"

Uncertainty fueled her torment. Either the KGB had forced the hands of her mother and brother, or her family members had, on their own, penned their sorrow and arranged for its delivery. Either possibility was unbearable. Maya needed protection from Laura Kensington and any other would-be messengers. I gladly accepted the challenge, even though I feared that Maya had no other use for me. Perhaps, with time, her feelings would run deeper than mere gratitude.

Maya gave me the address where she and Dmitri were staying — a carefully guarded secret — and warned me of heavy security. I promised to visit her the following night, to give her an update of my efforts. She promised to hold her bodyguards at bay.

I couldn't sleep all night, thinking of her. The next morning, I sought out two people. First, Laura. On the way to her office, I was jittery with fatigue and had the sense of being followed, even without any overt signs of it. When I arrived, Laura's secretary was in the anteroom. No one else was around. I entered Laura's office and closed the door behind me, feeling nervous and slightly silly. No one could hear us, but I imagined a bug.

Assuming the role of FBI agent, I interrogated her rapid fire, bait and trap. I was woefully inept. She gave me this explanation: "A little man with a Russian accent came up to me outside the theater and handed me those letters. 'Gee-ef dees to Volosova. Letters from family.'"

"A stranger?"

"Of course a stranger. You think I run around with types like that?"

"How on earth did he know who you were and where you were going?"

"I have no idea. It was a little creepy, I admit."

"And you didn't think it through. Anything could have been inside those envelopes! What was written on the outside?"

"Her name, that's all. Come on, Franklin. Cut out the Dick Tracy. It would have been cruel to hold back letters from her family. What would *you* have done?"

"Gone to the police."

"Not when the best interview of your career is waiting. You would have done the same."

"Maybe, but..."

"Your envy is showing. I got to her first, plain and simple. Got past the gatekeepers before you did. So there. Accept it."

I accepted it and didn't mind so much that Laura got the first interview because I'd been given something far better. Maya had made me her trusted confidant and protector. But I wasn't about to reveal this. "Your visit upset her greatly, that's all I can say." I turned to go. "I suggest you stay away from Maya to avoid causing her any further distress." It was a pitifully weak demand with nothing to back it up. Laura only smiled at me with shining eyes.

Feeling put down and inadequate as a detective, I went back to my office to await my second appointment of the day: Suzanne. I wasn't sure how, but I wanted to use her as my informant. She was the person I knew best in the company and the only one I could approach. She was also likely to be in daily contact with Maya, since they were at similar levels of virtuosity, and Colin had told Suzanne to "learn from her." There was resentment, to be sure, but I figured that Suzanne would get over it. She had a heart of gold, could see the business logic behind Colin's decision, and was confident enough to know that he hadn't replaced her. At thirty-four, she was an exciting, mature dancer at the height of her career.

I asked Suzanne how Maya was doing, and immediately, she sensed my interest and concern.

"Ah, you have a little crush!" She mocked me. "You have nothing to worry about. Maya is perfectly happy, except for that worm of a boyfriend, Dmitri."

"What's he up to?"

"Every time I see those two together they're spouting off in hot Russian, 'nyet' this and that. Nothing at all like their on-stage love affair."

I was heartened to hear this. A breakup in the works! In my obsessive state, I was sure this meant a chance for me. "Nothing violent, is there?"

"I saw him grab her arm once. She pulled away and cursed wildly in Russian."

"Your interpretive skills are amazing."

"Anyone could figure it out."

"Have you spoken to her?"

"Not much. But this morning, before class, we were in the studio together, sitting on the floor, banging out our new *pointes*. Her only complaint about defecting is that she has to get used to another maker. She claims her new shoes are inferior."

I thought nothing of this. Professional ballerinas need two or three pairs of *pointe* shoes every day and love to complain about them. A ballerina's "maker" is a cobbler who knows her foot intimately and handcrafts each shoe to unique specifications. The stiff toe box is created from layers of cardboard, glue, and fabric, stitched and nailed to a leather sole. Each ballerina has her own ritual for molding the shoes to her liking by hammering, floor banging, or mashing the toe boxes between sensitive hands. After a few hours of wear, the shoes are "dead." Limp and useless.

"Who's her new maker?"

"Stanley Graven. Sign of the cross." Graven's unique symbol was a Maltese cross, which he impressed on the bottom of every sole.

"Who's the old maker?"

"Don't know. The imprint is"—she deepened her voice—"a hammer and sickle."

I shuddered. "Comrade ballerina!"

"She still has about a dozen pairs from her old maker," Suzanne continued. "The box just arrived by air freight—a friend of hers in the Kirov smuggled them out of her dressing room in Paris. They're in the storage room reserved for the principal dancers. It's under lock and key, but she seems nervous to let them out of her sight. She puts on a pair only when she's feeling especially insecure."

"The great ballerina feels insecure?"

"You know. Homesick. And I think she's missing someone she left behind."

"Her mom and brother."

"Nope. I'm guessing it's a boyfriend. We all know Dmitri is just a cover."

"Well, sure, we all know about Dmitri, but how do you know there's someone else?" I tried to remove the adolescent squeakiness from my voice.

"I just know it. She hasn't said anything. It's intuition. That's something we women have, Franklin. Intuition."

In that moment I admired Suzanne enormously. She was compassionate and magnanimous toward her little sister, a girl ten years younger, who should have been regarded as a rival in the company. I asked Suzanne to look after Maya, to protect her from harm, to report back to me what was going on inside the studios and the theater.

But this was asking too much, and she resisted. "Why should I, Franklin? She's a big girl. She doesn't need a mama." Her eyes were on fire. She was vivacious and even more redheaded in her rage. But there was mockery in her emotion. She knew me too well. Why should she humor a man driven by lust? "Maybe she's homesick and lonely," said Suzanne, "but she made her decision and will have to live with it."

I enjoyed her honesty and was beginning to see, maybe a little bit, how I really felt about her. I squared my shoulders and acted the grownup. "Suzanne. I've known you half your life. You're the only real friend I have on the inside. I can't reveal all the details, but there've been some threats. You have to believe me. She needs someone to look out for her."

After further arm-twisting, she came around to the idea. I was grateful and thanked her with an embrace before we parted. Alone with Suzanne's perfume on my collar, I counted the minutes until nine p.m., the appointed hour for my visit to Maya's apartment.

NYBT was housing the Russians in a luxury high rise on the Upper East Side. When I arrived that evening, the uniformed doorman told me to wait in the vestibule while he summoned a scary-looking fellow in the lobby. I gave that man my name and purpose and showed him identification. Maya had preapproved my visit, and he waved me ahead. Another such man was standing outside her apartment door on the twelfth floor, and I repeated my demonstration.

Maya came to the door wearing a purple dressing gown, her feet bare. Behind her, on the living room floor, she'd left a basin of Epsom salt water and a towel.

Stripped of their pink satin adornment, a ballerina's feet are not always a pretty sight. Corns, calluses, blisters, bunions, and blood. If a shoe suffers a premature death in the middle of a performance, or if something else isn't quite right with it—a hard bulge, a broken arch, the tip of a nail protruding from the insole—the dancer must stay on her toes, maintaining the illusion of ease.

Maya's feet were no exception. I caught a glimpse of them before averting my eyes to the couch, where Dmitri was sitting. He stood. In reply to my greeting he said, "Hello," and gave me a blank look when I asked, "How are you enjoying your new home?" He nodded and said "Yes." In the awkward silence that followed, he said "Pardon" like a Frenchman and left the room. Timothy was right. The man didn't understand a word of English.

"Come and sit," said Maya, gesturing toward the couch. It was long and plush, with white cushions. I took one end and she took the other, tucking her battered feet beneath her. There were dark circles under her eyes. She gave me a wan smile, her vitality expended and left behind in the NYBT studios, where she'd had a grueling day of class and rehearsal. Sitting on the couch in the intimacy of her home, I didn't feel quite inside my own body as I regarded her tiny form across from me, a presence so diminutive yet momentous that she appeared translucent, of another world.

The goddess spoke: "Tell me that you talk to her. That woman."

I assured her that Laura Kensington would no longer be a bother. It was a bold statement at odds with reality, something I couldn't vouch for. I said nothing about my agreement with Suzanne.

"This is not interview," Maya said, waving her hand in a circle. "None of this, about the letters. You print nothing."

"I wouldn't dream of it." But how could she trust me? Even today, it astounds me that a defector from the Soviet Union, a person conditioned for a life of wariness and vigilance, would assign such a sensitive mission to a relative stranger. But I still had a boyish, innocent face, well into middle age. I'm sorry you wouldn't know it now, Alexis. I can't bear to look at myself in the mirror.

I told Maya: "I will do everything in my power to ensure your safety and your ability to concentrate on your art."

"Thank you. I am grateful."

We talked for an hour or so, more about her life than mine. Her words and gestures were veiled in a mood of profound sadness. With Dmitri nowhere to be seen, hidden away in another room, our discussion was free. Toward the end I remarked, "I've heard you're disappointed with your new maker."

"Pfft! Shoes are terrible. Pavel is the only one knows my feet." She looked off into the distance. Instantly, I knew there was something under the surface. Perhaps some of Suzanne's feminine intuition had rubbed off on me. "Pavel?"

"Yes, Pavel Shirokov. My 'maker' is how you say it. He knows my feet, the high instep, the short baby toe, the spreading metatarsal. He knows this. No one else." Her eyes had grown misty.

"I hear that Stanley Graven is excellent. If you give him some time, he'll get to know your feet just as well."

"I doubt very seriously." She jumped up from the couch. It was my signal to go. I had, of course, botched this meeting very badly. By mentioning Stanley Graven, I'd given away my connection to Suzanne. How else would I have known this detail?

Near the front door, she found the energy to come out of her funk momentarily. Charmingly, she rose up on tiptoe and kissed my cheek. "Thank you for that Laura person."

I was in heaven. "May I come backstage after your performance tomorrow?"

"If they let you. They watch the door now. Very careful.

After that other time, I tell them no one."

"Let no one in?"

"No one."

My heart sank again. I should have been elated to know that she was taking control of the situation. It was her assertion of that control against *me* that was so disappointing.

As I walked out the door, I didn't know it was the last time I would see her alone.

I hear a key turn in the lock.

Alexis has just gone, and I've gained a second wind. I ate a bit of dinner, had another stroll on her arm, and can face the night, alone. A single beam of lamplight falls upon this page.

In the dark again, I sit. Wednesday, June 14, and Sunday, June 18, 1972, the final performances of *Swan Lake*.

Don't think that I didn't try to see her again. After Wednesday's performance, I sought entry at the usual backstage door but was cut off, all my goodwill and insider status of no value. The following night, and the night after that, I went to her apartment building. The bodyguards were under strict orders to turn me away. A few times, in broad daylight, I visited the NYBT studios. Colin was not available. Neither was Maya. I took these rejections personally, although there was no reason to doubt that her instructions pertained to the world at large.

Twice daily, I contacted Suzanne for a report. "You worry for nothing," she said every time. On Sunday afternoon, the day of the last performance, she said, "Thanks to you, we're now the best of friends. She's a fascinating little thing! Doing just fine and so happy to be here. Maybe a little tired and stressed, but no sign of any goons on her trail."

"Are you *sure* she would tell you if there were any threats?"

"How would I know? We've been friendly for such a short time. But I do know this—she's on to you, Franklin!"

"On to me?"

"She knows you've been trying to see her. Every day. She mentioned it before class this morning. 'You know this man Franklin? Should I be worry for him?'"

"Worried about *me*?"

"You, sweetheart. I told her you're harmless as a kitten. Still, I would bug off if I were you."

Her advice fell on deaf ears. I was certain to keep trying, *if* I'd had the chance.

In the dark then and now, I see and feel everything again. At the Met, as the lights dim and programs rustle, the overture begins, and I wait impatiently for Maya to take the stage. For the last time.

In the third act of *Swan Lake*, Prince Siegfried is tricked into declaring his love for Odile, the deceptive double conjured by Von Rothbart. In the fourth act, the Prince returns at midnight to the *lac des cygnes* where he begs for, and receives, Odette's forgiveness. But they're powerless to overcome the sorcerer's spell. The Prince's betrayal has sealed Odette's fate. Come morning, she'll turn into a white swan again, this time forever. The despairing lovers cast themselves into the lake.

In the moments before her stage suicide, Maya's portrayal of Odette transcends the boundaries of despair.

Her swanlike arms flail limply, her knees buckle. I'm transfixed, in shock. This isn't the choreography. With a tripping run instead of a soaring leap, she casts herself into the lake and disappears. Dmitri follows with a *grande jeté*.

The apotheosis. In the final moments of the ballet, the lovers glide into the afterlife on a gentle, uplifting theme. As the strings beat out their quiet strokes, the stage remains empty except for the lake—rippling sheets of midnight blue fabric catching a moon beam. Behind a transparent backdrop, the lovers rise into the sky on a heavenly cloud.

Something is wrong. I choke out a cry. Around me, people are gasping. Dmitri is struggling to support Maya, holding her by the waist with one arm, his free arm overhead in fifth position. His face is stricken with panic. Limp and feeble, Maya is folded nearly in half over his arm, her torso arched back and arms flung behind her, *arabesque* drooping, *pointes* collapsed. With a final effort to lift herself up, she falls backward onto his arm with an audible rasp and a catlike screech.

My eyes are a blur of tears. Help me, dear God!

The grandfather clock strikes twelve. I've fallen asleep briefly, wanting to forget.

We were in the dark. The house lights were off when the curtain fell on a scene of panic. An army of police officers swarmed into the audience, taking us hostage. The lights flicked on, revealing pure chaos. Later, I learned the details.

In full costume, Maya's lifeless body was transported by ambulance to the hospital. Colin and Dmitri were fast behind in a taxi. As soon as they arrived, death was pronounced. Was Dmitri heartbroken? He'd just lost his meal ticket. Without Maya, the plum roles were no longer guaranteed. Was Colin heartbroken? Businesswise, he'd lost nothing. The contract was fulfilled, and Maya hadn't promised to sign another. Colin made sure he had the white swan costume and toe shoes in hand before leaving the hospital. These artifacts would fetch thousands at auction, and the company needed the cash.

Maya's death stunned the world and grew to mythical proportions with the discovery of a note on her dressing room table. "Pavel, this performance is for you. I'm wearing the last pair." Hasty translations of her Russian distorted the message into a suicide note. Her last performance. The last pair of shoes she would ever wear. Torn from her lover, ruing her mistake, Maya had publicly committed the ultimate act. She had gone to meet her maker.

But how? Rumors abounded. Depression and unrelenting physical demands beat her down to a wisp, making her susceptible to a hidden weakness. A brain aneurysm. A congenital heart defect. She'd starved herself and collapsed from pure exhaustion and dehydration. She had willed herself to die.

Several days later, the autopsy revealed the cause: cyanide poisoning. A horrible death by chemical asphyxia, its climax marked by the "death scream," an involuntary response to the internal collapse of her lungs. Questions were answered and others were raised by the medical examiner's strange findings. Not ingested or inhaled, the poison was injected into her left foot, the lateral plantar artery. Who would devise such a bizarre method of suicide?

The district attorney opened an investigation. Search

warrants were executed at the Met, the NYBT studios, and Maya's apartment. No syringes were found, but already a week had passed—plenty of time to destroy evidence. Sharp minds said, "The left shoe!" Colin was forced to relinquish the *pointes*, and here they discovered the instrument of her death: a tiny, hollow nail, designed to work its way through the insole and act as a syringe with the pressure of a well-placed *plié-relevé*. To Maya, the prick of pain would have been a small annoyance not unlike any other indignity a ballerina must endure from a negligently crafted shoe. The potent poison gradually worked its way through her body as her heart pumped, delivering death in the final moments of the ballet.

The mystery deepened when the soles of the deadly *pointes* were examined. They bore no symbol at all, neither Maltese cross, nor hammer and sickle.

The shoes were sent for analysis to uncover their maker, and the search for conspirators began. Someone had placed those shoes in the box, and someone had made sure that she wore them. No one was exempt from interrogation. Dozens of people were hauled into police headquarters. In France, depositions were conducted of Claude Fournier and others involved in the Paris "leap to freedom."

Immediately, I came forward with everything I knew, the names of the makers and their marks, and Laura Kensington's delivery of the letters. Laura was the person of greatest interest to the police. Repeatedly, they questioned her about the little Russian man we supposed was a KGB agent. A sketch artist made a drawing of the suspect, and it was printed on the front page of every newspaper in the country and across Europe.

Ultimately, Laura wasn't detained because she clearly had no motive to harm Maya. Nor did any of the other key figures. Not Dmitri (he needed Maya), or Colin (he hoped for a long-term contract), or Claude (he'd received his finder's fee), or Stanley Graven (he was pleased with the new, lucrative toe shoe account), or Pavel Shirokov (he loved her).

Or me or Suzanne.

Forgive me, Alexis, I must stop here.

This story is not about Maya. No, it is not.

How can I say this? You've seen the old newspaper stories and your father and I have explained some of it. I won't be guilty of another sugarcoating.

I go on.

A month after the murder, the public was aching for a culprit, someone to string up. Anonymous tips flooded in. Innocent men were detained on the basis of their slightest resemblance to the sketch in the newspaper. By then we knew that the shoes were made in the USSR, as confirmed by the inferior quality of the pink satin and other materials which were identical to those in the hammer and sickle shoes, a few "dead" ones that Maya had left behind. No question, Pavel was the maker, though his mark was missing. A motive was easily contrived. Heartbroken and angry at Maya for leaving him behind, Pavel became a willing participant in a KGB plot. A cry went out for his arrest, but it was impossible. The only extradition treaty on the books was of questionable validity, signed by the leaders of the U.S. and tsarist Russia in 1893. Even so, Article IV of that treaty relieved the parties of any requirement "to deliver up their own citizens or subjects." Pavel was safe.

I cannot remember the name of the detective who interviewed me. I've blocked it from my mind. He was scarlet faced, dogged, and persistent. I was afraid, I remember that. Afraid for my own sorry self, convinced that I was one of a handful of suspects who'd been allowed entry into Maya's private residence.

I told him: "Miss Volosova granted me a single interview at the NYBT studios. We ran out of time that day, and she permitted me a short visit to her apartment the next night to complete the interview." I indulged in a silent sigh of relief, having confessed the most damning fact.

"Do you have the clipping?"

At this, I balked and shivered. "Clipping?" In my gut, the emotion and guilty knowledge roiled: my shameful desire for a woman half my age, my promise not to print our interview, my belief in a secret mission to protect her. I felt childish and ineffectual. How could I claim the status of protector when I hadn't protected her? "I was still working on the article when she died. It was never printed."

The detective smirked. "How long does it take to write an article?"

"I was working on a special column, a long retro-spective, a life story."

He didn't look convinced, so I kept blathering. "I needed to do more research on defectors and artistic freedom, perhaps add some details comparing the daily routines of dancers in the two countries. For instance, Maya—Miss Volosova—made an interesting observation to another ballerina in the company, a complaint about the feel of her American *pointe* shoes. It was only a pet peeve because, really, she was ecstatic about being in this country.

She told Suzanne as much on the day she died."

"That would be Suzanne Violette?"

"Yes."

"She was the ballerina who told you about Volosova's *pointe* shoe complaint?"

I didn't answer, but my face must have said it all.

"She was the one with the victim before she died?"

"Well, yes, they were friends."

"Friends? But Volosova took her place in the company."

"Not exactly. Just a few performances."

I froze up, fearing that I'd said too much already, and I said nothing to explain, nothing to help her.

In the following days, I badgered other company members into telling me what they'd said to the police. The floodgates were open: many had seen the two ballerinas together, giggling, sipping tea, banging out their *pointes*, making trips to the locked storage room where they both kept their toe shoes. Someone even claimed to have glimpsed Suzanne in the company of a funny little man who looked very much like the sketch published in the newspaper.

Early one morning, I picked up the ringing phone and heard this: "Franklin! I've been arrested!" Suzanne was allowed a single phone call, and I was the person she called. I was that person because she loved me, and at that moment I knew that I loved her.

Shame enveloped me. Yet I said nothing to her about my slip during the interview with the detective, and I said nothing to the authorities about her innocence. The front page of the newspaper had a photograph of my beautiful Suzanne in police escort beneath the headline, "Ballerina

Accused of Conspiracy to Murder."

I found a lawyer for her. But I said nothing.

I visited her in jail. But I said nothing.

A grand jury was empaneled to hear the evidence and hand up an indictment. My brave Suzanne exercised her right to testify. Although the proceedings were secret, I imagined her testimony from everything she told me later:

Prosecutor: "Ms. Violette, tell us about the last time you spoke with the victim."

Zanni: "I visited her dressing room about fifteen minutes before curtain. I wished her good luck and a beautiful performance."

Prosecutor: "Was she wearing her *pointe* shoes?"

Zanni: "Yes, but they wouldn't be the ones…the poisoned ones."

Prosecutor (snidely I imagined, with a wink to the foreperson of the grand jury): "And how would you know that?"

Zanni: "She was wearing the shoes for the second act, when she makes her first appearance. She had different shoes for the third and the fourth acts."

Prosecutor: "And why is that?"

Zanni: "The shoes are pale pink for the second and fourth acts. They're black for the third act."

Prosecutor: "So, when you saw her last, she was wearing the pale pink shoes for the second and the fourth acts?"

Zanni: "No, just the second act. The shoes are dead after a single act and can't be worn again."

An unfortunate choice of words.

In all of this, Suzanne uttered not a word about my part

in forcing her closeness to Maya, how I put her up to all of it. She said nothing about my obsession, my repeated attempts to get to Maya. Wouldn't *that* have been a pretty motive for murder? The leering stalker failed to get the girl. But Suzanne, with her pure heart, knew that my desire was mere folly, a middle-aged man's last fantasy before he finally grew up. She did not betray me, unaware that I had betrayed her.

The prosecutor put the conspiracy charge to the twenty-three grand jurors for a vote. We won't blame them. They were ignorant of everything discovered twenty years later, after the fall of the Soviet Union. They didn't know about the memorandum between the First and the Second Chief Directorates of the KGB, outlining "The State's Problem of Defectors in the Arts." They didn't know about the design of the death shoe, like Sputnik, a glorious achievement of Soviet science, developed after Makarova's defection in 1970. By 1972 the design was perfected, just waiting for the next defector. While Maya was on tour in Europe, Pavel was innocently making a pile of her shoes, looking forward to her return. Immediately after Maya's defection, the Soviet authorities confiscated the lot as "property of the People," found a pair to which Pavel had not yet affixed his imprint, and inserted the lethal nail. An agent planted the pair in Maya's box of shoes in Paris, and during the days after her defection, made sure that a "friend" in the Kirov shipped the box to her in New York.

The rest of the plot relied on her love for Pavel's shoes and the certainty that she would eventually wear them all. It was mere chance—or was it?—that she happened to pick the fatal pair for the fourth act of the final performance of the season. Did she notice the difference in these shoes, the lack of a mark? After her death, the crooked scheme claimed another victim. Pavel heard the news and guessed that his shoes had been the instrument of her death. He committed suicide by hanging.

None of this was known at the time the grand jury voted to indict Suzanne of conspiracy to murder. And none of it was known to the judge (bless him!) who reviewed the grand jury testimony and threw out the indictment. In a packed courtroom, the judge proclaimed the investigation to be a witch hunt and the indictment a product of prosecutorial overreaching. The charge rested on the flimsiest of evidence that wouldn't hold up in court. Suzanne was released, but she was traumatized, unable to dance for two years. A career at its height was left in ruins from the humiliation of a cruel notoriety. When she returned, it was only to dance supporting roles for a few years before an early retirement.

Oh, how I loved her! Weak as I am, cowardly as I am, I loved her. We were blessed with a son, your father. I love you both. Alexis, you must believe that.

Instead of *Memoirs*, shall we call this book *The Confessions of a Ballet Critic*? Does it lessen my guilt to pretend that my sins were of no consequence? Zanni, kind soul, would have befriended Maya anyway. She was just as fascinated by her as we all were. On the day Suzanne was released into my arms, this is what she said to me: "After everything, I'm saddest of all that Maya is gone. She was pretty and funny and so exquisite to watch. She was a tigress and a homeless orphan. She was the real victim here."

And still, I said nothing. How I betrayed you, how I

made you suffer, Zanni! Did you know of my cowardice? Did you find me out all those years ago when I breathed not a word?

My hand aches, but my heart aches more.

I must write.

But I haven't the strength.

God take me! I'm ready to meet m…

January 25, 2015

A ray of light passes through the opening in the curtain.

With every new day, I grow weaker. It's time to write about Suzanne Violette, the most stunning ballerina the world has ever known.

�

The Cost of Ice Cream

A WOMAN PUSHED her cart through the produce section in the supermarket. At hand's reach, inside the empty toddler seat, she'd arranged the newspaper specials and her wobbly, flaccid purse. She moved slower than other women her age—she'd declined considerably since her husband's death—yet, at eighty-seven, she was still well and agile enough to shuffle through her marketing, provided the cart never got too full. And it never did, now that her shrunken body and appetite exerted only modest demands.

Still, eat she must. The senior bus had dropped her with three other ladies from their building, ones she didn't much care for, women with different appetites and tastes, so they'd parted ways in the supermarket, nothing to discuss. Her special friend, not feeling well that day, hadn't come along, but had given instructions beforehand: "I'll be fine, really I will, if I can just do some cooking later. Please pick up a chicken, a very small roaster, the smallest they have." She'd handed her a wrinkled five-dollar bill with the suggestion, "Bring back as much change as you can."

Thinking of her friend, the woman interrupted her own needs and fretted a long while in the poultry section.

Standing there, considering the chickens, she felt an itch under her chin and a drop of water on her cheek and remembered the plastic rain hat atop her head. Despite the annoyance, she wouldn't remove it while shopping. The effort—the untying and folding, and later the unfolding and tying up again—was more than she could handle, and she didn't want to risk tearing it, wasting the fifty cents she'd spent on a hat that could serve for at least three or four rain-storms. So many wet, miserable days, stiffening her joints.

Time grew short. Head blurry, she had difficulty keeping a schedule, and it made little sense to look at her watch, a relic from an earlier life that frequently went unwound. But she was reminded of the passage of time when one of the other women, one of the three, strolled by the meat counter with nothing better to do than remark behind her back, "You know, it's twenty-five minutes to twelve already," before ambling on again.

Pickup time was noon, and the store was busy, and decisions were tough, so she didn't need the added worry of time limits, especially since the bus driver was under strict orders never to leave without completing a head count, as if they were on a grammar school field trip. Six times out of ten it didn't matter anyway—he was the late one. Still, if he was made to wait for her, there would be the unpleasantness of encountering his narrowed, puffy eyes as he leaned forward to look down the bus steps, fat belly sandwiching the wheel.

The chickens, all of them, were too big, most of them more than five dollars, a few less. Her friend loved plenty of leftovers, sandwiches for days, but still, one of these roasters would be too much, wouldn't it? Half of it going to spoil.

Perhaps a package of chicken parts for less money, but no, that just wasn't the same as a roaster, and her friend did so love a whole, roasted chicken. She thought of her friend's face, the lopsided smile, marred by the stroke.

She put on her glasses, threading the stems under the rain hat and over her ears, and sorted through a heap of slaughtered birds, looking at the weights and prices. It took some time, moving them one by one, using two tremulous hands for each, placing them individually on top of the chicken breasts, ruining the butcher's deliberate organization and knowing she'd have to put them all back again. There, at the very bottom, was the least expensive one at a price of $4.26.

Her decision made, and the fowl reorganization accomplished, she pushed away and looked down. At the bottom of her cart, next to the chicken, was a single head of lettuce and two bananas; the rest of her shopping, and more decisions, still lay ahead. She needed a quart of skim milk, a can of tuna fish, and sandwich bread. Corn flakes, and a particular brand of cranberry juice were on sale, and she was sure, with careful planning, that the fifteen dollars in her purse would cover all these things, with the hope, in the back of her mind, for something sweet besides. Ice cream bars, vanilla with a hard shell of chocolate.

The usual items, the ones she always bought, weren't difficult. But, as so often happens, the sale brands weren't immediately visible. Time and again she consulted her newspaper, looked at the photographs, read the brand names and sale prices all typed neatly in small print inside the rectangular coupons bordered with dotted lines and little icons of scissors, trying to match the descriptions with what she found, thinking that the most likely cereal box seemed too small, convinced that the appropriate juice brand was out of reach on the top shelf, finally asking, nicely, a tall gentleman, if he could reach it for her. With time surely expired, she made one last stop in the frozen section, picked the sweet she wanted, and started for checkout.

She would be late, she knew, and she wasn't a spiteful person, but after all, how many times had *she* waited? How many times had she finished her shopping on time, only to stand outside with melting ice cream, waiting for that man to return from a trip to the donut shop?

At checkout, she chose the shortest line, settled in place, and looked around for the other women from her building. They seemed to have disappeared, nowhere to be seen, but presently she spied two of them, emerging together from a checkout further down, bagged groceries in their shared cart. They'd gone together and had finished together. The third woman was some distance off near the exit door, sitting on the window ledge next to a cart with two full bags, her expression set in a grimace of waiting, waiting for them. The other two were now slowly pushing toward her, arranging their cart in the aisle out of traffic's way, deciding where to sit—this side or that?—pulling skirts in around thighs and lowering themselves one notch at a time. With a final jolt, they were down on either side of the first woman on the ledge. Three crows, perched and waiting. Through the floor-to-ceiling plate glass window, the old woman saw the bus driver, just pulling up.

A woman pushed her cart through the produce section of

the supermarket. She moved with the speed and dexterity of youth, sinewy strong at forty from regular exercise. Her cart was near capacity, the added items threatening to topple. She always shopped for produce next to last, even though it was the first section in the store, to prevent squashing the tomatoes and bananas under a pyramid of beverage cartons. Frozen foods were last, a successful plan if the wait in line wasn't too long.

She moved quickly with little thought, accustomed to the weight of the cart and the weight of maintaining multiple lists in her head, adroit in the art of accomplishing the impossible in five minutes or less. Apples, oranges, bananas, broccoli, beans, potatoes, lettuce, cucumbers, carrots. She needed every kind of fruit and vegetable, added to the mound of every other kind of food, maximum ten percent junk, the treats, rewards, and bribes. Cost didn't matter. Food was food, and it must be purchased in sufficient quantities and eaten up and more bought and eaten every couple of days without stop, the money not a concern, not when it came to food anyway. The children, now ten and thirteen, their mouths opening on bottomless wells, didn't stop eating and she wouldn't stop buying. It made little sense to study bargain brands and sales. She hadn't the time for it, and the few dollars saved in nickels and dimes could easily be made up elsewhere. One less trip to the movies.

With two half-gallons of ice cream balanced on top, she searched for a line and found the best one, behind an old lady wearing a dime-store rain cap, only a few items in her cart and one other person ahead of them both, going through checkout now. She debated, glanced about for acquaintances or neighbors, and finding none, picked up a tabloid from the rack near checkout.

Five minutes later, in the middle of a two-headed baby, she became aware of her mistake. It was the old woman's turn, just eight or ten items in her cart, but she was the impossible kind, the type of person to hold everything up. To begin with she was slow, having difficulty leaning into the cart to retrieve her groceries, and to compound the delay, she interrupted this work after placing just two items on the conveyor. A problem had arisen with regard to a chicken.

"Do this separate," the old woman was telling the man, pushing a dripping chicken along the conveyer to the scanner. "This is a separate order."

"Okay," said the clerk, that single word betraying a heavy accent. He might have understood or not, might have simply been in the habit of mouthing "okay" to everything, for he bagged the chicken and scanned the next item on the conveyor, a head of lettuce, without closing out the order.

"No, no," admonished the old woman. "The chicken is separate. Here." She was holding out a limp bill, hand trembling. "Give me the change separate."

At last the clerk seemed to understand, and he voided the lettuce from the sale as the young mother, behind the old woman, glanced about at the remaining checkout lines, wondering if she could, even at the eleventh hour, find a better one. But in the midst of this search, another customer pushed a heavily laden cart up behind her, making an escape all the more awkward.

"Please," said the old lady as the man scooped at the coin tray in the register. "Put the change in the bag with the chicken." He turned and attempted to press a fistful of silver into the old woman's hand, but she refused it and reached for the bag, fumbled with the sticky plastic and opened it with a rustle. Her glasses were thick, distorting her eyes into the likes of insect globes under a microscope lens. "In here, please! Put the change in here."

The clerk deposited the coins and the old woman laboriously, with arthritic hands, attempted to twist the ends of plastic into a little knot, while the clerk turned to the register and ripped off the receipt. "Here," he said, holding the bit of paper in midair next to the woman as she concentrated on the knotting activity. "Here," he kept saying, as she pushed the chicken bag to the very end of the counter.

Finally, she turned to him. "Oh, dear!" she said, with a look of dismay. "I'm afraid that must go in the bag too! That *must* go in the bag!" She took the receipt, reached for the bag, and attempted to unknot her careful work, while the clerk scanned the lettuce again and stood waiting.

Hearing the metallic clink of change in the bottom of the chicken bag, thinking of the coins resting in a pool of blood and juices, the mother of the ravenous children remembered a day years ago when her daughter, too young to understand, reached up for a raw poultry leg on the kitchen counter. She had pushed her daughter's hand away, and now she felt a similar urge toward action but suppressed it, remaining silent and watchful. The clerk waited, the mother waited, each of them glancing now and again at the groceries in the old woman's cart.

Frustrated and failing in her efforts, the old woman settled on stuffing the paper receipt, twisted and crumpled, through a small hole at the top of the bag, then turned to her cart. She sighed and pushed a whisper-fine crinkle of gray under the edge of her hat before leaning over the cart for the remaining items.

The younger woman thought of helping, thought of the awkwardness involved, the difficulty of squeezing alongside and around her own cart in the narrow aisle to position herself for the task, thought about the issue of permission: whether she should ask first or simply pitch in with a cheerful comment of entitlement, hoping to appear bene-volent rather than selfish and intrusive. Either way, she risked a response from the old lady, something faltering and time consuming, perhaps indignant or unpleasant. Any time gained in the helping would be squandered in uncertainties over protocol.

The old woman's breathing came harder now, and her hands shook with the effort under the pressure of watchful eyes. She didn't seem angry or bitter, only flustered and worried, perhaps growing tired of life, making her fragility appear all the more delicate and worthy of careful consider-ation. Patience was required—the young mother under-stood. Old people and children required patience.

Tabloid still in hand, she twisted her wrist to glance at her watch. Quarter past twelve. Distracted, now without any hope of learning the fate of the two-headed baby, she placed the magazine back on the rack and punched a finger into the side of a cardboard ice cream container, testing for softness. The clerk scanned the items as they came, stopping after each one to wait for the next: a quart of milk, two bananas, a loaf of bread, a can of tuna fish, and a box of ice cream bars.

Slow as it was, all seemed to progress smoothly, yet an aura of foreboding hung in the air. Two items remained in the cart, and the old woman hesitated, becoming paralyzed with confusion or indecision. She reached for one item, a plastic bottle of juice, then abandoned the effort and reached for her newspaper instead. Placing it on the counter, she pointed with a knobby finger. "This is the coupon for the juice," she said, "and this one's for the cereal," then turned around and reached for the bottle from the bottom of the cart.

The clerk, having difficulty looking at the old woman, glanced everywhere else, his eyes momentarily resting on the mother, next in line. He gave an embarrassed little smile as his eyes met hers, but he looked away immediately, speaking into the air: "Cut it. You must rip it out. The coupon."

The old woman, absorbed in her task, reached for the cereal box and didn't seem to hear the clerk: "You must…"

The younger woman worked hard with her patience. What a silly rule—cut out the coupon!—and what a lazy clerk, failing to do this small thing for the old woman while she struggled with the cereal box, lost her grasp, and let it slip from her hands to the floor. At last, the young mother was presented with an appropriate Good Samaritan deed. Released into action, she squeezed around her cart and stooped to pick up the box, placing it on the conveyor. The two women, in silence, exchanged pleasant expressions and nods, a light shining from the bug globes of the older one.

In the interim, the clerk had deigned to examine the newspaper specials under his nose and flashed gleaming eyes between the coupons and items on the conveyor. "Sorry," he said. "These coupons. No good."

The old woman, flustered and bent, leaned into the

counter and peered down through her lenses, holding the frames back with three fingers to keep them from sliding off her nose. "What's that?"

"This." He pointed to the juice coupon. "Wrong brand. And this." He pointed to the cereal coupon. "Wrong size. You have fifteen ounce, but you need the twenty-two." She looked at him in confusion. "The bigger size," he said, louder.

"I looked at every one, and these match the pictures. See here?" She pointed.

"No, no, that is not. Different brand, you see? And read this! Twenty-two ounce, it say right here. See?"

"But if these aren't right, you don't have the right ones on the shelf. I looked. How can you advertise something you don't have?"

"I don't know, maybe we had it before."

"How can you do that?"

"Look, lady." He scanned the items. "The computer say nothing else. See. Juice, $3.59, not $1.99. Cereal, $2.69, not $1.19. See?"

"$2.69? But how can the smaller cereal be more than the larger cereal?"

Yes, the young mother thought. Yes, how can it be? This quibbling over pennies!

"Not on sale. Look, if you want, I get the manager."

The old woman said nothing, eyes downcast, then glanced out the front window before turning to the clerk. "Add it up. Maybe I have enough." She opened the clasp of her purse and pulled out a wallet. "How much is it?"

"$17.69."

"Here." She handed some bills.

"This is $15.00. You need $17.69."

"That's all I have."

"Not enough." He shook his head.

"With the coupons though…?" Her voice trailed, feeble and defeated.

"I have to take something off here." He swept an arm about, motioning.

The ice cream, the younger woman thought. The ice cream should be taken off, the most expensive item and the least healthy. Butterfat to clog old arteries. That's what should be done, a certain voice said, while a competing image came to mind: the old woman sitting alone in a yellowing kitchen, gnarled fingers ripping into the paper wrapper, trembling lips opening for the ice cream bar, a messy bite, a smile, shingles of chocolate sliding down past balled-up knuckles, landing on the tabletop.

Without further thought, the young mother reached for her wallet and searched the billfold for singles while her rational self, tired of grappling with the larger issues, refused to focus on the propriety and consequence of her actions. What did anything else matter? Intrusion or not, she wanted the old woman to have everything she desired, and quick, before the ice cream melted into waste!

"Maybe I can help," she said, leaning forward with three bills in her hand.

The old woman looked at the money with a question in her eyes.

Suddenly embarrassed, the younger woman hoped for a way out, but it was too late to retract the offer. "What I mean is," she said, "it's such a shame about the coupons. Here, why don't you take this? Please."

To her surprise, the old woman did not protest. She opened her hand for the bills, and their fingers brushed for the briefest instant during the transfer. "Can I send it back to you somehow? Maybe I should get your address."

"No, don't think of it! I want you to have it. This is good food here."

"Well, thank you," responded the old lady and looked no further upon her, turning to the clerk with the extra money.

And the transaction, its completion, went smoothly after that.

The old woman's friend, after all, did not seem to mind about the cost of the chicken. "I'll have plenty of leftovers," she said, looking pleased. "There's so much here, why don't you come to dinner tonight?"

"I will," said the old woman, noticing then that she'd been hoping for an invitation. Evenings, at dusk, just when she closed the blinds against creeping grayness, she was reminded of so many things. Her husband lying abed, stick thin and frail, and better times, his face animated, sitting across from her at dinner.

Back in her apartment after making the delivery, she thought of the ice cream. She'd placed it in the freezer before going down the hall with the chicken, and now, after a long chat with her friend, the ice cream would be hardened up again, recovered from that ordeal in the checkout line and the bus trip home, the many minutes of exposure to higher temperatures. She thought for a minute and didn't see any harm in having an early afternoon treat. It wouldn't spoil her appetite for the chicken dinner, hours later. No, it wouldn't.

She took the package of six ice cream bars from the freezer and labored at opening it. The cardboard flaps were always glued tight. So tight. She fumbled and pressed and pulled without effect until, in a sudden spasm of strength, she ripped the cardboard box open, scattering the six bars in a hodgepodge on the kitchen table. She paused to regard the disarray, and her eyes filled with tears. The box was ruined.

She carried the paper-covered ice cream bars to the freezer two at a time—two and then two and then one—leaving the last one on the table. By then her tears had spilled over and were flowing from under the rims of her glasses, down her cheeks, soaking into crevices of worn skin.

Unable to move, she stared at the ice cream bar on the table. Her eyes shifted onto the broken cardboard box, the tiny vase with three wilted daisies, the plastic napkin holder. All these things were resting on her little square table with the two chairs shoved underneath. Two chairs.

The ice cream would taste delicious, she knew, but just then couldn't bring herself to believe it. She felt queasy, unable to receive it. Leaving the ice cream bar on the table, she shuffled into the bedroom, and without thought, went to the bedside stand and picked up her favorite framed photograph. She stared down into it. His eyes held encouragement, and so she returned to the kitchen, determined to have her treat, and sat down at the table, where she propped the photograph in front of her, just beyond the ice cream bar.

Her tears had stopped but her cheeks were still wet, and her mouth wasn't eager, as it usually was, for the sweet taste. She gazed down into his eyes, big and brown and warm even in this fuzzy photograph, which wasn't a true likeness and didn't adequately catch the depth of his character, or so she'd thought at the time, now unable to trust her memory completely.

"Something happened today," she told him. "Maybe that's why I can't eat the ice cream."

His eyes encouraged her to say more.

"We were about to get on the bus and the store manager came up. He came right up to me! He was following me from the checkout and he said, 'Lady, please don't do this again.' And I said, 'Do what?' And he said, 'You know, this is the third time, and I'm worried the customers don't like it. This is the third time you've done this.' He was talking so nasty. I didn't understand, but now I remember. He was right, there were other times. But he thinks—oh, I know it from the way he was talking!"

Her lips trembled, and she felt the tears coming again. Still, he looked up at her with that warmth, a frozen second of his life. *Kitten.* His favorite name for her.

"Edgar! Have I? Have I done this on purpose? I'm always so careful with the coupons!"

I love you, Kitten.

She touched the paper wrapper, pulled the ice cream bar toward her, hesitated, and looked deeply into his eyes, wanting to know where they'd gone, wanting to go there with him.

Eat the ice cream, my love. The woman wanted you to have it.

She pinched the end of the wrapper and started to tear it, still not wanting to eat.

Kitten, you deserve this. You deserve so much.

Water dripped from the end of her chin onto the paper, and she tugged and ripped until it lay completely exposed: the perfect shape of the ice cream bar, the oval edges, the hard, smooth shell of chocolate. She handled the stick, lifted the bar, and bit into it, tasting nothing but the salt in her mouth, but she took another bite and swallowed with a lump in her throat, and bit again and again, doing it for Edgar, eating until the ice cream was gone.

When she was done, she looked down at the empty stick, feeling unsatisfied.

Later this evening, with her friend, the chicken would taste better, she thought.

ॐ

Fractals

MINERVA THRIEBOLD IS a tenured professor in the mathematics department of a formerly women's (now coed) private liberal arts college in New England. Isabella Baggio is one of three backup singers for a popular male entertainer on the cruise ship circuit and lives in Miami when stateside.

At the age of four, Minerva developed a dislike for her name and methodically repositioned the letters into every possible combination of seven, six, and five letters. She settled on Verna and proclaimed it. Her parents, Lucy and Brill, did not resist, although Minerva had been named after Lucy's favorite grandmother. Years later, Lucy was throwing out old toys when she found Verna's name combinations on a piece of paper wadded inside Mr. Potato Head's hat. In that childish handwriting, Lucy discerned a foreshadowing of mathematical genius, a grasp of algorithm.

Isabella, from the time she was an infant, was known as Bebe, a nickname created from the two b's in her names. Her mother, Sharyn, reflexively adopted the pet name during an episode of gentle cooing with her newborn. "Isabella Baggio, b – b – b – b!" she repeated, making a sound that put a smile on the baby's face and seemed to capture her sunny, sweet disposition. The spelling was later simplified to "bb" after the fashion of ee cummings, the mother's favorite poet.

In 1969, Verna and bb were sixteen. In 2004, they are both fifty-one. Verna and her husband Kent have been together for twenty-four years and have two teenagers, a girl and a boy. bb is, and always has been, single.

If their lives were the subject of a simple geometry lesson, they might be two lines in a plane, not parallel, required to intersect once, never to meet again.

"A fractal is a fragmented geometric shape we can split into parts which are each a reduced copy of the whole. This is a property called self-similarity." Verna moves the mouse and clicks, projecting an image of a romanesco onto the screen in the dark classroom. The olive-green vegetable, a cross between broccoli and cauliflower, displays the pleasing symmetry of repeating pattern. "Fractals, or approximations of them, occur in nature, like this romanesco."

Verna is not entirely present in her lecture. This morning she received an e-mail on her office computer at the college, a big surprise that, in the abstract, should have been interesting and exciting. But the intervening decades have marked the sender, imbuing her message with an aftertaste. Verna is left feeling sad and resentful, beset by involuntary thoughts. *Too little too late. Go away.*

Lines of sun pierce the closed Venetian blinds in the classroom. Seduced by the muted light, she intones, "A mathematical fractal is generated by an equation that undergoes iteration, endless feedback based on recursion. Can anyone think of an example of infinite recursion?"

An eager male hand shoots up in the gray. She points. "A spiral, infinitely winding into the center," he suggests, more or less sure of himself.

"Not always. It depends."

Another hand goes up. "Mirrors facing each other," says a girl. "The reflection inside a reflection inside a..."

"...reflection, inside a reflection inside a..." The class takes up the chant for several iterations and dissolves into laughter, a surrender to impulse driven by the fresh, April afternoon seeping in through the slats.

Professor Thriebold, for all her gravity, is known to allow, on occasion, a complete youthful surrender to the beauty of math. She laughs along and forgets.

Lucille Mae Fish grew up on a farm in Ohio, and Edward Brill Thriebold was the son of a San Francisco surgeon and a wealthy Nob Hill socialite. Lucy and Brill met while undergraduates at the University of California, and upon their graduation in 1951, both just twenty-two, they married and chose to make their home in Berkeley, where they raised their only child Minerva, born in 1953.

That quiet, pale girl with dirty-blonde hair and full-moon eyes lived her life from infanthood to the age of fourteen immersed in the soothing self-satisfaction of textbook learning. She was at the top of her class, master of the pop quiz, multiple-choice, and standardized test, a natural leader of the "smart" group in a time when pedagogues were not trained to conceal the intellectual differences among children.

Verna did not shun her classmates, but neither did she

seek them out. She was too socially insecure to be forward but always had a friend or two, never as smart and without anything else about them sufficiently intriguing to make up for it. This is how it was, until bb came along.

It was 1967, the Summer of Love. In an unknown, faraway place, the recently divorced Sharyn Baggio assumed a new identity, "Zenith," and journeyed with a younger man into that brewing explosion of a town Berkeley, bringing along her two girls, bb and eleven-year-old Ernestina. Zenith's new lover had swept her away with his dream of making a pilgrimage to the epicenter of Flower Power. He didn't come to participate in peaceful antiwar demonstrations but to experience the movement's tantalizing offshoot, the credo, "turn on, tune in, drop out." The man's name was Ray.

On April 6, 2004, Isabella sits in the light-filled, pastel-colored living room of her modest bungalow ten blocks from Miami Beach when a name pops into her head. She believes the name might have meant something to her at one time, but it has faded into the file of forgotten regrets and died with that part of her she successfully buried and laid to molder, fertilizing the greater, stronger part she's coaxed up to the surface, the part that has survived. There is no one left to recognize the traces of death that remain at the core of her being because her sunny side has been reborn, blooming up from the decay.

The familiar name percolates to the top with a cheery sort of, "I wonder whatever happened to...?" She goes to her desk and lets her fingers wander to the Internet browser where she finds Minerva Thriebold, a woman who has kept her full maiden name as her professional name, a professor of mathematics. Isabella understands the words on her screen to represent a valid identity, the larger projection of the smaller girl of sixteen she once knew. She explores the college website, finds the e-mail address for Professor Thriebold, and sends a thrilled, heartfelt message, replete with exclamation points. She refrains, however, from adding a happy face.

The Summer of Love, for Verna, meant its opposite, the beginning of a three-year bumpy escalation to the end of her parents' marriage. She was witness to restrained squalls with frustrated grabs and shoving, followed by sickly-sweet reconciliations. Stone cold silences. Political arguments, Lucy the rational, cautious one, Brill the socialist firebrand. They would forget about their child and then suddenly remember, acknowledging her existence with guilty, darting eyes.

At one time, their love had been overpowering. Lucy made a huge statement when she left a life of corn ears and alfalfa to follow her intellectual dreams to a distant university where she committed herself to a man with a socially unfamiliar past. Lucy and Brill's differences and their shared pursuit of careers in social research were enough to bind them inseparably against the tug of family roots.

But then the '60s took hold, and Brill became ever more strident and anti-establishment and resentful of his own easy beginnings, angry and ashamed of his parents' wealth. Lucy reacted, retreating into her mind, into the past and the tranquility of wind-blown acres of grain, family meals around the oak table, fundamental values, respect.

Verna escaped into her books and couldn't wait for the summer to be over and her freshman year at Berkeley High School to begin. On that September morning at 8:00 a.m., she walked into first period English and chose one of the tottering wood desks in the back row. She usually sat in the front where she could receive her academic due, but her behavior had started to show the signs of a new insecurity, the creeping influence of family strife. Her choice of seat that day was provident, for bb plunked down in the wobbling desk next to hers in the back.

Mr. McGraff had not yet opened his mouth when bb timidly glanced at Verna, dared to hold her eyes, and suddenly broke out in a smile, an intense flash of meridian light. "Hi!!!" she bubbled with her voice full of exclamation points, as it always was and always would be.

With one look, Verna guessed the new girl was a C-plus student. It didn't matter. Of greater interest were bb's unknowable past and her enigmatic arrival. The attraction was mutual, a simultaneous desire for outlet, to speak of everything except what must be forgotten and supposed not to exist, and here they were, magically sitting together, finding each other in the exact moment of need.

There could be no doubt as to bb's sincerity. The proof was in her physical beauty, which far surpassed Verna's plain features, a disparity that established the certainty of their deeper affinity. bb was the poster-lovechild hippie with waist-length ebony hair in full natural curl, wearing patched bellbottoms and a raw-edged, leather fringe vest over raglan-sleeved paisley. Her smile carried the promise of sublime love and beauty, transcendence.

Verna was taken. From that day forward, they were inseparable.

Lucy and Brill were so completely immersed in their own misery they hardly noticed Verna's increasing absence and the changes in her behavior. Her grades never suffered. School had become somewhat too easy for her and home life somewhat too difficult, leaving a void to be filled.

bb lived just five blocks away. Verna started following her home after school, sometimes to stay, sometimes to stop off on their way to bigger adventures. She came to know every crack and assaultive weed in the concrete walkway leading to that small single-story in the Berkeley flats. A choking screen of overgrown bushes obscured the front door. Directly inside that door was a cramped living room in plum and mustard colors, the air often thick with the marijuana and cigarette smoke of long-haired men who slouched over congas and guitars, their long-haired women skulking in the shadows, attached to cow bells or tambourines.

To the right was a narrow hallway leading to three tiny bedrooms and a bathroom, and straight through the living room was the kitchen with its pungent odor of tanned cowhide. The grimy countertops and dinette table brimmed with the tools, raw materials, and wares of Ray's leather business, Stingray Designs: fringe vests, belts, and Confederate rebel hats. Leftover signs of the munchies would be strewn about, baking tins with crusted brownie residue or blackened pots with an inch of cold stew.

The first time up the front walkway, as Verna was swallowed by the bushes hiding the secret door, a flash of panic hit. This was her first impulsive act of rebellion, an after-school visit she hadn't revealed to her parents. That day, the living room held three men. Leading Verna through, bb cast a shade of dark curls down over her eyes as if she might, in this way, make it into the kitchen without being noticed. A man's voice, forced and silky, came up from the floor where he was sitting cross-legged on the dirty shag carpet with a guitar resting in the deep diamond between knees and crotch.

"Little flower," he said. "Made a new friend at school?" One of the men glanced at the girls with sleepy eyes, the other was stuffing a bong.

bb stopped and turned. "This is Verna," she announced to the room with her sunny smile, avoiding his eyes.

The inquiring man regarded Verna, letting his gaze slip here and there, finally settling on her face. Her eyes grew wide and he laughed. "She tell you who I am? bb can forget her manners." His hair seemed wet or maybe greasy, combed close to his head, ending in snakelike waves at the bottom of his neck. His blue eyes, closer to gray in the dim room, were gripping, mesmerizing.

"This is Ray," said bb.

"Isabella's stepdad," he corrected, and waved his hand to shoo them away. "Go on, baby munchkins, and get some cookies and milk."

Verna gladly followed her friend out of that living room and into the kitchen, where they scrounged for a snack within the morass of leather pouches and sandals bearing imprints of peace signs, yins and yangs. The refrigerator held a few cans of beer, ketchup and relish, a single bagless hotdog roll.

"Doesn't your stepdad have to go to work?"

"He makes all this stuff at home." bb laughed and twirled in a circle, letting her Indian cotton dress balloon and settle again on her slim, braless form. Verna felt instantly comfortable to be with another girl as flat as herself in a room away from the prying eyes of men and boys. "Bitchen!" Verna said, trying bb's favorite word.

"Yeah. And then he tries to sell it on the weekends."

"Far out! Your stepdad is pretty cool." The words spilled automatically, like an obligation.

bb smiled vacantly and said nothing, her face a picture of studied absence deep within. Verna couldn't understand that look, but it made her regret what she'd just said. In time, she would figure out that Zenith was the breadwinner, allowing Ray to falter and b.s. at the flea markets where he bartered his wares for a high or netted a few coins after expenses.

bb rummaged in a cabinet. "Here, you want this?" She smiled brightly and held out a box of Cocoa Puffs, but her little sister Tina appeared from nowhere and laid claim: "Hey, mine!"

bb held the box up in the air and demanded, "Give me a hug first! Come on and give me a hug!" As Tina came for it, bb lunged, picked the girl up, and spun her around in a dazzling burn of love! Where did all this love come from? It exploded in a burst of hard brown pebbles onto the floor!

Just as quickly, bb dropped her sister and the box and took Verna's hand to lead her away while Tina scrambled for the sugary bits on the floor. They escaped to bb's room and shut the door. It would be their cocoon, a cozy squeeze on all sides with the paisley bedspread tacked to the ceiling in air-filled scallops and the walls covered with posters of the Doors, Beatles, Rolling Stones, and Grateful Dead.

They spent the afternoon applying mascara and eyeliner while Verna answered bb's questions about certain kids at school. Later, bb put the Sgt. Pepper LP on a pink turntable and started to sing in a voice that was full, clear, pure, and easy. Verna joined in. She had but one artistic love, and that was the study of music, mostly classical. She played the piano and loved to sing and could hold a tune but struggled to listen to herself, to make sure she didn't go sharp. Whenever she became worried about losing pitch, her volume would plummet to near nothingness.

There was no such worry that afternoon as her voice rode on the stronger current by her side. She dreamed of timeless music—hymns, madrigals, and chorales—and by the end of the afternoon, she'd convinced her new friend to join A Cappella, an after-school club.

"Fractals are infinitely complex. Take this one, for example. You see it here as I zoom in at different levels of magnification. In the next few weeks, we'll explore some of the techniques for generating fractals: iterated function systems, both deterministic and non-deterministic, random fractals, escape-time fractals. Strange attractors."

The slide collage devolves into a fast-paced light show as Verna clicks on image after image, a fern, a cloud, a crystal, a Koch snowflake, cauliflower, mountain range, river network, branching pulmonary vessels, tree limbs, a fractal flame like wispy smoke. The flashing images take her back. She sits again on that long, slick seat in the boat-like

Chevrolet, pushed up against the passenger door, Zenith driving, bb center, the three of them bumping and sliding in the dark toward red taillights and green traffic lights smudged on a rainy windshield. She strangles on smoke from Zenith's cigarettes, and now the burning roach is passed from mother to daughter, and from daughter to daughter's friend, click, click, click, a Sierpinski triangle, Mandelbrot set, chaos game—color, angle, pattern, shape, infinity, vortex. They step into the Fillmore in San Francisco and push through an intermittent, strobe-lit crowd of tie-dye in a cavernous space, walled in splashing colors. They twitch and undulate, a thousand separate souls immersed in the rasping anger of Janis Joplin.

Wait! Where did they go? Pressed on all sides, Verna is surrounded and alone, stripped of bb's love, Zenith's protection. Dizzy and paranoid, a pinprick of light, she pushes through the squirming bodies, halts, and circles. Fright chokes her neck, wobbles her knees. Why would anyone want to feel like this, to be in a place like this?

There? No. There! "bb!" And as she yells out, voiceless in the din, Zenith's arms reach up from behind. Verna turns and looks down into the face of the petite woman with the deep, sensitive eyes and accepts her embrace. In her ear she feels the startling, husky voice.

"Verna."

"My goodness, Verna, this must be you! You were so smart—I always knew you would make it to the top! Do you remember me? From way back when, Berkeley High? I live

in Miami now, but most of the time I work
on cruise ships. I'm a vocalist! Remember A
Cappella? Please write. I'd love to know
how you're doing! Maybe we could get
together sometime and catch up?

"Luv, Isabella"

Her finger moves to "send" but remains frozen. The
missive isn't complete. Again, she poises herself to type but
stops, feeling the sudden sting of a buried dagger. Internal
training takes hold, the deep breathing sets in. She waits it
out. *There now. My gosh, how ridiculous!*

"P.S. You might remember me as 'bb,' but I
don't use that name anymore!!!"

As freshman year wore on, they talked endlessly about boys
and pretended to hope, yet knew, that they would never
have boyfriends. bb was so beautiful it puzzled Verna that a
boy hadn't taken her away. At the same time, it was unthinkable because there wasn't an inch of space between
them to allow anyone else in. The only time they were apart
was late at night.

They suspected that sex was prevalent within a certain
set of their classmates. This was not said bluntly but expressed with eye contact and suggestion. "Free love" was
the standard, and it came to hang a weight around their
necks.

Verna was secretly convinced of a societal expectation
that she lose her virginity as soon as possible. The absurdity
of this, for a girl of fourteen, was not apparent to her.
Embarrassed to admit it, she had overheard her parents

making love, less so in recent times. First on her "to do" list was calculus homework, last was sex, right underneath cleaning her room, but on the list nevertheless.

There were no rules, advice, or guidance from her parents, but just as well, because she couldn't possibly discuss this subject with them. Imagining that bb and Zenith had long, female conversations, she was jealous. Zenith was so unlike other mothers. She would coolly suggest their next adventure, mysterious and unknowable behind her cigarette smoke and gray-green eyes, slivered in a protective squint with every drag. Surely bb was able to talk to her, and maybe Verna could too, if she needed to talk, but she'd convinced herself of no such need. The facts and evidence of expectation and obligation were unavoidable, blazoned on the face of the world.

Zenith had a fulltime clerk-typist job and was never home during the day. The three of them were together only on their special Saturday nights when Ray was off at some other house jamming. Those were the evenings filled with dense smoke, swimming heads, pounding music, and trips to Denny's at three a.m. Tina was considered too young to come along. Verna wasn't quite sure where she stayed on those nights.

In A Cappella they were learning "Ode to Joy," Beethoven's 9th. On the few occasions they went to Verna's house, she would play the record and they would sing what they'd learned, knowing that it could never be as great. Everything had a gap between real and imagined—free love too—that was what Verna suspected. She couldn't ask bb outright what she believed about sex, afraid of the probable response, a sunny smile with an "outasite!" Afraid, maybe, that bb would say she'd actually done it, as impossible as it was.

They were not supposed to be self-conscious about the outlines of their own bare nipples poking through the cloth as they observed more dramatic development under the blouses of their classmates. They dropped joking hints about their endless wait, and as it turned out, they would keep waiting forever. Their bodies were alike in this way, but what did it matter to bb, who was so completely beautiful? In candlelight and incense, they styled each other's hair and took turns running the brush bristles along bared arms and backs to feel the exciting tickle.

Often enough, Verna suggested they go to her house, but they usually ended up at bb's. She wasn't sure why. There was an invisible pull. Ray would be in the living room nearly every afternoon, jamming and smoking. They would receive his sidelong look or a "munchkin" comment on their way to bb's room.

Only once did he walk into their secret sanctum without knocking. bb did not utter a protest, but a small ripple of emotion passed through her body.

"Lady Guinevere. Tell me your secrets!"

He closed the door behind him and sat on the bed next to bb. She scooted away an inch, stoking his attention. The dilated pupils in his glittering eyes pulled their space into his trip on something stronger than pot. A hand went to bb's shoulder, and she gave an embarrassed laugh. He massaged her neck, took up a curl on his finger, and wound himself into it, staring at her profile. "Ray!" she said under her breath with another little laugh. Verna was on the floor by the turntable looking through a stack of records, averting her eyes, feeling hot and unsure.

"What's the trippy news from Berkeley High?" he asked, drawling the last word.

"Not much."

"That singing club you go to. Sing me something." The lock was coiled around his finger, and her head tilted slightly toward him under the pressure.

Verna's senses perked. She sat up, shifting from the side of her thigh onto her knees.

"We haven't really learned anything," said bb.

"Oh, you have, I've heard you!" He was unwinding the hair now, releasing the pressure, so maybe it was nothing after all, but Verna's accelerating heart wouldn't slow down. She jumped up and began to sing "Ode to Joy"! Ray turned suddenly and dropped his hand as if taken by surprise to see her there in the room with them.

bb sprang up and joined her. Their voices swelled, obliterating the threat of bad karma, becoming stronger together, bright and clear as Ray lost edge and substance. Smiling vaguely, he listened for a while, then stood up with a slight pitch to the side and left the room.

It takes several days. She fights with herself about responding, but knows that she will, perhaps must. How can she not? How can she fail to release even a tiny bit of what would have been a gush, an open torrent of relief, anger, and love that would have been impossible to stanch thirty years ago, or even twenty? The tread of time has diminished the relief, anger, and love to just anger and love and then anger and then resentment and then a dull ache and then indifference.

But respond she does, in a middle-aged voice that neither of them ever could have foreseen, choked with suppression and filled with little white lies that maybe bb — no, Isabella — won't be able to detect in her new, apparently oblivious and incomprehensibly distant persona which so nakedly refuses to take responsibility.

"Isabella, How interesting to hear from you.
Good for you, that you've been able to take
up a career in singing."

She almost adds, "to make use of your talent in this way," but she can't go that far, to be so hideously hypocritical! A cruise ship!

"As you can see, I'm a professor of mathematics. It has been an enjoyable and fulfilling career."

At this point, a word or two about her family might be appropriate, but she can't bring herself to involve Kent and the children. There's nothing in Isabella's note about her own family. And so, she just ends it.

"Thank you for your note.
"Best regards, Verna"

In June of 1968, the country was reeling from two assassinations. As freshman year came to a close, Verna was looking forward to a summer of secret rendezvous with bb and Zenith, trips to be-ins and rock concerts and volunteer work for the UFW. In a private meeting, Verna's father had approved the part of the plan that included pamphleteering and picketing with the Mexican farm workers. In those days,

Lucy and Brill were never in the same room at the same time. Separately, they had each met Verna's closest friend but seemed unaware of her importance.

On the morning of the last day of school, after Brill had gone to work, Lucy announced, "We're leaving on Saturday."

Verna was eating a slice of wheat berry toast. She kept chewing, unable to see her mother's face due to an involuntary habit of tilting her head down, a subconscious acknowledgment of shame. "Leaving?"

"We're going to Ohio, to visit my sister and your cousins."

Her chest tightened. Once, when she was nine, they'd gone to visit Aunt Denise, Uncle George, Kathy and Hank, the most boring people in the world on the loneliest, most expansive stretch of big-sky farmland she'd ever seen.

"Without your father," Lucy added.

"When're we coming back?"

"Not sure."

"A week?"

"Oh, longer than that. We'll be gone for some time."

That piece of toast, the good, nutty taste of it, was seared in memory, a contradiction.

That afternoon in bb's room, there was dramatic hugging and sobbing, wild plans of running away, and hopeless wailing at the futility of it. They made promises to write and to think of each other every minute of every day they were apart. And they would, and they did.

Verna didn't know that the Ohio days of 1968 were to stretch into the whole summer, a planned, trial separation between Lucy and Brill. Not aware of this, Verna remained frantic for only a few days in the beginning, then gradually succumbed to the oddly calming effect of the big sky. Tractors and acres of corn. Mashed potatoes and tumblers of frothy milk. The farm stand. Hank and experiments with French kissing. They agreed it wasn't really incest because Hank was Uncle George's boy from a previous marriage, but the taboo was great enough to restrain them from doing anything more.

Most special were the afternoons sitting alone under a huge willow, reading bb's letters. They arrived once a week, those impossible-to-fold stacks of paper rolled and shoved into business-size envelopes. In cheap blue ballpoint, the handwriting was large and round and open and uniformly slanted, neatly resting on each line of both sides of the wide-ruled binder paper. If Verna had been blind, she could have read the lines with her fingers, tracing deep impressions of passionate prose etched into the pulp.

> "Oh Verna! We saw the People yesterday in Golden Gate Park and they sang 'I Love You'!!! It was so bitchen!!!"

and

> "Where does the universe end???"

and

> "Do they have cows and pigs where you are?"

and

> "I'm lying on my back in bed counting the paisleys. I'm up to 279!!!"

That calm feeling under the big sky was owed in part to her unshakeable belief that bb was in that little house on the Berkeley flats, waiting for her to come home.

*   *   *

Not long after sending the reply e-mail, Verna receives a letter. Instantly, she's transported back to the farm. The paper is different, ecru stationery bearing the logo of a cruise line, but the quality of the pen and the handwriting have not changed. Childish, round, and careful, a rejection of darkness and maturity, the finite components of a complex, reiterative pattern.

> "Dear Verna, It was so great to hear from you!!! Is this crazy? In May I'll be working a cruise line with a stop in Boston!"

So, the suggestion is laid. Verna might resist, might dwell in false analogy to geometric principle, concluding that a second meeting is impossible. Instead, she resigns herself immediately to their unavoidable reunion and launches into the business of its arrangement. The diversion is enough to keep her mind away from a suspicion that she still harbors a lingering, hidden yearning to lash out.

Verna returned from Ohio a week before the first day of sophomore year. The homecoming was as dramatic and tearful as the parting. Children of today might not understand. An overwhelming fear will take hold in anticipation of hearing a voice again, coming eye-to-eye again, after months of physical and vocal separation and endless days of hanging in reverie on a written exchange. A sudden realization! Freed from the inhibition of physical presence, eye contact, and body language, the flow of thought had been unleashed. She remembered all those things she'd written to bb this summer. Confessions about Hank. Descriptions of the fights between her mother and father. Dreams of becoming the greatest mathematician of all time. Envy of bb's hair and eyes.

With trepidation, Verna telephoned and froze up at the sudden intimacy of bb's voice in her ear. Nervously they made arrangements, an immediate meeting, and bb was waiting out on the sidewalk in front of her house as Verna rounded the corner. Their eyes locked and they ran, each taking her own half of the block at a sprint, and they flew into each other's arms!

Another year together had begun, in many ways similar to the last, but changed by the aura of growing unrest in the nation, the accumulation of unpleasant knowledge in their young minds, the temptation of false gratification, the glorification of anarchy, the oppression of too much freedom. Their experiments were deeper, darker, more dangerous and exciting. Verna suffered from doubt every time, before and after. They hitchhiked. They talked to strangers in the park. They smoked pot without parental supervision and snorted coke with. Zenith taught them how. They laughed and cried and felt every wonderful soaring emotion of adolescence, the panicky passion of complete inseparability.

Yet a transparent veil of inhibition separated them. Verna could see something on the other side but did not understand her friend any better. She was too busy hiding from herself, unable to utter the most painful thing. From the day of her return, it was clear that the summer apart had done little to mend her parents' relationship. bb also was hiding, leaving Verna uneasy and ignorant of how she could take the painful journey behind bb's eyes which, often, did not smile with her mouth but opened into a vast, impenetrable obliteration. Perhaps Verna's eyes said the same.

The girls covered up their secret unknowns with a mask of teen exuberance. Still, they were able to feel the depth of their souls in each other, sharing something beyond words.

A week before she takes to the sea, Isabella receives a letter. She's overjoyed to get it, not put off in the least by the businesslike tone. *My goodness, Verna was always so organized!* There's a date, a time, and a place for their reunion. An adventure! So neatly planned.

Isabella glows with a smile that's more or less permanent under the influence of countless swaying performances in eveningwear, singing the backup fragments, with innuendo, to "I Heard it Through the Grapevine." The men often look at her as they sit at tables covered in white linen, so handsome and safe, holding hands with sweethearts or wives or paramours while they allow her to smile at them from her diaphanous perch, beautiful and distant.

Since that day, a month ago, when she sent off that e-mail on a whim, a few things have come back slowly, especially some of the emotions she felt when Verna, so long ago, went off across the country, leaving her behind with...him. Twice, a summer and a year.

What, really, did she feel about Verna then? What does she feel now? She's never been angry at another person in her life, but if it's anger or betrayal, or anything else that requires forgiveness, she must have forgiven it by now. Yes, that must be it, but when? On a date uncertain, a sunny day before the sunny day that Verna's name suddenly came to mind, free and clear.

Now there's no threat of a bad feeling to swallow her up. No isolation. No fear. No self-hatred. No panic. Just a blinding white light. And something to look forward to—a new adventure for two old ladies!!!

On an afternoon in May of their sophomore year, Verna and bb cut class and went to the university campus where they stretched out on the green and made daisy chains. Mascara and daisies were bb's trademarks, thick black lashes and a halo of flowers nestled in the cushion of lustrous curls.

Although Brill and Lucy both worked at the university, Verna had the impression they didn't know of her wanderings to the campus during school hours. And if Zenith and Ray were aware of bb's playing hooky, they weren't the kind of parents to do anything about it.

That day, something was up, they could feel it. The California Highway Patrol was in town. They'd ducked a few officers on the way to campus, but their route hadn't taken them through the area of greatest concentration. In the background, they heard a voice over a loudspeaker in Sproul Plaza.

The sun shone oddly through the black coating on bb's lashes as she gazed down at the flowers in her hands. "Did you hear about People's Park?" she asked Verna.

Brill, in one of his moments of parental instruction, had spoken of it with shining eyes when Lucy wasn't around. Verna both liked and disliked him when he got like that. His energy and zeal were catching, but his absorption in what he was saying removed him to another universe. The citizenry of Berkeley, he told her, had claimed a bit of university property, where they'd planted shrubs and flowers, creating a park. There was governmental resistance. This was the part that excited Brill the most.

Verna repeated this bit of information and asked bb, "D'you think that's what they're talking about?"

Her friend jumped up and reached down to grab her arm. "Come on!"

When they got to the plaza, they pushed in at the outskirts of a huge crowd a moment before the speaker cried out, "Let's take the park!" Verna's pounding heart was climbing high in her chest when, suddenly, they were swept up and carried away, two flies on the elephant's tail. A single being of muscle and throat and hair pushed out onto Telegraph Avenue, chanting "We want the park! We want the park!"

Their girlish voices combined with the rest, and in those first moments, the intoxication of purpose gripped Verna with a pride she'd never felt before, to be marching alongside college students with intellect and just cause, and now, wouldn't they—she caught herself—wouldn't *he*, wouldn't her *father* really be proud of his daughter! This unspoken admission declared itself within the jostle of strangers surrounding her, breaking it loose. She was surprised to discover a need for him exclusively, not for her mother who already loved her, of that she was sure. Lucy had been the one to take her away while he stayed behind, without protest, and then said so very little when they returned. He didn't really love her. No, he did not.

But the beauty and righteousness of the moment very

quickly turned ugly and rotten with fear. A block ahead of them, at the front of the crowd, a swarm of uniformed officers in riot gear bore down on them, wielding bats and cocking rifles as their captain made demands by megaphone. This was no demonstration but the beginning of a melee. The students were picking up whatever came handy, a book, a rock, a bottle, even garbage out of a receptacle, taunting and threatening to hurl these things.

The girls stopped dead and turned to each other. bb's eternal smile hovered like a ghost keeping company with the stubborn vacancy in her eyes, something familiar. Verna felt the shock of a new thought without having time to connect, to understand, to remember when she might have seen that look in her friend's eyes before. At this moment they had to act, to be in it or out of it as they found themselves uncomfortably close to the ugliest things that seemed about to happen. "Pigs!" she heard. People were on rooftops throwing things down. A scuffle broke out. An officer brought down a bat.

The girls stood immobile, trapped in ice. Verna's eyes inched left and right, and then she saw him, a man who looked like her own father and was, in fact, her own father. He pulled his arm back like a baseball pitcher and let something fly at a policeman, who deflected it with his riot shield, making a noise she could distinguish even within this ruckus. The noise of her father's rock was the loudest noise of every noise that combined in the mix of decibels making up this hell. The sound of his rock said violence like no other rock, and she wanted none of it.

Canisters shot out from the bank of cops, catching the sun, exploding in acrid plumes of smoke. Brill was caught in a cloud and he whirled, clutching his eyes, twisting blindly in circles. He threw his hands down, looked up, and started to run wildly, dodging an officer in pursuit. He was headed straight toward her. Could he see anything through the sting in his eyes?

Gunfire sounded.

"Let's go!" They turned their backs on People's Park and broke into a sprint, heading west, toward the bay.

Later, they found out that a man on the roof had been shot and killed.

How dare she appear out of nowhere like this.

Verna is on her way to the coffee shop, fighting the desire to turn back. Her impulse is to drive to her office where she can be completely alone, although it's a Saturday and she should be with her family. Her sanctuary, always, has been the world of concept, theory, and logic. On tough days, she reclines on the couch in her darkened office behind a locked door, formulating new hypotheses and theorems, lulling herself into an alternate reality. And this is one of her toughest days, May 15, 2004, the anniversary of People's Park.

At dawn, the significance of the date found light as she struggled to wake up, drenched in sweat, running, nowhere to go. She could smell the tear gas again and see her father's face.

Brill, of course, had seen her, and just as she'd imagined, he was proud of his girl. He bragged about it to Lucy when she bailed him out of the city jail. At that moment, feeling a pang of mother's love, Lucy began to formulate her plan for the second and final escape to Ohio. They couldn't go immediately, had to let Verna finish out the school year, but the extra month gave Lucy time to work out the details. At all costs, they needed to get out. Away from Brill, away from Berkeley, away from that girl who was bringing Verna down. Indeed, Lucy had guessed enough to smell trouble, not too late, she hoped, to save her daughter.

This time, they settled in their own small house on the edge of nowhere. Ripped from what she'd known, Verna was not in the mood to make new friends, and she turned again to books, immediately enrolling in summer courses at a junior college. For companionship, she clung to bb's fat letters, dwelling in a distorted dream of the past.

Come fall, as she wandered solitary through the halls of a new high school, she remained connected to her friend in the written word. Long distance telephone calls were never contemplated in those days, yet there was a belief in lasting friendship without voice or touch. Before long, Verna would return to Berkeley to see her father, maybe at Christmas, or if not then, no later than spring break, and bb would be waiting there, snug in their cocoon.

As the year wore on, the letters dwindled but never ceased as Verna was steadily drawn into the joy and comfort of her intellect. It became clear that junior year would be her last, and she sent off applications to colleges. She could not be interrupted in these academic pursuits for a visit to her father, who'd done little to maintain the lines of communication. The man who could fight for a park couldn't seem to fight for a daughter.

Lucy was the one, finally, to arrange a return. She had legal matters to attend to in Berkeley, but more important, she believed in the value of fatherhood and in Verna's need to see her father. She made plans for a summer trip to Berkeley, where they would stay with friends.

When she announced it, a mad excitement overtook Verna. It wasn't about her father. She was angry at him and didn't much care to see him or their old house where he still lived. The real attraction was bb.

Three weeks in advance, she sent off a letter and almost immediately started her daily run to the mailbox, looking for a response. During those days of waiting, she took an inventory of her stockpile of letters in the drawer where she'd saved every one, finding, to her surprise, that the most recent was a single page dated nearly two months ago. A bad feeling crept in and descended full force on the day she opened the mailbox to find her own letter returned, unopened and banged up, stamped "addressee unknown."

She did not believe in that smudged, purple-ink message applied by an ignorant postal clerk. She had to see for herself.

On a June afternoon, a year after their last hug on the cracked walkway, Verna took that path again up to the front door of the little house in the Berkeley flats. The bushes had grown bushier and the weeds taller, with a realtor's sign sprung up in their midst. The house was locked and empty. She knocked anyway, just to hear the confirmatory echo bouncing back. The occupants had disappeared without a trace.

The night before, in her old house, she'd been shocked to see Brill looking so changed with his unkempt, shoulder-length hair and eyes nearly gone to madness. But she didn't feel shock now as she stood in front of bb's empty house, and that meant there was something predictable in this situation. She was angry. Not at her friend—that would come later—but at herself for letting bb slip away.

In their year apart, with her head clear of forced substances and false dogmas, the first iterations of Verna's essence had taken root. She'd discovered the beginnings of her adult person, her preference for lucidity, prudence, responsibility, and restraint. Tranquility could be eked from boredom, results from hard work.

In the methodical way she had about everything, she commenced a search during that week in Berkeley. Most people she asked were unaware that bb had left. A high school acquaintance had heard that the family moved to Oregon. Another thought that bb had run away, and the family had gone to look for her. There were rumors of bad trips and overdoses. The people who remembered anything realized they hadn't seen her since sometime in the spring. A secretary at the high school confirmed this. In mid-April, bb told her favorite teacher she'd be dropping out. The next day she was gone, leaving no forwarding address.

In the midst of these discoveries, Verna humored her mother with another uncomfortable visit with Brill. He smiled and bounced and exclaimed inappropriately. She didn't understand half the things he said. Something had snapped in him, and he would never be the same.

It was a relief to return to Ohio, where the search for bb continued from afar. Verna wrote to everyone she could think of. Fear controlled her actions, she couldn't deny it. Something bad might have happened.

But the world didn't stop because of it. She survived the rest of that summer when she turned seventeen, went to college and grad school, and lived the beginning and middle of the rest of her life. Time dissipated the fear, uncovering a belief in bb's continued sunny existence on this planet. And with that belief came the certainty of betrayal. The stark facts proved it. Between the two of them, only one had the ability, easily, to find the other, possessing knowledge of an address in California and an address in Ohio.

Thirty-four years later, all her searching for naught, Verna sits in a coffee shop in Boston, across the table from the newly materialized desaparecida. They are two women in middle age, each infinitely complex.

Verna's recent lectures swim in her mind. *In recursion, the function being defined is applied within its own definition, defining an infinite statement using finite components. In this process, components are repeated in a self-similar way.* If this is so, and if, when they were both sixteen, they discovered a common subset within each of them, experienced a natural convergence, a fated intersection, then why had they evolved in this way, spinning off into beings so utterly at opposite poles?

She can't fix the hideous dichotomy on exterior appearances alone because she and Isabella have metamorphosed very predictably, like time-lapse photography. The years are in their faces as they gaze upon each other again, the woman who was true, and the woman who was not.

Verna is thinking this way, knowing that something so crass would never enter the mind of the woman across from her. Isabella sits prettily unaware. Verna sits to judge the new betrayals she observes as they vie with that huge one from the past for her attention. There is the backup singing and the hair color and the biggest, most obvious betrayal, a protruding surgical alteration underneath Isabella's clingy jersey. But the sexuality is packaged, controlled, synthetic, sunny, wholesome. She is what she was so many years ago, the blankness in the eyes removing her corporal self from the dirtiness and defilement of her surroundings.

And Verna knows what Isabella can see sitting across from her on the other side of the table. A dowdy, graying, bookish, owl-eyed professor, staid, respected, and ostensibly mature. Is the anger visible or as carefully hidden as she'd like to believe?

In mind-numbing avoidance, they continue where they left off, speaking around the edges of the glacier that sits on the table between them. They take turns reciting their respective CVs in broad outline, each leaving a glaring blank for 1970. Verna is acutely aware of the omission and assumes that Isabella is equally aware behind her glistening smile—has she had cosmetic dentistry?

Verna shows snapshots of her children.

"Oh, they're beautiful! Just like you. I'll bet you're a wonderful mother!"

"Well, I try. It *is* difficult these days. I worry about them, of course."

"I'm sure you do."

"Children must be protected. From so many things. Car accidents, violence in the schools…" She attempts to read something, anything, in Isabella's confident composure and celebrity smile. "…sex and drugs." Nothing.

"My goodness, what a challenge!"

The past cannot be provoked to the surface, and

barrenness does not seem to concern Isabella, secure in her singleness and childlessness. But wait, what is this?

"You remember Tina?"

"Of course. Your little sister."

"She has two girls, a little younger than yours. Twelve and fourteen. They still live in California, in Concord. Here, look!" She pulls out a wallet with the school photos of the two nieces, and Verna can see the love in Isabella's eyes, the same love she saw that first afternoon in the kitchen, the big rush and hug and soaring emotion.

"They're beautiful," says Verna, feeling softer now, more open, allowing the next question to come without forethought. "How is Zenith doing?"

"Zenith?" Isabella has retracted into the void, staring back without responding, evoking sudden regret in Verna. Her own mother Lucy, at age seventy-five, is still a vibrant Ohio farm girl. Her father Brill, with whom she maintained a distant, intermittent relationship over the years, died in 1996, in a questionable, solo car accident.

"Sorry. It's been so long since she stopped using that name! My mom died two years ago."

"I'm sorry to hear that."

"Lung cancer."

"I'm sorry."

"Yes, I miss her."

It is the first point in their conversation when the eternal smile fades and a hint of deep sorrow emerges. The sorrow is completely healthy, a feeling evoked by the memory of a very close departed loved one, the kind of person who gave of herself during life and is guilty of no serious transgressions against the living. And it's the kind of sorrow that Verna cannot say she felt at the death of her own father. And it's the kind of sorrow that renews the anger she's temporarily forgotten and spurs the next question from her mouth, cruel and unthinking.

"How is your stepdad, Ray?"

Isabella squirms and slightly blanches. She looks down at her hands. This is a direct hit, but maybe it's the reason she's traveled the distance of space and time to appear in this coffee shop in Boston to face Verna, her sole witness.

"Ray." She gives that embarrassed little laugh from so many years ago when he unexpectedly entered her bedroom.

Verna remembers the glittering, dilated eyes, the finger wrapped in bb's curl.

"My mom left him, a year later."

Verna doesn't ask. It is the unspeakable year.

Isabella shakes her head, still looking down. "He wasn't a nice man." She speaks gently, in a controlled, schoolteacher voice, the sides of her mouth turned down. "No. He wasn't very nice. Not very nice at all."

The sterilized contempt is chilling.

Verna breaks into a sweat, her heart racing. A creeping dread rises from her gut, announcing her devastating mistake, the faulty moral judgment.

Isabella looks up, and what is this in her eyes? It presses through the studied blankness, a message surfacing from a finite component in the depth of her core.

You know what I'm talking about! Don't ask! Don't ask!

Verna won't ask, just as she didn't so many years ago. She has an urge to run, but when the running is away from oneself, there's nowhere to go. "Excuse me," she says, pushing up from the table, overcome by vertigo. Just before she falls, the deep, sweet blackness rushes up to meet her.

෫ා

Pianissimo, Fortissimo

THEIR VOICES SPOKE to me, flowed through me. I uttered them softly, *pianissimo*. I shouted them bravely, *fortissimo*. I had my favorites, but they were never enough, and new ones came to me, quietly begging, loudly demanding. One by one I chose them, never letting go of the old ones, my favorites. Each new one gave me something the others could not: his own way of moving me, telling me how to feel and affording me the luxury of wordless expression.

These were my thoughts when I first met Bowen, but I didn't say them, for I've always had difficulty speaking, using my own voice to express myself. My chosen circle was ever-expanding yet closed to outsiders not of their world. So I thought. But all I said to Bowen was, "I'm afraid."

He understood. "If you're devoted completely to them, for me it would be like saying, 'I'm devoted only to myself.' That's ridiculous. We all need something else."

He was right. And he cured my insatiability while I continued to enjoy them all, hearing their voices and letting them flow through me, letting them use me to speak.

One day early on, when we were still at Juilliard, I was

surprised to see him pick up and play, well but with mistakes, at least five different instruments. "I play them all badly but hear them all perfectly together," he told me. Then he handed me some music. "Play this," he said. "You'll play the theme perfectly while I hear all the other instruments perfectly, in here." He tapped his temple with his forefinger, just under a blond curl. After I played it, he sat down to write, adding strings, brass, woodwinds, percussion.

From that day on, we were together in every free moment, the few, our union spiritual more than tangible. I played, he composed, eleven, twelve hours a day. In between, we found each other. There was more of him to find than there was of me. His music was his voice. My music was theirs. But he said, "You exist in it. Otherwise, it would be nothing, sound like nothing. Parts of you are there, and I can hear them." I was grateful for his faith in my existence, for I'd not been able to find it on my own.

Two years later, an orchestra performed the composition that Bowen first asked me to play. Finally, I was blessed with the sound he conjured so easily in his mind.

I'm on tour again.

I walk onto the stage wearing anonymous black, my dark hair pulled away from my face, falling straight down to the middle of my spine. Whether alone or with an orchestra, I have no separate existence. My body should not be seen. I'm no more than an instrument of the voice speaking through me.

The people in the audience fade into gray. If I think of them or play for them, I'll fail. The composer, his voice, fills my mind, and I'm completely faithful to him in that moment and throughout our evening together. I'll play him, *pianissimo, fortissimo,* and everything in between.

On my first bow, a small one, the applause comes to me like a distant gust of wind high in the trees, something that won't ruffle my aspect or disturb my purpose. I sit and adjust myself on the bench, lift my hands above the keys, and wait for my cue, his voice saying, "Now."

But before he speaks, someone in the front row coughs. I hear the cough. I shouldn't hear the cough. I've never allowed myself to hear the sounds the audience makes. But I hear it and suddenly it's me, Victoria Burgess, sitting in a black dress at a piano on stage.

People from another world summon me, and I turn to look. They wait. They cough, rustle programs, fidget with suits and skirts, cross, uncross their legs. I'm alone on stage or in front of an orchestra, I can't remember. Suddenly deaf to the voice that guides me, I struggle to recognize it. Am I to play Rachmaninoff's Rhapsody on a Theme of Paganini? Ravel's Piano Concerto in G? Chopin's Ballade No. 2 in F?

Turning back to the piano, I raise my hands and let them fall into a snarl of disconnected phrases. I'm stunned but continue. My fingers are twisted and curled, playing none of the right notes, but playing. Then they become limp and mushy, unable to play at all. No strength. I cannot move them. Then pain. Then nothing for a long while.

Time, a lot of it, has passed; I have no way of judging. But now my hands feel something. No longer mush but straight as boards, my hands are bound tight. Nothing should ever bind my fingers in this way. They must remain relaxed and softly curved in moments of rest.

I resist, suspecting the worst. My fingers, long and slender, smooth and curved, nubs for nails, have nowhere to go. Once fleet and exact, they stumble and fail.

I struggle to understand, but not very hard. There's a truth here I don't want to discover.

Their voices come to me, begging, fearing the loss of their medium. First Bach, with his mathematical exactness. Then Brahms, with his romantic intonations. Then Mozart, with his precise playfulness. Then Chopin, Bartok, Liszt, Ravel, Debussy, Prokofiev, Haydn, Beethoven, Rachmaninoff.

But most of all I hear one voice, Bowen Tanzer's. His phrases play in my head, surprising me with their ironic twists, always ending the same way: turning a blind corner in the near distance, suddenly facing me head on, beckoning me back.

Bowen is standing above me, looking down. He smiles, but his forehead is bunched with lines of concern. I've seen him sit for hours, fingers tapping, forehead bunched over staff paper as he composes, but never looking quite this way. His smile now looks like a conscious device, intentionally pushed onto his lips from a perceived need—a need that would never arise in the course of his work. Only in relation to me.

I smile back, but my thought is, "Why are we smiling?" His face is all I see in a shimmering bowl of bright light. He stands above me. Something odd.

"Bowen," I say, hearing nothing. I'm sure my lips have moved, yet I hear nothing.

"Don't," he says, his fingertip touching my lips. The universe revolves around that spot of warmth on my mouth, sending my eyes back into my head under heavy lids. No part of me exists but the place he touches.

Another long time, maybe not so long.

I open my eyes. He's still standing above me with the same smile.

"Bowen," I say, this time hearing my voice. "Something's wrong. Something happened."

He shakes his head, but not to negate my words, and closes his eyes tight in two straight lines. When he opens them, his face has the same smile, the same bunched forehead, and a single tear traveling slowly down his cheek, past his mouth to his chin, a droplet hanging suspended in time, then plummeting, smashing into atoms on my nose.

I never really awaken completely. The first several months are spent in pain, more mental than physical. The scene is replayed again and again in my head. My arm swings freely, unhindered by the slight pull of my briefcase. I've been careful not to overload it with music; the extra weight isn't good for my hands, their strength to be guarded, preserved. I carry only my current work, Beethoven's Sonata in F Minor, the "Appassionata."

I'm humming the *andante* movement as I cross the plaza at Lincoln Center. At Broadway I pause before entering the crosswalk, stopping to look, right, left, both ways I'm sure, right and left as always, and I step out lightly into the street, still humming, but a car comes from nowhere and I'm in the air.

Air is all around me but there's none to breathe. The briefcase flies away from me, pulled from my hand by an unseen force, and I'm flying after it, suspended above the ground with my arms stretched long, my internal music changing suddenly to the final movement, the *allegro ma non troppo*, as I anticipate the blow of concrete. My arms reach long for the other side of the street, and in this tangled moment of perception I imagine unscrewing them from their sockets like doll's arms and throwing them free to the other side. But instinct takes over as the ground comes up to slam me. My arms, my hands, break my fall.

I owe my life to my hands. But is it a life anymore? There's no hope and never has been any hope I will ever play again, my wrists and fingers broken in so many places that they've healed stiff and useless. Daily I bend and flex and curl them, not to play or in any hope of playing, but simply to relearn what I must to survive, to dress, to eat, to bathe. To touch Bowen.

I cry daily, sometimes hourly, but hide it as best I can.

Bowen sits, hour after hour, forehead bunched, fingers tapping next to staff paper. He scribbles, erases, scribbles, crumples the paper and throws it. He doesn't fill many sheets.

Finally, I say, "Bowen. I'm weighing you down. You should be free of me."

He looks at me, his eyes tired and sunken. "That's ridiculous. I can't live without you." His voice sounds tired because he *is* tired, tired of struggling for the perfect con-sonance that once filled his head, but he doesn't mean it to sound unconvincing. Like it sounds.

My lip quivers despite hours of practice with the words

I must say. Finally, as always, the words fail me. I can't use my voice to express my thoughts. How can I tell Bowen that he proved my existence, something I always doubted? He found my very being and showed me where it lay. Through the composers' voices I could speak. That existence is gone, the one Bowen discovered and loved.

I say nothing more. But he knows.

"There are other ways," he says at last.

"What ways?"

"Other ways to express yourself in music."

"There's nothing. Every instrument takes fingers."

"You should lecture. You have so much to give."

I almost laugh. "Me, lecture? I can hardly talk to *you* about music."

He looks down at his empty page, unable to meet the truth in my eyes. He knows his suggestions are made in vain.

Then I speak again, more than I'm used to, my voice shaking. "People talk about music. They lecture. They write. But it's meaningless. You know that. Do you think Beethoven can be heard and understood by me talking about his music? Do you think his voice can be heard through my words? Of course not. His music has to be played and listened to and felt. That's the only way music communicates."

Bowen looks at me again, his face just like it was on the day I opened my eyes in the hospital. All these months and his expression hasn't changed—that tiny, forced smile, meant to be reassuring. Reassuring for him or for me? His lips grope, then emit sound, a small, painful gasp. "Victoria." His eyes squeeze into those two straight lines and open again. "There's a way for you. Somehow, I know this."

Bowen finally completes a short piece of music, his first since the accident. I've made progress, now able to hold my spoon like a chimpanzee, able to dress myself through the wonders of Velcro.

He smiles more than he has, a smile turned inward in self-congratulation for his small, yet momentous, achievement. With that slender grin, he shows me the music. I can hear the theme in my head but not in his way, the thirty instruments combined in thunderous sound.

Taking my stiff right hand, he leads me to the piano. We sit together on the bench. He places the music on the stand and starts to play.

His hand misses. "Damn! That's not it." He plays, misses again, but keeps on.

I'm shaking by now, sitting on my hands to keep them from the piano.

He stops in mid-phrase, turns to me, looks at me hard.

"I can't hear it without you," he says. "Play."

Our eyes are locked in awareness of my hands, hidden from view under my thighs. The blood, what little I still feel, is pressed out of them.

"Play!" he says again.

I have to do something. I extract my right hand, my "good" one, and raise it above the piano, letting the blood flow back into it. My index finger is poised, tremulous. I let it fall on middle C, lift it again, down on F. A weak, impious sound. My finger rests on F, then slides off into my lap.

"Play!" he yells, his cheeks two balloons of red. "I can't

hear it without you. Play it!"

Paralyzed, I can't respond. I think he's going mad. Of course you can hear it without me. Of course you can, Bowen. Why this torture?

He stands, starts to pace, then breaks down in the middle of the room and drops to his knees, letting go a howl, a ripping, primal sound. I've never seen him do this and I'm scared.

He howls and sobs. He's breaking down completely and for the first time. All this time he's shown nothing but that forced smile, that single tear in the hospital. All of it held in until now.

I can't look at him, and I turn to the music, trying to focus, feeling the heat of my insides elevate to a rolling boil in my abdomen. It pushes upward on my diaphragm and tightens my throat into spasm, then just as suddenly washes everything clean and open. A hand straightens my spine, another lifts my chin, completing the inner passageway, my column of sound.

I sing! Middle C, then F. It's Bowen's voice, my own mixed with his, the notes purely felt, more beautiful than I've ever heard them coming from me. I sing, on and on, feeling his voice deeply within me.

My voice rises above his painful sobbing. He lifts his head to regard me in astonishment. Quietly he stands and returns to the piano. By now I'm completely immersed, our voices united as he listens by my side.

When I'm done, my eyes remain on his music. I'm afraid to look at him. We wait a long time, the room absorbing the sound I've made.

He takes my chin gently with his hand and turns my

face to his. "You've changed it," he says softly, like whispering in a church. "You made me see."

My chest swells and exhales in warm release.

He smiles like he used to, relaxed, without pretense. "This is my first piece for voice. Your voice."

࿇

Like Love

"OUR WIVES ARE cheating on us," the man said.

Harold, telephone to ear, tried to visualize a face. He'd failed to catch the name but recognized the voice as belonging to a man he'd met, very briefly and for the first time, about a month ago at a City Ballet fundraiser. The only image coming to mind was a perversely stiff handlebar mustache, waxed at the ends into tight curlicues, something that would cause any soft-skinned creature, woman or child, to cringe whenever the man pressed in for a kiss.

"Are you still there?" the man asked. "Did you hear what I said? This is a serious matter."

"Yes, sure, well. You say they're cheating."

"Cheating on *us*. To be more explicit, they're having sex." Cheating usually did mean sex, Harold knew, and he also supposed he knew what the man meant. Still, the words only grazed the top level of his mind, not fully penetrating as he wrestled with the visual image he needed, a more complete picture of this man, and now, of his wife. "Who are they having sex with?" asked Harold absently. "Or should I say, with whom?" concerned that "whom" might have a plural form he'd forgotten.

The man gave a snorting laugh which became, all too quickly for Harold, a derisive guffaw. "With each other, of course."

"Of course," said Harold, now catching a glimpse of the wife and husband together, wondering how he could have remembered the man first, or rather his handlebar, without simultaneously envisioning the wife. The two of them had stood six inches apart while sipping champagne at the black-tie affair, exuding such a feeling of overbearing largeness. Not large-magnanimous, but large-overweight and tall—and loud—the wife oozing over the edges of a slick, compressive gown, like the spongy raw dough in one of those pop-open canisters.

Harold, I want you to meet someone. Claire had engineered the meeting from opposite sides of the room, Harold allowing his wife to drag him, reluctantly, into this couple's presence, where he suffered their tactless airs while glancing wistfully around the banquet hall.

Harold must have fallen silent again, for the man said, "You have *nothing* to say about this? They're having an affair, I'm telling you. With each other."

"Um-hmm."

"Two women, two middle-aged women with grown children, doing God knows *what* together. You have no opinion on this? Two *middle-aged* women. You know what they look like. My God! Secret meetings, luncheon dates, and rendezvous. I know they've done it in my bed, probably yours too. Can you imagine? I've just found out, but I'm sure they've been at it for months."

"What did you say your name was?"

"My name?" He fairly yelled before expelling a noise of

exasperation, a burst of air pushed from his lungs. Harold almost felt the hot breath coming through the telephone receiver, bringing to mind another image of this man. How could he have forgotten until now? That cigar, an expensive one no doubt, but still a cigar, sticking out the corner of the mouth, nesting under that thick canopy. It remained unlit, but still, it gave off such an offensive odor of tobacco that Harold had been shocked. The gall—threatening to smoke a cigar at a benefit dinner! Any refined or courteous person would never engage in such behavior, but perhaps the unwritten rules didn't apply to the likes of this man, one of the wealthy benefactors.

Harold couldn't remember the man's occupation, or lack of one. In either case, he certainly possessed a sizeable fortune, something far beyond Harold's means, which had strained considerably under the weight of his unlikely contributory position of "Patron"—an obligation assumed strictly out of respect and support for his daughter Ronnie, a demi-soloist with the ballet company.

"My *name*, for God's sake!" the man jabbed. "Our wives have been seeing each other for *months* now!"

The oblique insult to Harold's memory knocked something loose, sending the wife's name floating up from a dark curl of brain, where it had been stored along with other information he was in the habit of ignoring. "Your wife. Dolly?"

"Yes. Dorothy."

"And, forgive me, I *am* quite bad with names. You are...?"

"Stanley Bridgeman. *E.* Stanley Bridgeman." The "E" emphasized and set off, like the gold lettering Harold imagined on the man's desk and wall placards.

"Ah, yes, and—that's right! Your son dances with City Ballet? Freddy?"

"Frederick. E. Frederick Bridgeman."

"Forgive me. My daughter has spoken of him as Freddy." Harold could see the entire family now, the son's prominent upper lip like the father's, *sans* handlebar. "You know my daughter, Veronica? She danced in *Pas de Quatre* last year. Did such a beautiful job, and she's only eighteen. Your Freddy, Frederick, is about the same age? Or a little older?"

Another exasperated burst of air. "I can't believe this! I've just told you our wives have a sexual relationship and you have no opinion on it. No reaction at all. You'd rather talk about the ballet while they flee to the Isle of Lesbos to live in a den of hedonism and selfish pleasure. Is it proof you want? You don't think I *know* this? Big red "C's" are scribbled all over Dorothy's calendar, and it's "Claire" this and "Claire" that all the time, and the credit card bills—have you checked your credit card bill lately? Spas and luncheons at hotels. My God, do you have any idea what happened here the other day? In my bed, on *my* side of the bed, a pair of pink panties! I'm sure you'd recognize them because they certainly weren't Dorothy's. 'Here,' I said! 'Here, what's this?' She took those panties in her hand and looked at them so carefully, as if this were such a mystery. Finally, she said, 'Oh. Those must be Claire's!'"

Harold imagined it, Dolly—such a large woman with a big red mouth and too much perfume—holding a dainty pair of pink panties in her gorilla hand. Yes, Harold remembered those hands now, one on the champagne glass, the other waving fake, plasticky painted nails through the air, the fingers big and long and distended like an ape's. This woman was having "sex" with his own petite Claire. Reportedly.

"Well, I can't say that I've checked Claire's panty drawer lately—"

"My God, you're blind to this!"

"—and I find everything you're saying very interesting, but my opinion, if you really need it, is simply this. I'm not sure what your wife is up to, but I can say that the thought of my wife and yours together, in the manner you suggest, is absolutely absurd."

"Blind!"

"But I must say, I credit you with a lively imagination, and—" *And what?* "Thank you for the call."

At least the man had the sense to call Harold at his office. Possibly he'd searched the wife's address book, which likely contained only the cell and home numbers next to Claire's name. Too risky to phone Claire's fool of a spouse at home, he would have thought, and it was easy enough to look up Professor Harold Murkle at the university. As luck would have it, Harold had been alone in his office, between meetings with students, when the call came. Now, long after the unexpected conversation had ended, Harold was unable to quiet the man's voice.

What a marriage those two must have! Awakening slowly to the implications of the call, Harold couldn't get over his growing sense of pity for the man. Obviously that Stanley Bridgeman, with his "E." and all, was a kook or an alarmist, a man suffering from some deep insecurity with regard to his wife's affections. And what a strange manifestation of his fear—an obsession with homosexual liaisons! Why not suspect a "Charles" or "Christopher" as the big, red "C," a man who enjoyed seeing Dolly's abundant rear squeezed into microscopic pink panties?

E. Stanley, what an imagination you have! Maybe a midlife crisis of some kind or a misplaced anxiety. That was it—Dolly, the victim of Stanley's misguided homophobia. Wasn't the son a ballet dancer? A natural subject of parental concern about sexual orientation. Not that Harold subscribed to that view, and he'd certainly keep an open mind if Ronnie ever took up with a male dancer, but perhaps it was enough in E. Stanley's case to provide a basis for suspicion. No wonder the man's imagination had cross-circuited with all his worries about Freddy—his namesake, E. Frederick—that boy with the long upper lip and close-set eyes. Rather effeminate looking, as Harold recalled.

These thoughts worked on Harold's countenance, leaving a trail of grimaces, frowns, and grins as he finished up office hours, three meetings with students. These three were indistinguishable from any other students he might have seen at this time of the semester last year or ten years ago, each one concerned about his or her grade on the midterm exam in Art History 101A. One student, a pugnacious boy (about the same age as that E. Frederick), negotiated hard like a used car salesman: "This is definitely a B, not a C. If you change it to a B, I'll give you an extra credit paper this week."

Virtually anyone if not Professor Murkle, a recognized expert in the field of Impressionism, could see that the boy's exam merited nothing higher than a C. No, the Professor wasn't about to besmirch his reputation for tough but fair grading on this one. "Can you explain then, just explain" (the boy's face pouting with adolescent belligerence) "what exactly is the difference between my exam and a B exam? Just *what* exactly?"

Harold looked at that face, knowing what he knew and knowing what the boy didn't, certain that an explanation would be futile. Never would this student understand the refinement of opinion and subtlety of insight that were required for a "good" answer—yes, "B" meant something better than average—to the exam question: "Identify two highly-acclaimed Monet landscapes; for each, discuss the actualization of technique and emotional effect."

Of course, Harold could have gone into the issue in depth. An explanation for his grading decision existed, fully supported by a yardstick of standards embedded in his consciousness from years of training and a sensitive intuitive cognition of artistic media. Subjectivity was involved; no way to get around it. He wasn't teaching something exact and objective like calculus or biology. But how could a mere boy ever accept that his subjective opinions were immature and inadequate? Why should Harold attempt an explanation of the underlying reasons for his opinion which, among men of his own stature and learning, was indisputable?

And so, he told the boy: "Go look at Monet's work again, steep yourself in it completely, compare the paintings to the descriptions in your essay and then come back and convince me, if you can, that you've given me more than just an average paper. Your words must attempt to rise to the level of that mastery in the work. You've given me a superficial mimicking of textbook phrases. It shows some knowledge, an average understanding, no more. Go back and try harder next time. That's all I can say."

Harold managed an encouraging smile, for he didn't harbor any malicious feelings for the boy, didn't really wish him to fail. And the student actually went away looking as though he'd been dealt a fair deal. At least he was gone without another word, almost the same way that E. Stanley had suddenly fallen quiet at the end of their conversation an hour earlier, in immediate response to Harold's unyielding and facially rational expression of opinion.

No, you didn't convince me, E. Stanley. Go back and try again. You didn't convince me.

And that's what Harold kept reminding himself all the way home.

As usual when Claire wasn't busy with a special exhibit, she was waiting at home for Harold, ready to pour wine in the den while dinner cooked in the oven. Red tonight—a clue about the meal to come. He was in the habit of one (small) glass before the meal and one during, just enough to aid the digestion and loosen the conversation.

Not that their conversation needed help, nothing like the artificial assistance required by those Bridgemans, who'd looked quite rosy-cheeked and damp on the brow at the benefit dinner last month. Obviously, that pair needed the lubrication of intoxicants to aid their faltering lines of communication and assuage their unease with one another.

But Harold and Claire were alike in so many ways, from interests to temperament, that even their moments of silence—and there were quite a few of them, now that Harold thought of it—were comforting and anxiety free. If anything, the sole tension between them, slight as it was, emerged from their varying fields of interest and expertise in the art world: Harold, the impressionists, Claire, the post-modernists.

They were quiet people but enjoyed a gentle communication that came with their special understanding and appreciation of art, its emotive force working subtly on the passions. Yes, that was Claire—a quietly passionate woman, delicate, intelligent, and tasteful. Nothing at all like that garish, fleshy, painted ape.

Harold watched Claire as she filled each wineglass exactly three-quarters full, a tiny smile gracing her lips. Nothing devious in her face. It contained no secrets, no hint of a hidden, double life. Her expression told everything: a serene enjoyment of simple delights and complete satis-faction with her life. And with Harold? He imagined her on the bed lying beneath him, eyes closed, that same smile turning the corners of her mouth at the start of their intimate exchange, its breadth and depth growing with the swell of her pleasure.

You know what they look like. Yes, Harold *did* know, and he liked what he saw, suspecting as well that he was supposed to, at some point during middle age, become disinterested in his wife's naked body, discretely turning away when she walked through the bedroom in bra and panties, making love only when urgency required in the pitch dark while fantasizing about younger flesh. These kinds of feelings were supposed to happen at some point, weren't they?

But Harold thoroughly enjoyed every glimpse of Claire's nakedness, as thoroughly as if they were both still twenty-five. At times she even accused him, with that little smile of hers, of following her into the closet when he knew she was about to change clothes, and of wandering into the bathroom while she was soaking in the tub. He never denied the accusations but responded with a smile of his own.

No doubt that E. Stanley had never experienced anything so delicious as a lifelong carnal interest in his wife. In all likelihood, the Bridgemans hadn't enjoyed sexual relations for months or years now, providing the source of E. Stanley's fears. But Harold and Claire were still quite active; why, they probably surpassed the national weekly average, whatever that might be, for healthy fifty-two-year-olds. Statistics must be out there, somewhere, and Harold decided, even as he sought to remember the day of his last intercourse with Claire, to do a little research in a library or bookstore, when he had the time.

"Enjoying your life of leisure?" he asked, taking the glass of cabernet from his wife. Immediately, he feared that his question might sound like an accusation when, really, he was quite pleased that Claire's position as assistant curator at the Modern afforded her large stretches of time to devote to family and personal interests. She worked long, hard hours only when a special exhibit came through, and the last one, a Botero collection, ended over a month ago.

Claire didn't seem to notice Harold's self-doubt. "Completely," she replied. "I played tennis this morning, doubles with Nanette, Denise, and Dolly."

"Tennis with Dolly?" Harold conjured an image of a tennis-skirted Mrs. Bridgeman.

"Yes, she has a court right in her backyard, lucky girl. And later in the afternoon, I dropped in on Ronnie. I still can't get used to the idea she's gone."

Harold remarked the melancholy note. Was this it? A hole in Claire's life? Something in need of a plug? "Yes, hard to believe she's gone," he said and looked at her, hoping to catch her eye and connect. "Our baby," he tried. "Still so young."

"Hmm. Hard to believe." Claire, her face still touched with serenity, looked beyond her husband's gaze. "But the apartment was the right thing, no question about it. She practically lives at the studio, and now she can just roll out of bed, grab her bag of toe shoes, and be there in five minutes."

"Yes, more convenient for everyone." Convenient? Claire reacted, and Harold saw it there, momentarily, her disappointment at his insensitivity. Since when were decisions about children based on convenience? This was their little girl, Veronica, suddenly gone after eighteen years. And now Harold had a new thought: not just a child, but a female presence was missing from Claire's life. He took a fortifying sip before speaking. "It seems this one is going harder for you—harder for us—than David."

"Well," she looked at him briefly, "the second and last child, I suppose."

"But for women, for mothers that is—not that I buy into pop psychology—separation from the son is supposed to be the most trying."

"It's been four years since he left, after all."

"True."

"Time changes things." Their eyes met, and he saw the

time that had passed between them. "And now," she said, still looking at him, "with Ronnie gone, the house is *completely* empty."

Harold froze, watching Claire through the pulse in his eyes, which made a throbbing frame for her face, alternately gray, then grayer. Pressure rose in his temples, and he looked down at the glass in his hand, noticing with surprise that he'd nearly drained it. "I miss her too," he said truthfully, knowing he hadn't as much as Claire.

They lapsed into a prolonged silence before speaking again, choosing mundane topics. During their meal together, the pressure in Harold's temples grew. He rarely suffered from headaches and was puzzled at this one. Claire seemed the same as always, the touch of sadness he'd detected earlier easily replaced with her gentle smile. How could he possibly mention that nonsense with Bridgeman? It might have been good for a laugh between them, but Harold feared the laughter would hurt his throbbing head, threatening to burst at the temples.

After dinner, he helped Claire with the dishes, then announced he was going to bed. Claire mistook his behavior for something else, and moments later, slipped into bed beside him, wearing her sheerest nightgown. Harold barely noticed the gauzy peach apparition through slits of swollen eyes, coming fully awake only when Claire nestled her head into his chest, her hair brushing his chin.

She wanted him, wanted a man—her husband—not a plump female friend. Her gesture, something that should have been heartening, only increased the pain in Harold's temples. He stroked his wife's soft crown, sending more pressure into his own. The room spun around them. Don't you wish, E. Stanley? Don't you wish that "E." stood for Edmond or Ellington instead of Eunuch? Dorothy doesn't want you the way my Claire wants me.

But he felt only pain, not arousal, and he could think of nothing else but his headache. "I'm sorry, Claire. I'm afraid I just don't feel very well tonight."

She lifted her head to look into his eyes, concern in her own. "You're sick?" She touched his forehead like she used to touch Ronnie's and David's, school mornings during flu season.

"Quite a headache is all."

"Hmm." She laid her head on his chest again but in a different way, holding back some of its weight for herself. "Maybe you should take a day off. Stay home tomorrow."

"Let's see how I feel…"

"I don't have much planned. I can call Dolly in the morning and cancel —"

"Dolly?"

"I invited her to lunch is all. Our house. But we can do it another time."

"Don't. Please don't cancel anything on my account."

In the morning, without specific, conscious recollection of the Dolly luncheon, Harold's headache remained intolerable. It was all he could manage to pick up the phone and call his secretary. Appointments and office hours would be cancelled, a sign put on the lecture hall door for his afternoon class. Measures to which other professors resorted occasionally — but not Professor Murkle, not in the fifteen years of his tenure and eight years of assistant professorship before that. All for a headache! An embarrassing absence but necessary just the same.

He was sickened all the more at the idea of facing college sophomores. He remembered the conversations he'd had with students the day before, the words he'd used to justify the grades he'd given. Glib, superficial, and pat. No better than the students' essays, their sentences and paragraphs developed with a marketing plan in mind, what would sell for an A or a B. Where was the depth of insight, the evidence of his wisdom and age? Where resided the reasons behind his judgment and opinion? Buried, resistant to articulation, as good as nonexistent.

After Harold had laid the telephone receiver down, Claire gently asked whether he was finished so that she could call her lunch date and cancel.

The wife's name went unspoken but resounded in Harold's throbbing head. He would not avoid this; he would see and judge for himself. "No," he stated firmly in a whisper to minimize his pain. "I'll stay out of your way," he added, knowing that he would not.

"Oh, it's not that," said Claire. "It's not a matter of *you* bothering *us*. It's the other way around. Dolly tends to be quite—how to put it? Demonstrative. Not a relaxing sort to have around when you've got a headache. She doesn't tiptoe."

But Harold's insistence was clear despite his near silence, and Claire knew his inflexibility well enough not to protest further. She wasn't to make a phone call, wasn't to change a single thing or even mention to Dolly, beforehand, that her husband was home sick. Dolly had been invited and was still invited and would come, despite Harold's condition.

Precisely at noon, the doorbell rang long and loud under the firm pressure of an insistent finger, sending Harold bolt upright from the bed into a revolving room. He was fully dressed and as immaculate as he could manage under the circumstances, still nothing he could do about the bloodshot eyes and his need to squint against artificial light.

As if the bell were less than noticeable (Harold couldn't remember when it had sounded so piercing), Claire yelled out from the kitchen, "Dolly's here!" before going to the front door. All morning, rich aromas of special foods had come creeping, invading Harold's sick room, and now he couldn't help noticing another new thing, an unusually exuberant quality in Claire's voice.

"I'm coming," said Harold, tottering into the hallway. There was Claire, emerging from the kitchen, on her way to answer the door. She turned back, cheeks flushed, and looked at him. "Harold! You should be resting."

"I'll just say hello. Don't want to be rude."

Claire gave a slightly disparaging look—was there something underneath, a secret to cover?—before moving into the entryway and laying her thumb on the latch. Slowly, she opened the door to reveal, squeezed into the framework, the plentiful figure of Dolly, topped with a beaming face and a lipstick-free smile. Harold had difficulty reconciling this Dolly with the image he'd been carrying. She wore a simple dress providing sufficient coverage, and her hair was free floating, clipped back at the sides, unlike the stiff-sprayed off-the-neck hairdo she'd worn at the benefit dinner.

"Darling!" exclaimed Dolly, shifting a large, pendulous handbag on her shoulder before extending the long fingers of her right hand. Claire accepted the hand and closed in for a European sort of kiss-kiss on the cheeks before Dolly looked up, noticing Harold lurking behind in the hallway. She seemed surprised, not rattled. "Professor! How nice to see you again!" She walked past Claire for a polite handshake with the husband. "No classes today? A school vacation day? So many odd little holidays now that I can't keep them straight!"

"No holiday," he said. "Just a day to rest."

"Harold is suffering from a monstrous headache," said Claire, her eyes bouncing between her husband and her guest.

"You poor man!" Dolly reached again for Harold's hand, this time to deliver a motherly, healing squeeze. Her hand was bigger than Harold's but without the apish feel he'd anticipated. He glanced down as she withdrew it. The fake, painted nails were gone, and her natural ones were trimmed smoothly into short, squat ovals. "How is it feeling now?" she asked. Harold felt comfortably enclosed, like a cool pat of butter worked deep into the center of an oven-warmed dinner roll. Dolly's large mouth, with lips soft and pink, might have opened wide to admit him.

"Getting better," he lied, discovering in the same moment that his lie had become the truth.

"You might just go off and take a rest, if you like," Claire suggested.

"By all means! Don't stand on ceremony for me!" said Dolly, giving Harold a double-eyed wink and Claire a gentle squeeze on the shoulder.

"Well, thank you, but I'm fine enough to have some lunch, if you don't mind. I didn't eat breakfast..."

"No, you didn't," agreed Claire.

"And something smells very good."

"My goodness, something *does* smell wonderful. Just heavenly! Claire, you always go to such lengths—we don't deserve it, do we Harold?"

"Oh, but you do," said Claire, looking at Dolly. Harold remembered that look, and an image suddenly came to mind from the first day of the Botero exhibit, nearly three months ago: Claire at the museum, gaping in awe at a painting of a rotund woman. How long now? *I'm sure they've been at it for months.* He turned to Dolly, surprised to see a North American facsimile of a Botero painting in the flesh, a ripe plum of a woman exuding the lush fullness of life. Someone who gave of herself and filled the emptiness in others.

He stared, frankly stared, unable to rip his eyes from her, no longer seeing that abhorrent mental image but a warm-blooded woman, drawing him in. Perhaps he saw and felt what Claire did, and perhaps he should have felt uncomfortable for himself, or for Claire, or for his marriage, but oddly, he felt only fascination and wonder along with a medicinal tranquility, as if the aspirin he'd taken had been laced with something stronger.

"Everyone's so hungry, we might as well sit down," Claire announced. Dolly gave Harold the look of a conspirator about to enjoy a taboo delight. He became embarrassed and looked away. They followed Claire, who set out for the dining room, bypassing the kitchen table. A deliberate choice, Harold knew, sensing that the reason had nothing to do with the formality of the dining room but a need to indulge in space. Dolly required it and had the capacity to fill out a room to its four corners. Harold accepted this now without question or offense.

For an awkward five minutes Harold sat alone, feeling useless and ignored, while Claire and Dolly made several trips between kitchen and dining room, laying the table, bringing the food, drinks, and condiments. Their conversation flowed incessantly along with their movement, most of the talk coming from Dolly's mouth, most of the physical contact initiated by her. Dolly was in the habit of touching, just about anywhere it seemed, Claire's arm or hand or shoulder.

Harold's eyes followed them. Each time they left the room he leaned sideways in his chair to see as much as he could before they disappeared completely into the kitchen. There was a touch at the small of Claire's back. Constant chatter, liquid and easy. The words didn't matter. Harold didn't hear the words but was swept into their comfortable intimacy.

A closeness between his wife and this woman had developed somehow, right under his nose these last few months. What kind of intimacy was this? He'd seen other women acting this way together, touching and talking. Half the female sex must be in bed together, is that it, Bridgeman? When did a touch mean something more? Did the eyes give it away? Dolly's eyes were shining, gleaming with powerful emotion, a *joie de vivre*, or maybe love. Could it be lust? What about the excitement in Claire's eyes? Something quieter, but full of possibility.

Still, everything seemed too open. Wouldn't a cheating spouse try to hide that look, try to avoid touching her lover in front of her husband? Not if she lacked a sense of treachery, guilt, or deceit. Women, creatures of love, accustomed to the tactile sense, were allowed to kiss and hug. After all, what more could this giant teddy bear really do to Claire in bed? More than kiss and hug, perhaps, but all those other things?

All of a sudden the women were sitting down and ready to stay, Claire at the head of the table with Dolly and Harold on either side. Dolly stared at Harold across the table with wide, inquisitive eyes. "Is that how you see it, Professor? You two must have such wonderful discussions about this! I'm so honored to be in the company of renowned experts!"

He looked at her, bewildered. Fuzziness had replaced the sharp, jagged pain of his headache, making an impressionist's blur of Dolly's round face. "Pardon me?" he said, aware of bustling activity around them. Claire, not waiting to ask what they wanted, busily filled their plates with several kinds of food.

"Where do you draw the line between subjective and objective criteria? I've always been so fascinated with this question! How can the experts agree on the greatness of certain works of art when it seems like such a subjective decision? Are we not individuals, after all, with different tastes and sensibilities?"

Harold sat, stunned, while Dolly twisted a liberal forkful of linguini, opened wide, and fully enclosed the pasta ball within her succulent mouth, clamping lips tightly around the neck of the fork to aid its shiny-clean withdrawal. She breathed in deeply while chewing with rolling, big cheeks, looking at him expectantly, certain of her entitlement to a profound response.

"A difficult question, yes," managed Harold. To buy

time, he bit into a mushroom-filled puff pastry and chewed slowly.

Dolly, at length, swallowed and suddenly looked flustered. "How insensitive, taxing you with all these questions when you're suffering a headache! Please forgive me."

"No, no, not at all. I'm feeling quite better. Maybe it's the food."

"Yes, the food. Claire, you've outdone yourself! This is superb." Claire, quietly chewing, beamed her response. "Harold, you're a lucky man, eating like this every day." And as if to prove her point, Dolly inserted another large roll of pasta into her mouth, letting a stray sun-dried tomato dangle, then drop from the edge of her bottom lip onto her plate.

"Well, perhaps not every day," said Claire.

"No. But, yes," said Harold, thinking that his wife's cooking appeared and smelled different today, but actually tasted very familiar. These were some of Claire's favorite dishes. How many times had he forgotten to compliment her? "I *am* very lucky, indeed." He looked at Claire, and she, for the first time that day, returned his gaze and lingered.

Without actually willing it, his eyes filled with love and appreciation, feelings he couldn't very well hide despite the confusion of his thoughts. Her eyes widened and contracted, as if to catch and hold his love, brightening her gaze and communicating something in return. Her own love for him? Reassurance? Recognition of their inviolable union? She seemed oblivious to the presence of that woman sitting next to her, that Dorothy Bridgeman. Dolly. Who's Dolly?

No more than three seconds elapsed, but for those three seconds Harold erased those interfering Bridgemans and felt completely alone with Claire, fully confident of her love and fidelity—a firm, intuitive belief, no more—until their privacy suffered an intrusion from the, however so briefly, forgotten guest.

"Oh, Claire, something has come up and we *must* change our tennis date for next week." Dolly stuffed a mushroom pastry into her mouth before diving under the table for her handbag. Chewing, she heaved the bag up onto her lap, and without looking, dug deeply inside until she found what she needed: a fat, well-worn, leather appointment book with a thick red marking pen stuck in the middle. She placed the book on a bare spot of table, and it fell open where the pen had bent the pages, exposing the current week of dates. Harold couldn't help noticing two big red "C's," one on the current date and the other yesterday, undoubtedly the doubles tennis match.

Dolly flipped to next week. "Wednesday is just no good for me, darling." She passionately inked over a big red "C" with her pen, leaving a dark wet spot, blood red, soaking through to the other side. "Is Friday possible?"

"If it's one of our early ones, yes." So, there'd been early ones, and therefore some late ones as well. "About ten?"

"Perfect!" Dolly nodded her approval and marked a new "C," closed the book, and set it on the table beside her plate.

Harold's fog continued, unabated. *Secret meetings, dates, and rendezvous.* But this one was hardly secret, and those big, blotchy C's, bright red or not, meant nothing at all next to the near certainty of Harold's three seconds with Claire. And hadn't the headache vanished entirely? He chewed and thought, his internal tumult slowly working its way upward as Dolly and Claire resumed their chatter, a blur of unintelligible sound.

Suddenly, he sat up taller and spoke, cutting Dolly off in mid-sentence. "Getting back to your questions, Dolly..."

She looked at him in surprise.

"About art, that is. I've been thinking lately, more than you might know, about the very issues you raised."

"Oh?" Dolly beamed, like a bright student. The women waited, Dolly filling the moment with another forkful and another spontaneous touch, resting her fingertips atop Claire's hand on the table. Harold saw the touch and tried, this time, not to compare it with something else, not to analyze, describe, judge, or explain it. He longed to know, simply, what it was, just like he'd always known things, assuming the reasons could be found—just like he'd always known Claire and had taken her love and fidelity for granted.

"These questions come up frequently in class, and I do my best to explain." He felt his lie and looked away from Dolly to regain his composure. When he turned back to speak, his eyes shifted from Dolly's intent expression, to Claire's serene smile, to the food on his plate, the walls, the ceiling. "Actually, I've set down a number of criteria in a treatise I wrote, what, eight years ago..."

"Twelve," suggested Claire.

"Yes, twelve, entitled *Impressionism: The Masters*, which discusses all those objective qualities in a work that contribute to its greatness, like innovation in technique and perspective, novel or relevant subject matter, the consonance of style, subject, and mood, nuances in shading, original combinations of color..." Harold babbled uneasily, feeling all of his so-called objective criteria drifting away from him like ripples in a stream. "These are the intellectual justifications for our opinions. But there's one thing," and his eyes finally came to rest on Dolly's, "that's harder to put into words. And it's something just as important, but it's completely subjective. Maybe we're all enough alike in basic ways that we come to agree on the greatness of a certain work of art just because it touches us all in the same way—hits the same emotional key."

Dolly gulped her most recent mouthful, removed her hand from Claire's, and lifted the napkin from her lap to dab at greasy lips, sighing deeply. "Artistic greatness, like love," she said, squelching a dainty burp behind her napkin.

Harold and Claire looked at her quizzically.

"You just *know* when it's there."

She allowed the words to hang among them before gesturing, in a pious way, opening her hands palms upward, one toward Harold, the other toward Claire, while they kept their eyes fast on hers through a moment of unifying silence.

At length, Harold and Claire pulled their eyes away to behold each other at the altar. He touched her hand, much the way Dolly had, while searching for another intimate three seconds, hoping to go beyond, to show his wife the depth of his commitment to her. "You're right," he acknowledged Dolly, keeping his eyes on Claire. "I could say it's Claire's smile or her intelligence or her cooking or her gentleness. But, none of that really explains it. I just knew when it was there, and I still know it."

Claire flushed but looked pleased all the same. She said nothing, but he didn't expect it from her, not in front of Dolly. Instead, he searched his wife's face and found the certainty he needed, the light of love and feeling in her eyes. The fog lifted.

Smiling, he shifted his gaze to discover Dolly, fighting tears. "If only Stanley would say something like that!" She sniffed. "We all know it for ourselves, don't we, but wouldn't it be nice the other way around? Wouldn't it be nice just to know when love is returned? But it's all such a matter of faith."

"Oh, but he *does* love you," said Harold, thinking of E. Stanley's fretful admonition. Why would the man be so worried if he didn't love his Dorothy? And what a shame that she didn't know it, hadn't yet experienced the bliss of complete faith the way Harold had, only seconds ago, Dolly herself an indirect cause of it. He saw her perplexed look and added: "I mean to say, I'm certain that he must feel very deeply for you. At the benefit dinner last month, it was so evident."

"You're very kind! My husband has been so pre-occupied lately, but that's nothing to concern you." With tears threatening to spill, Dolly became very busy, dabbing at wet eyes with her napkin while scooping up her appointment book with the other hand and diving for her purse. She rummaged around under the table, apparently pushing the book into her handbag.

An "Oh!" and suddenly she was up again, dry eyed and cheerful. She leaned toward Claire, touched her arm, and whispered loudly, "Remind me later, dear. You left something at my house. I have it in my purse."

Harold's ears perked up. The pink panties? Evidence of sex, or a hasty change after tennis? Claire only smiled pleasantly, while Dolly's attention returned to her plate, the tasty remnants soaked up and consumed with a bit of bread. Harold looked on, feeling intuitively certain of an innocent explanation, more than ever aware of his inability to claim certainty.

He gazed at his beautiful wife, the woman he loved and had known for half his life, realizing that today, just today, he'd discovered how much he didn't know about her, how much he wanted to learn! Did she feel as strongly about him? *All such a matter of faith.* He'd seen the love in her eyes, had faith in that much.

And the rest would come, they would grow closer and stronger. He would have faith in that.

෨

Dear Reader,

Thank you for taking this journey with me. Reader input was essential to the creation of this story collection. Let your voice be heard! Return to your online bookseller and post a reader review of any length on the webpage for *Your Pick*.

For news about my books and life, visit my website vskemanis.com and look for V.S. Kemanis on BookBub, Goodreads, Facebook, Instagram, YouTube, and Twitter.

Wishing you many wonderful adventures in imagination,
V.

Opus Nine Books

All works published by Opus Nine Books are dedicated to the nine members of the family headed by John and Kate Swackhamer at 3 South Trail, Orinda, California —a large world under one small roof.

℘

www.ingramcontent.com/pod-product-compliance
Lightning Source LLC
Chambersburg PA
CBHW031228120726
47905CB00002B/515